Ease

Stephen Intlekofer

One Tribe Press
Ellicott City, MD

One Tribe Press
P.O. Box 2414
Ellicott City, MD 21041
www.onetribepress.com

Publisher's Note: This is a work of fiction. Names, characters, places, and incidents are a product of the author's imagination. Locales and public names are sometimes used for atmospheric purposes. Any resemblance to actual people, living or dead, or to businesses, companies, events, institutions, or locales is completely coincidental.

Ease/Stephen Intlekofer. -- 1st ed.
ISBN 978-0-9965586-2-4

For Lauren and Isla

The disciples said to Jesus, "Tell us how our end will be."

Jesus said, "Have you discovered, then, the beginning, that you look for the end? For where the beginning is, there will the end be. Blessed is he who will take his place in the beginning; he will know the end and will not experience death."

—Gospel of Thomas

Part I

{ 1 }

LET'S ACCEPT THAT I AM YOU so we can experience this together.

{ 2 }

What Is Past Is Past

A ND NOW IT'S TIME to proceed, again. We sit with ourselves calmly throughout...

Over the months and years leading up to all of this, I'd been slowly drifting away from any particular purpose for my life. The past was beginning to resolve into a set of reliable mental categories, and the future yawned out in front of me with a (mostly) comforting sense of inevitability. I had flashes of hope and anticipation, often on a daily basis, but these moments invariably receded into a state of complacency mingled with a vague restlessness. Nothing about any of this was unpleasant, really. It was just habitual.

Then, suddenly, as I was wandering near my apartment one summer evening, a rock flew past my head and clattered away down the sidewalk, and the course of everything was altered. I heard a loud cackle somewhere above me.

"What the hell are you doing?" I yelled up at the perpetrator, a scrawny little kid standing on the edge of a rowhouse roof.

"Fuck you!" he screamed back, his hands cupping his mouth for effect.

We stood there staring each other down for a few seconds until he reached into his swollen pants pocket for what I assumed was another rock. I wrapped my arms around my skull and darted into an alley on the other side of the street. An older man in a rumpled white suit was already taking refuge there, a cigarette dangling from his bottom lip.

"For what it's worth, I just called the cops," he informed me resignedly.

"Good," I said. "That kid's like 10. It's ridiculous."

"City life," the man mumbled.

"Indeed," I replied, shaking my head.

"Who else wanna fuck with me?" we heard the kid yell from the rooftop. "I'm gonna show you all what's what."

"Oh no you're not either!" yelled the man in the white suit, suddenly springing to life and yanking the cigarette from his mouth.

"Where you at old man? Show your face!" the kid screamed back.

"Hell no!" the man bellowed into the air. "You got the upper hand for now standing on that roof, but the cops are about to come and pull your ass down!"

"Let 'em come!" screamed the kid. "I don't give a fuck!"

After a brief period of consideration, I decided I didn't need to wait around, so I walked to the opposite end of the alley and turned the corner. A cop car sped past me as I strode up the sidewalk.

{ 3 }

The Moment

WHEN I WAS IN NINTH GRADE, I had to leave the main school building and walk to a separate trailer for French class. I would count the steps from the main building to the trailer. Let's say it was 100 steps total. Around 50 steps in I would think, I'm halfway there. Then I'd take 25 more steps, cutting the distance in half again. Even five steps away, there were more steps to go, and there was always a halfway point.

I repeated this ritual every day I walked to class (I was bored in high school), and it got me closer to grasping the concept of a *moment*. A moment wasn't a set amount of time—it was malleable, containing infinite possible semi-moments inside it. Later I was confirmed in this when I read about Zeno's paradox and the endless journey from one point to another. To my adolescent mind, this demolished time as we know it, but sadly this epiphany had no bearing on daily, mundane reality. We were all just servants of the clock.

That summer evening as I marched up the sidewalk, the representation of time was still there in the length of my body's shadow on the concrete, but that would soon disappear for me completely.

{ 4 }

The Office

DURING THE FIRST FEW WEEKS after the rock incident, I had a growing intuition that some core piece of my internal reality had shifted, although I had no idea which piece. I also began to have an inexplicable urge to quit my job, which was a reasonable job, a job I liked well enough. I tried to dismiss the urge at first, but I soon felt like I was being almost violently compelled to act. So one night in mid-August, after a few glasses of bourbon, I made the firm decision to quit as soon as I reasonably could. I'd do it abruptly, with no notice. As for the plan after that, I had no clue.

In the office the next morning, I turned one of the blind cubicle corners and almost ran smack into a short-haired woman I'd never seen before. She appeared to be about 45 or so, with green eyes, a plain black scarf, and an ankle-length dress. Was she Mennonite? The shallow split-second judgments the brain sifts through...

"Oops, sorry. Damn blind turn," I said, smiling.

"Not a problem," she said, smiling back. "Uh oh, you've got a bit of a spill."

I looked down and saw that I now had coffee all over my shirt.

"Crap. Yes I do."

When I looked up again my new acquaintance was already well past me, her dress swishing rhythmically as she walked away. I sighed and tried to remember what day it was. Monday? Tuesday? Didn't I have a meeting at 10 or 11? Should I do something about this goddamn shirt? I just let it be and shuffled along to my desk in the middle of cubicle forest. Soon enough this would all be over.

My cubicle neighbor Rod was on the phone asking his wife to pick up something for the house from Bed, Bath, and Beyond. It had obviously devolved into an argument, as most conversations between Rod and his wife tended to do.

"No, it broke last week so we need a new one," he said irritably. "It won't even turn on at all anymore... That's right, I broke it. Of course I did!"

I tuned him out and pulled up my Outlook calendar. No meeting at 10, and it was Wednesday. I heard Rod slam down the phone and his face soon materialized above me, the wide and deep-set eyes peering down at me from atop the partition.

"I envy you. You don't deal with this shit anymore."

"Not for nine years," I replied, leaning back in my chair and staring up at a broken tile in the ceiling.

"I admit, there's good stuff in there still," said Rod. "I think we're at like 80-20 bad-good though."

"Ouch. Gotta at least get that back to 50-50 somehow," I said, chuckling.

"Do you miss it?"

I considered that for a second. Shit, that was the meeting I was thinking of—lunch with the ex-wife at noon.

"No, not the way it was. But I'm different now, and she's different now. She's actually nice to me again."

"Ha!" Rod scoffed, and plopped back down in his chair. "No one ever really changes. Just go to your high school reunion. I went to my 20-year in May and everyone was the exact fucking same."

"I've tried to avoid that," I answered flatly.

"You scared?" came the flippant response.

I ignored this and thought about what I'd say to Marion at lunch. It had been about six months since we'd seen each other, and I'd done exactly nothing with myself. Should I tell her about my "plan"? She'd chuckle at it, no doubt, but would likely stop herself from laughing outright. She'd developed a certain level of mercy toward me since we divorced.

{ 5 }

The Fly

S HE WAS WAITING FOR ME TO RESPOND, but all I could focus on was a water droplet sinking down the side of my water glass.

"Sure, I'm happy," I replied slowly. "I guess I'm happy. I'm restless. You know me."

"Yes, I know you," she said with a hint of a smile.

"I've changed a bit though, over the past few weeks. I think I'm ready to take some kind of leap. I've prepped myself for it."

"What do you mean by that?"

"Breaking myself down a bit. Removing layers."

She grinned knowingly and took a sip of water. Her wide green eyes, which had always hypnotized and unnerved me, latched onto mine.

"Layers, huh? And what have you found behind them?"

"Not sure yet," I answered. "Maybe nothing."

"Does that scare you?"

At that moment a huge fly settled on my hand, and then quickly flew to the rim of my water glass. After a few seconds, it inexplicably dove straight into the water. I watched in silence as it struggled to escape.

"What did you say?" I asked distractedly.

"I was asking if you were scared," Marion replied patiently.

I glanced over at her, and then back down at the floundering fly.

"Yes, but not all the time," I began. "Mainly at night, when my mind is thinking, cycling, feeling like something is coming, or rather, my body feels like something is coming, and my mind is trying to sort it out."

"What's coming?"

"The leap. I've already mentally quit my job in preparation."

Marion leaned back and chuckled, no doubt recalling many of my other similar declarations that had led nowhere.

"What does mentally quit mean?"

"That I've decided to walk out when the time is right, without a word to anyone."

"Seems a bit short-sighted. What if you need another job?"

"I won't," I replied without thinking. "So how's the kid? Miles, right?"

"Good, good," she said, laughing at my abrupt change of subject. "He's a true character. An old soul. He's almost six now."

"Good lord."

We'd divorced nine years before, almost to the day. She'd never mentioned wanting to have children.

"Can I meet him sometime?"

"Sure," she said. "I'd love for you to meet him. I'll call you Uncle Byron."

"Next week?" I asked.

"Sure, why not?"

She seemed a little taken aback by this sudden push to see the kid, as was I, frankly. Why the rush? I couldn't think of a reason for me to care so much other than pure curiosity. Any spawn of Marion's would have to be interesting, at the very least.

"I'm glad we did this," she said.

"Did what? Had lunch?" I asked.

"Well, yeah. Considering how things have been. Or how they were, anyway."

Her eyes were searching my face intently, as they were wont to do.

"Me too," I said. "But let's not worry about any of that anymore."

It suddenly felt so tedious to cling to any of the old shit.

"Amen to that," she replied, smiling.

{ 6 }

Gliding

L EAVING THE LUNCH WITH MARION, I decided to skip out on the rest of the day at work. On impulse, I walked into the first place I saw where I could grab an alcoholic beverage, which happened to be a Ruby Tuesday. The place was fairly dark and only about a quarter full, it being 2:30 PM on a Wednesday. The bar was empty except for the bartender, who was staring down at her phone intently. I sauntered up slowly and sat on a stool. I stayed as silent as possible to test how long it would take her to notice me. After about three minutes, she glanced up from her phone and blushed deeply.

"Oh man," she blurted out. "How long have you been sitting there?"

"Ten minutes," I lied, with my serious face.

"Damn, I'm so sorry," she said, genuinely embarrassed.

"Kidding," I replied. "Only a few minutes. It's my fault for being so quiet."

"Nope, still my fault," she said, grimacing. "What can I get you?"

She was probably about 28 or so, with short reddish hair and narrow blue eyes that darted around the restaurant. Her mouth was slightly crooked, which was especially noticeable when she smiled.

"Hmmm," I sighed exaggeratedly. "Let's see..."

I glanced at the beers on tap and rapped my fingers on the bar.

"IPA?"

"Good choice," she said, smiling, and then walked over to pour me a glass.

She returned and placed the beer in front of me on a restaurant coaster.

"Cheers," I said, holding up my glass, which she then ceremoniously clinked with her glass of water.

"I bailed on work this afternoon," I said with a smirk.

"Cheers to that," she replied, chuckling. "What are you going to do with yourself?"

"Well, I'm going to sit here and drink this beer and talk to you for a bit, if that's OK."

"That's fine by me."

"Beyond that I don't know."

I sipped my beer and stared down at the thin ring of liquid on the coaster underneath.

"So how did you end up in this job?" I asked.

"Do you really want to know?" she asked skeptically.

"Yes, I do."

"Well, I left college and had no idea what to do, basically. My friend started waiting tables here and recommended me. That was about five years ago, when I was just kind of drifting around not doing much of anything. I didn't really think about whether it was something I wanted to do—it was just a job. I specifically asked if I could work at the bar."

"Why?"

"Don't know. I guess I didn't feel like running around bringing people food. Plus I like to talk to people."

"So do I, sometimes," I replied.

"Sometimes?"

"Yes, only sometimes. I like talking to you, because you seem to know how to listen."

"Do I?" she asked, smiling and blushing a little.

"Yes, you do. "

"That's good to hear."

I decided to move on to whatever the next stage was going to be.

"Assume you're never going to see me again," I said. "Which means you can tell me whatever you want."

"OK," she responded with some uncertainty.

"Think back as far as you can remember, back into childhood. Give me a memory, can be good or bad."

She laughed nervously and took a sip of water.

"OK, let me think."

Her eyes stopped darting around for a moment and fixed on the barstool next to mine.

"I have one," she began. "I must have been about seven years old. I was at my grandparents' house in North Carolina. It was an early summer morning, right after the sun came up. I always used to play outside before breakfast when I was there. They had a pond on their property, with ducks, and that day I was sitting cross-legged by the pond, watching the ducks glide around. I remember there was a little bit of mist on the surface, which made it very mysterious. Then, over on the other side, a boy walked up to the edge of the pond, sat down, and started staring right at me. I had never seen him before, and it kind of creeped me out, but I just sat there without moving, staring back at him."

She paused for a moment, waiting to see if a customer was going to sit at a table or come to the bar. He sat at a table. I took a sip of beer and waited patiently.

"After a few minutes the boy stood up," she continued. "He cupped his hands over his mouth and yelled over to me, 'Hey! Who are you?' 'Who are you?' I yelled back. He just laughed and sat back down. I remember thinking it was all very weird, but I still didn't get up to leave. I'm not sure how long we sat there like that, but eventually my grandmother called me in for breakfast. I got up to go, and the boy stood up and waved at me. I waved back and then walked away, back to the house."

She looked at me and grinned.

"So that's the memory. Good enough for you?"

"Yes... definitely." I said, smiling. "Did you ever find out who the boy was?"

"No. I asked my grandmother and she said it was probably the neighbor's guest or something. I never saw him again."

"Well thanks for telling me."

"You're welcome. Now it's your turn."

"OK," I said. "I have one for you. You mentioning your grandparents got me thinking about this one."

I took another sip of beer and adjusted myself on the stool.

"So I was about eight years old, lying in the back of my grandmother's car. She had a big green Lincoln. My grandmother was in the passenger seat—my mom usually drove when we all went out together. My mom was grabbing something from inside the house, and from the back seat I was watching my grandmother try to light a cigarette with a series of matches, each of which would blow out a split second before she was able to seal the deal. My grandmother smoked unfiltered Chesterfield Kings, about a pack a day, from the time she was 16 until a few years before she died of emphysema at 82. She only used matches to light them, never a lighter. I remember watching by the counter in the grocery store as she'd ask for two cartons of Chesterfields. She'd always ask for a few extra books of matches to go with them."

My new friend was now staring at me intently, her left hand cradling her glass of water.

"On this day she just couldn't get her goddamn cigarette lit," I continued, "and I remember being amazed and slightly disturbed by her determination as one match after another blew out. She simply would not be stopped from lighting what was probably her tenth cigarette of the day, to be followed by ten more. And twenty more the next day, and twenty the day after that, and so on. I thought to myself how ridiculous it all was, how much willpower she spent doing this. Completely meaningless. And I knew she was just killing herself with them anyway. She eventually lit this particular cigarette, and that was that. End of memory."

There was an awkward moment of silence as the story was processed.

"Ah, memories," she said finally, chuckling. "Thanks for sharing that, as depressing as it was."

"My pleasure," I replied with a mischievous smile. "I should also say she was an amazing grandmother to me. I remember she would put a bowl of York peppermint patties in a drawer, barely hidden. My cousins and I knew exactly where to find the bowl, and we ate them every time we went to her house, but no one ever talked about it. The bowl was mysteriously refilled every time we came over."

I paused and took another sip of beer.

"I have a bowling memory for you too, if you want to hear it."

"Sure," she said. "I love bowling memories. They're the best."

"Well, I once bowled a 260 game when I was 16, at all-night bowling in an ice storm."

"Is 260 good?"

"Oh yes, it's very impressive."

"So that's all there is?" she asked, smiling. "That's not even really a memory. It's just a statement of fact."

"That's it," I said, grinning. "That's all you get."

We gazed out over the nearly empty restaurant floor, stretching out the moment.

"Well, what should we talk about now?" she asked serenely.

"No idea," I replied, circling my finger slowly around the rim of my glass. "You decide."

{ 7 }

A Walk

I USED TO GET CONFUSED AND OVERWHELMED by the sheer volume of perspectives in the world. Many billions of people, all considering the world on a vast spectrum of frequencies, concerned about survival, perpetuation, comfort, opinions, personas, beliefs, as much verification as possible. Is every perspective its own equally valid reality, or is accessing the entire collection at once the only way to experience things as they really are?

Now, where I am, it all makes a bit more sense.

That day, I left the restaurant around 6 and decided to take a walk down by the harbor. I'd had four beers, so I was a bit tipsy, and I began to steadily release my focus so I could do some objective observation. People-watching in Baltimore was always edifying if you let yourself release into it and switched off all judgment.

Ease

The first person I focused on was a thin, haggard older man leaning against a trashcan at a painfully awkward angle. He had a scraggly white beard streaked with brown tobacco stains, wore a weathered Orioles baseball cap, and smelled strongly of piss. A half-eaten hot dog sat forlornly in a wrapper on his lap, and he was staring at the ground mumbling under his breath. I tried to catch what he was saying, but I could only hear the word "yesterday" repeated a few different times, somewhat despondently.

I soon found myself walking behind a self-satisfied young couple dressed immaculately in fitted pastel-colored clothes and sunglasses. They were earnestly discussing where they were going to go to eat that evening.

"Ryan and Jill said that place was amazing," the woman said.

"Yeah, but we don't always agree with them. Remember the disaster at Salt?" replied the man.

"I know, I know. We could just try it out though."

I quickly broke off from those two and ended up behind an older man with a young child. The little girl was pulling on the man's shirt, screeching for ice cream.

"But I waaaaant it Granddad..."

"But Carmen, you had ice cream right after lunch, and now it's almost dinner time."

"But I don't want dinner. I just want ice cream."

"But that's not what people do, silly. They eat dinner and then dessert. Ice cream is dessert."

"No it's not, it's just ice cream. I can have it whenever I want. My mommy said."

"I don't think she said that," the man replied with commendable patience.

"I'll get what I want. You'll see," the girl said, folding her arms and stopping on the sidewalk.

I passed by them and continued on my way. Eventually I sat down on a bench facing the harbor. I leaned back and gazed up at the late summer sky, my eyes following a jet's slow contrail toward the sun.

"Well, shit..." came a soft, frail voice beside me.

I turned to see a short, emaciated woman who must have somehow sat down on the bench without me noticing. She seemed to be in her 70s or thereabouts, and one of her shoes had a large sole on it to compensate for one leg being much shorter than the other. A pair of fitted crutches was resting by her side.

"What was that?" I asked her.

She turned and stared at me unblinkingly with large, piercing blue eyes surrounded by swirls of wrinkles.

"I said, well, shit. I'm just tired of it."

"Tired of what?" I answered, taking the bait.

"Being here, I guess," she said more gently. "Nothing more to do."

"I'm sure you have more to do," I replied.

"Naw. I'm old. Crippled. Tired. Seems like I've been around forever and nothing changes. I'm ready to head out now."

"Ah," was all I could think to say.

She sat back on the bench and stared out at a tourist boat on the water.

"When I was young, my life was better. I saw things differently. I felt hopeful."

"But not anymore?" I asked.

"No, not anymore."

She paused and we sat silently for a moment. A baby started crying loudly behind us.

"Don't you feel like it's all a tease?" she asked.

"What do you mean?"

"We see beautiful things, transcendent things, and then they're gone, and we're back in the muck. And there's so much more muck than beauty, especially nowadays."

"It sure seems that way sometimes," I said, to appease her.

"It all feels like a big joke to me," she went on bitterly. "But goddammit, when did we ask to be put here? We never asked. It was foisted on us."

"By who, do you think?"

"By God, the devil, what have you," she answered, waving her hand dismissively. "Does it matter?"

"Not really," I answered with a slight smile.

"It's OK though," she said, softening a bit. "You either accept it or you don't. You buy in or you don't."

We sat silently for a few seconds, absorbing the peculiar ambiance of the harbor. She then abruptly began the laborious process of rising to her feet. I stood to help her, but she shooed me away.

"Well, it was good to meet you," I said.

"Really?" she asked with a wry smile. "I do thank you for listening, in any case."

And with that, she turned her back on me and ambled slowly away. I watched her wind her way through the crowd for a few minutes until she disappeared beyond the Chipotle across from the aquarium.

{ 8 }

The First Dream that Teaches

THAT NIGHT I HAD A DREAM—the first of a curious series. It began as a convoluted reimagining of an evening about 15 years before, soon after Marion and I met.

We were in a restaurant. In "real life" it had been a Japanese restaurant in the city, but in the dream it was completely dislocated, at some moments floating in the sky, and at other moments buried underground at the end of some sort of passageway. Marion was eating a squirming octopus tentacle, and I was eating some sort of soup with rice grains floating on the surface. As surreal as our surroundings were, our conversation was a fairly accurate replay of the one from all those years ago.

"When I was a kid, I thought I knew what life was about. It was about playing, eating, and sleeping," said Marion. "Eating and sleeping were the necessary evils that allowed more playing to happen."

"Totally," I replied, smiling. "My best friend until I was about 10 was named Jeremy. We'd just call each other and the only thing we'd say was 'Hey, can you play?' Literally, that's all we said on the phone, ever. Then we'd hand the phone to the nearest adult so they could work out the details."

Marion's eyes were shining brightly and changing color every few seconds. Her whole body was trembling and radiating.

"Then you get older and you hit all these subtle milestones that begin to make you jaded. Like when you first get homework, or when some adult tells you about how hard it is in the 'real world.'"

"Fuck all that," I said, laughing.

The scene abruptly changed to our apartment about five years later. We were fighting.

"If you can't figure out why I'm pissed, I don't even know what to say," she said ominously, stalking away from me toward the bedroom.

"Is it because I didn't call to let you know where I was?" I asked, exasperated. "It just seems ridiculous that you should be so mad about that. I forgot. Everything was fine. I thought you were just here relaxing."

"Yeah, I'm annoyed you didn't call, but it's so much more," she said, trying to remain calm.

By now, the bedroom had detached from the apartment and was floating on some sort of lake.

"OK," I offered, "tell me what more there is."

"I don't want to get into it right now. I'm really tired after this shitty day and I'm sick of explaining things to you. You never listen. You tell me things will change and they never do."

Her voice now had a strange, distant echo to it.

"I do listen. I'm listening right now, and I'm trying hard to figure out why you're so pissed at me. It seems like you're always pissed at me."

"I'm not always pissed at you. You love to say shit like that."

"Well that's what it seems like."

"I just feel like you're living this selfish existence in your own little world with no concern for me..." she said, her voice trailing off.

Suddenly we were both lying under a tree in the center of a rolling field. It was springtime, and the early evening light was pulsating through the leaves above us.

"I feel perfect right now," she said with a small sigh.

"Me too," I replied contentedly, settling deeper into the grass.

We just lay there breathing and listening to the breeze for what seemed like hours. In the dream, I even dozed off a few times, both hands resting on my chest. I would turn every so often to look at Marion, who was surrounded by a thin veil of white light. The light seemed to be pouring slowly out of the top of her head, surrounding her like a mist, and she was inhaling and exhaling it with deep belly breaths.

"Do you want to find out what it's like to die?" she asked suddenly.

She turned to look at me, her eyes wide and lit from the inside.

"Do you want to find out what it's like to die?" she asked again, more firmly.

"Sure," I said calmly.

At this point the dream finally ended, and I abruptly woke up in my bed, panicky and covered in sweat. I sat up and leaned back against the headboard, trying to slow my breath and my pulse. My body was thoroughly electrified. I sat completely still and let the energy move up through me and out the crown of my head. As it slowly departed, I felt a strange peace descend and encase me.

{ 9 }

Work

A S I OPENED THE DOOR TO ENTER the company building, the short-haired woman from the day before appeared behind me. I held the door for her and smiled. She thanked me but didn't seem to recognize me, which, ridiculously, pained my ego a little. I took this non-recognition as some sort of omen. As I walked through the lobby, I decided that today was the day I'd leave.

How to do it? I was thinking I'd just slowly and quietly gather up my stuff throughout the morning (there wasn't much), then go buy a backpack at lunch and pack it all in there. Then around 2 or so I'd just walk out. When I got to my desk, I started pushing things together on one side—my books and notebooks, my pictures, random business cards, pointless little trinkets I'd acquired over the last six years. Six years... good lord. During that time, I'd worked with plenty of folks in the company I truly liked, but saying goodbye to anyone would defeat my goal of an abrupt, mysterious departure. What about Rod, though? I at least had to say something to him.

Just for fun, I opened up my Outlook calendar and looked at the meetings scheduled for the next week. There were at least two distinct reality paths open to me at that moment. I could stay and live out this calendar, or I could leave and allow all of this to simply evaporate.

"Rod, you there?" I said, my voice raised to project over the cubicle wall.

"Yeah," came his answer. "What's up?"

"How's the wife? Did she calm down?"

Rod's head dutifully popped up above the partition.

"Same old shit. We argued for like two hours, she went to bed, and I stayed up drinking Rolling Rock and watching TV."

I laughed and shook my head.

"I'm telling you man," he said. "You're lucky you're not dealing with this bullshit anymore. I know I tell you that every day, but it's true."

"I know it's true," I replied, chuckling.

After a few seconds of silence, I came out with it.

"I'm leaving, Rod," I said firmly. "Today."

"What? Leaving the job?"

"Yes, but don't tell anyone until I'm gone. I'm leaving after I get back from lunch."

"What are you gonna do?"

"I don't know yet. I have enough saved up that I can travel for a bit. We'll see where that leads."

"Have you told Julia?"

"No, I wasn't planning to."

"But she's your boss, dude. She'll be so pissed if you just walk out."

I paused and considered that.

"Yeah, she probably will be."

"Well damn man," Rod said, with a tinge of sadness. "I'll miss you, I really will. Who's gonna listen to me complain about my life?"

"Someone else will move into my cube, probably within a few weeks. You'll make friends with them. You make friends with everybody."

This cheered him up a little.

"I do? Thanks man."

"I'll keep in touch," I lied. Well, half-lied. Maybe I'd talk to him again, sometime.

"No you won't. No one ever keeps in touch with work friends when they leave a job."

He was right.

"Well, good luck anyway," he said. "Send me a picture or something if you see some cool shit when you're traveling."

"OK, I will," I said, smiling.

Rod peered down at me for the last time, shook his head mournfully, and vanished back to his seat. I leaned back in my chair and gazed up at the bank of fluorescents above me. It was almost time for lunch.

I began to rethink my decision to leave Julia in the dark. I probably did owe her the courtesy of letting her know. It would let her get all the HR stuff started, plan for who might take my spot, etc. She was a decent boss, left me alone for the most part. My grand gesture of simply walking out without a word was starting to seem narcissistic and juvenile.

{ 10 }

Leaving

EVERYTHING WAS PACKED AWAY in my brand new black backpack, which was sitting on the floor next to my chair. I was feeling more and more comfortable with my decision as I filtered through emails for the last time. There was an office party the next day to celebrate some company milestone. Also an urgent meeting at 9 AM about a new project coming in. I declined that invite just for kicks.

It was almost 2 now, the time I'd decided to leave. I would head to Julia's office first, and then straight out the door. I shut down my computer and just sat still in my chair, absorbing the random sounds of the office for the last time. Mouse clicking, keyboard typing, one-sided phone discussions, mundane social chatter, feet walking ever-so-purposefully on the carpet.

At 2 PM sharp I stood up and made my way to Julia's office, trying not to catch anyone's eye along the way. Her door was shut, but she saw me through the glass and motioned for me to come in. She was engaged in a heated discussion about some manuscript that was due but hadn't come in, and she pointed for me to sit while she finished up. After a minute or so, she abruptly hung up and swiveled her chair around to look at me.

"Byron, what's going on? You want to chat about something?" she asked, her eyes narrowing.

"Yes," I began nervously. "I'm leaving the company."

Julia leaned back and sighed, shaking her head.

"I had a feeling. When do you plan to leave? Two weeks? A month, hopefully?"

"Today."

"Today?" she asked incredulously, glancing at my backpack. "You mean right now?"

"Yes," I answered. "Sorry about the short notice."

"It's the shortest notice," she said, laughing but pretty clearly annoyed. "Why are you leaving? Another job?"

"I'm actually going to travel for a while, I think."

"Well good for you," she replied, smirking.

I wasn't sure what to say next, so we sat in silence for a few seconds.

"It's OK," she said more gently. "It's OK, thanks for telling me. We'll miss you."

She paused and looked up at the ceiling.

"I sometimes want to get out of here too, particularly on days like this. But I don't. I've accepted my role, I guess. Nothing to do about it at this point. Fuck it. We probably won't see each other again, will we?"

She gazed at me quizzically.

"Good luck to you, seriously. I've always liked you."

"Thanks," I replied, feeling a bit more relaxed. "You've been great to work for. My reasons for leaving are purely personal. Nothing to do with you or the company at all."

"So what's the real reason you're leaving?" she asked, leaning back in her chair.

"Well, long story short, I had a sort of premonition recently. I feel like I'm being pushed to take action, like there's no time to waste. It's hard to explain."

"A premonition? What do you mean by that?"

"A strong intuition. That's the best way to describe it, I guess."

"My uncle died recently, unexpectedly, and a few weeks before he died he told me he had a premonition that it was going to happen. He used that word—premonition."

She paused, flicking her fingers.

"He wasn't that old," she continued. "Died in his sleep two months ago. No one knows what caused it, exactly."

"Sorry to hear that."

"He was an odd duck. The last time I talked to him he kept going on about this guy named Saint Germain. You heard of him? Supposedly some master of alchemy who lived for hundreds of years."

"I think I've heard the name," I replied, surprised by this turn in the conversation.

Julia sat motionless for a moment, staring at the wall behind me.

"Well, I should probably get back to work," she said, abruptly standing up to walk me out. "I've got some kind of meeting at 2:30 I think. I'll take care of all the HR stuff, of course. Typically you're supposed to do an exit interview, but fuck it."

She smiled and opened her office door for me.

"Good luck, seriously," she said again. "I'll probably never see you again, but hey... have fun."

"Thanks so much," I replied, smiling. "Good to have known you."

I walked out of her office, down the hallway, and out through the lobby for the last time. I felt simultaneously light and heavy. A dark current of doubt was beginning to flow beneath the surface. What the hell was I doing?

{ 11 }

What Now?

F OR WHATEVER REASON, I left the office and drove straight to the Horseshoe, the new casino that had just opened at the south end of the city, down by the two stadiums. As I pulled into a parking space in the garage, I made the decision to simply release the past and the future. I turned my car off and sat staring at the dashboard. So began the rest of my life.

When I got inside, I went straight to the ATM and took out $300. I'd make that my limit for the moment. Which game first? I'd go for the illusion of control and play some blackjack. I found a $25 table with three other players. Two of them were stewing silently and looked strung out already, at 3 PM. The third player was a tall, rail thin man wearing a dark green suit and a black cowboy hat. He tipped his hat at me when I sat down. The other two didn't look over—they'd obviously been losing.

"Been a cold table," the tall cowboy said. "I was about to leave til you showed up. Let's see if you change the luck."

"I'll do my best," I said as the dealer tossed out the cards.

I won ten hands in a row. My table companions started winning too, not every hand, but the majority. Even the disheveled pair was getting a little giddy, with one of them clapping his hands loudly after every dealer bust. Everyone was drinking quite a bit as well, which was helping the mood.

"We've turned this thing around, goddammit!" proclaimed the cowboy, after yet another hand where every player won. "You mad now, my dealer friend?"

"Nope, not at all," the dealer said, smiling and shaking his head. "I don't give a shit, like I told you earlier."

In the end, I won about 25 out of 30 hands, including a bunch of split/double down wins, and I walked away from the table up almost $500 on top of my $300. My companions at the table all begged me to stay, but I was suddenly longing for a game of pure chance—roulette.

I sat down at a $25 table. There was one other player, a small elderly man wearing a navy blue track suit. He had a hearing aid and wore incredibly thick glasses, and he was drinking what appeared to be a full glass of straight whiskey, no rocks.

"Is that whiskey?" I asked him as I sat down.

"What?" he yelled back.

"Are you drinking whiskey?"

"Oh yes, Jim Beam," he answered. "Always do."

"OK, great," I said, chuckling. "How's the table?"

"How is what?" he asked, leaning toward me. "How's the table? Oh, running bad. Real bad."

"I turned around a blackjack table just now," I said with a dose of tipsy swagger. "Let's see what I can do with this one."

I plopped down $100 on 17, and another $100 on black. The old man seemed to like my style, as he followed me with a $25 chip on each. The dealer spun the wheel. It hit black 22, so we were still all even.

"All even," the old man said. "What now?"

I threw down $300 on black. The old man whistled softly and put $50 on black. The dealer spun and the wheel hit black 22 again, incredibly. I was up $300, and the old man was pleased.

"OK, what now?" he said, taking a big sip of whiskey.

I threw down another $300 on black. The old man tossed $50 again right behind me. The wheel spun and hit black 17, my original bet. I was up $300 more.

"Shit son, you really do turn a table!" the old man cackled.

I took all this as a sign. I picked up a handful of chips and counted them. $350. I put it all on double zero.

"Are you serious?" the old man said, cackling some more. "OK then..."

He put down $25 on double zero with me, and another $50 on black. The dealer spun the wheel.

"No more bets."

I gazed peacefully up at the mirrored ceiling and watched the ball begin to settle, popping in and out of the numbers. Red 16, popping out to black 24, popping out again to black 29, then finally coming to rest on double zero. I froze.

"Holy shit son!" the old man squealed with delight.

I quickly calculated. I was up around $12,000 on this spin alone. The old man had made a quick $800. The dealer shook his head, grinning.

"That's nuts," he said as he counted out a stack of $1,000 chips for me. "What now?"

He was just as curious as I was about what could happen next. I glanced over at my companion. He was waiting patiently, cradling his whiskey glass. He wasn't doing anything until I made my choice, of course. There was a small but growing crowd of people watching now as word of what had just happened quickly wound its way around the floor. I had no idea what to do, no intuition whatsoever. I was blank. No thoughts, just mere sensation. Everything slowed to a crawl and time disappeared. It was a pure moment, stretched out like a membrane.

"What now?" I asked the old man unconsciously.

"What do you mean, asking me?" he said, laughing.

"I have no clue. You decide."

I picked up two $1,000 chips and let them rest in my palm. Zero again? Yes, zero. I put them both down on zero—single zero this time. I had to change it up at least a little. If I lost, I would still be up a lot, but this was a good test of how absurd the path might be for me from now on. The old man put down $50 on zero, and five other onlookers also threw down $25 chips, one chip each.

"OK, here we go," said the dealer, pulling on the wheel.

Around it went.

"No more bets."

Again the ball bounced around from number to number. The crowd craned their necks and I deliberately blurred my eyes so I could see next to nothing. Eventually the ball came to rest and I refocused my eyes. Green—double zero, again. A deep shiver ran through me. I quickly gathered my chips and strode off, edging my way through the crowd.

"Where are you going, son?" I heard the old man yell. "Come back, let's play some more!"

I walked to the cashier and placed all the chips in front of me on the counter. I was up around $11,000 total. Watching the cashier count out the bills, I took a long breath in and out. The post-dream calm from earlier that morning began to settle over me again.

{ 12 }

The Kid

WHEN I GOT HOME, I immediately called Marion. I told her nothing about the job or the casino, I just asked if I could possibly meet her and Miles somewhere the next day, if they were available. For some reason, I felt like I needed to see this kid, talk to him, before I embarked on my nebulous journey. She told me the morning was open, and we agreed to meet around 10 at the Towson mall.

That night I slept deeply, and I woke up in the morning unable to remember any of my dreams. Lying in bed, a spot of sunlight hitting the wall just above my headboard, I was filled with an indefinable calm I had rarely, if ever, experienced. Everything felt perfectly situated.

Marion and Miles were waiting right by the door as I entered the mall. Marion smiled and nudged Miles forward to meet me. I held out my hand and he shook it limply. His eyes fixated on mine, never dropping for a second.

"Why aren't you at work?" Marion asked. "It's Friday."

"I quit yesterday," I replied calmly.

"So soon?"

"It was time. The impulse came to me and I just followed it."

"Well congrats, I guess?"

"Thanks," I said, smiling. "Yes, it's good. Things are very good."

"Question for you—will you watch Miles for about a half hour? I'm getting my nails done. Just made a spontaneous appointment. If you don't feel comfortable with it, that's fine, I'll just take him with me and we can meet up after."

"No, it's fine. I'm happy to take him. We could go to the Lego store."

I looked down at Miles, who was still staring right back up at me.

"Want to go to the Lego store?"

"Yes," he answered.

"OK," Marion said, leaning down to give him a kiss. "Mommy will see you soon, OK? You'll hang out with Byron for a little while."

Ease

Off she went, and Miles and I were left alone with each other. He looked very much like her, with the same wild black hair and deep-set green eyes.

"Who are you?" he asked me suspiciously.

"I'm your mom's friend Byron," I answered.

"Did you ask my mom if you could see me?" he inquired sternly.

"Yes. I was just interested to meet you, to see what you were like. I knew your mom a long time ago, and I wanted to see what her kid would be like."

He considered this for a few seconds.

"What do you want to talk about?" he asked, softening a little.

"I don't know yet," I admitted. "What do you want to talk about?"

"Do you think you're supposed to meet me?"

"Yes, I think I am," I answered.

"Why?"

"I really don't know. Maybe you have something to tell me?"

"Like what?" he asked.

The conversation was definitely heading down an unexpected path, but I didn't resist.

"Maybe you know something I don't know," I said. "Something that maybe I need to know."

"You're glowing," he said, breaking into a smile.

"What do you mean?" I asked, amused. "Where do you see it?"

"All around you," he replied. "Your head and your body."

"Well why do you think I'm glowing?" I asked.

"Probably cuz you're almost at the end," he answered matter-of-factly.

My breath suddenly grew shallow and I felt like I was going to fall over. I pointed to a nearby bench.

"Let's go sit there, OK?"

"OK," he said calmly.

I made my way there as best I could and plopped all my weight down on the wooden slats. In a few seconds, my body began to return to equilibrium.

"Are you scared?" Miles asked.

"Should I be?" I asked, trying to project calm.

"No," he said, patting me on the shoulder with such gentleness that it nearly brought tears to my eyes. "You don't need to be scared at all. It's just natural. You'll come back."

"What do you mean, come back?"

"You'll come back here, but it won't be the exact same you."

"How old are you?" I asked incredulously.

"Five. Here I'm five."

"How old are you somewhere else?"

"No age," he responded, his unflappable gaze again fixated on me. "Well, all ages, kind of."

My head was swimming and I felt slightly dizzy. I took a few deep breaths as I watched a mother and daughter buy pretzels at Auntie Anne's. This glimpse of normalcy calmed me a bit. Miles just sat on the bench patiently, waiting for me to say something or take him to the Lego store.

"Where is somewhere else?" I finally asked.

"It's hard to tell you," Miles answered. "Right now I don't know enough words."

"Is it somewhere far away or is it close by?"

"It's not far or close," he said. "It's different than those."

"Am I going there?" I asked hesitatingly.

"Probably soon," he answered. "Do you think I could please get a pretzel?"

More normalcy, thank the lord.

"Sure," I said. "Let's go get one."

We walked up to the counter and I bought us each a pretzel. I got Miles a lemonade to go with it, and we returned to the bench to eat. We sat in silence for a bit, chewing away. Miles seemed very pleased, and I began to feel that now-familiar peace descend again. I made a pact with myself right then not to overthink any of what was happening, as much as that was possible given my sort of brain. I was finding that whenever I started to logically dissect anything that was occurring, a wave of doubt and dread swelled to the surface. But if I simply let it all wash over me without trying to isolate or understand it, there was peace.

"Do you think my mom is done with her nails yet?" Miles asked.

I looked down at my phone. It was already 10:30.

"Soon. She should be almost done now," I said.

"I don't need to go to the Lego store," he said. "We can just sit here and wait for her if that's OK."

"Sure, that's definitely OK," I replied.

"You can ask me more questions if you want," he said, reading my mind.

"OK, let me think of one," I said, smiling down at him.

"You're still not scared?" he asked.

"No, I'm not scared."

"Good."

"Are you ever scared?" I asked.

"Sometimes, but only for a few seconds. Then I remember that everything's fine."

He paused to take a sip of lemonade.

"How are you boys doing?" interrupted Marion's voice from just behind us.

She walked around the front of the bench and tore off a piece of Miles' pretzel.

"Yum. I looked for you guys at the Lego store. You decided to just get pretzels and hang out here?"

"Yup," I said. "Just talking and relaxing. We're friends now."

"Good," said Marion, grinning. "Miles, are you and Byron friends?"

"Yes," he answered. "We've always been friends and we always will be. I didn't remember him at first but now I do."

"Oh, really?" said Marion, laughing.

"Yes," replied Miles, leaning his head against my shoulder.

I just smiled up at Marion, pleasantly baffled.

"Thanks for getting him a snack," she said.

"My pleasure."

Miles stood up and handed Marion the last small part of his pretzel.

"Shall we walk the mall?" Marion asked.

"Fine with me," I answered, rising to my feet.

We proceeded to stroll through the four levels of the mall from bottom to top, stopping from time to time for Miles to examine a stimulating store window. I was happy just being with these two, and I simply relaxed into the oddly familiar flow of the situation. Any tension or resentment that Marion and I had been holding onto from the past was now seemingly slipping away. Some other type of bond was forming in place of that old one—something indefinable. At one point she reached out and gently grasped my hand as we walked. Miles didn't seem to notice, or more likely he did notice and just thought of it as a perfectly natural thing for friends to do.

"Well, here we are," said Marion when we reached the set of doors where we'd first entered. "We're going to head home for lunch. What are you going to do now that you're free?"

I paused to invent an answer.

"I think I'm going to just get in my car, hop on 70, and drive somewhere a good distance away out west," I said, as if it had been my plan all along. "I feel like I need to explore."

"Leaving today?" she asked.

"Probably," I answered impulsively. "Maybe even right now."

I thought of the large manila envelope filled with cash that was sitting in my trunk, hidden.

"I'm happy for you," she said with a tinge of melancholy. "I think you've always wanted this."

Miles walked over and gave me a quick hug around the leg. I hugged him back.

"Bye Byron," he said. "I like talking to you."

"Same here, Miles. I'm glad we're friends now."

Marion wrapped her arms tightly around my neck and pressed her lips against my ear.

"I love you," she whispered.

"I love you, too," I answered softly.

And for the moment, that was that.

{ 13 }

Where to...?

A S I WALKED TO MY CAR in the parking garage, I decided to just leave town right then. I'd head to 70 and start driving without a particular destination in mind. I had no clothes or toiletries with me, but I did have the money I'd won, so I could buy whatever I needed. I-70 begins (or ends) at a park-and-ride on the west side of Baltimore and runs all the way to Utah—over 2,100 miles away. Every time I got on 70 leaving the city, I had the deep inclination to just keep on following it indefinitely. Now it was time to do it. I'd start at the very beginning.

As I was circling the park-and-ride to get on the interstate, I suddenly felt so unsettled that I stopped the car and got out. It was around noon, and the late summer sun was beating down on all the empty parked cars. I was the only person in the lot. A massive thunderhead loomed off in the distance to the west. The air was heavy with the typical Maryland humidity, and there were cicadas droning away in the nearby woods, with one rising to the forefront to replace another in a continuous cycle. The undercurrent of dread was forcing its way to the surface. It began to course through the length of my body, and soon became so intense that I could barely breathe. I bent over at the waist and gulped in several deep breaths, trying to suppress the overwhelming urge to vomit. My heart was racing, and I was dizzy and sweating profusely.

After a few minutes of this agony, I finally began to feel a bit of a release. I stood up straight, closed my eyes, and breathed in deeply. Solidity was returning. I watched waves of soft light sway against my eyelids, and the dread slowly cycled back down to equilibrium. I opened my eyes. A station wagon had stopped beside me and a grey-haired woman was staring at me intently through her open passenger-side window.

"Are you OK?" she asked loudly.

"Yes, thanks," I answered, smiling to put her at ease. "I'm good. Just a very minor panic attack."

"Oh my," she said, pursing her lips and shaking her head. "That does not sound fun. You know, when I feel anxious, I think about lying outside in the grass on a perfect afternoon, looking up at the clouds. That usually helps it all just float away."

"That's great advice, thank you," I replied, straining to be polite.

"Also kitties. They help. I have three at home and they just relax me so much."

"Ah yes, cats are very calming."

"Also chamomile tea," she said. "Try that too."

"I will, thank you," I replied, edging back toward my car to try to escape.

"My pleasure. I do hope you feel better soon. Good-bye now."

She smiled broadly and drove off, leaving me alone again in the parking lot. I sighed deeply as I opened my car door. Continue? Yes. There was no choice now.

{ 14 }

Flip Side

ABOUT AN HOUR INTO THE TRIP, around Frederick, it began to storm. Traffic slowed to a crawl as the rain and wind lashed the windshields. Soon hail arrived as well, and most people decided to just pull over to the side of the road to wait it out. I stupidly tried to keep driving even though I could see maybe five feet in front of the car, but eventually I decided to stop under an overpass. There was already another car under there, along with two motorcycles. After a couple of minutes, a stocky man with a leather jacket and a long grey beard left one of the bikes and walked toward me, motioning for me to roll down my window. I hesitated for a moment, but then complied.

"Hi," he said loudly over the roar of the wind.

He placed one hand on the top of my door and leaned down to look at me.

"Hello," I said suspiciously.

"Hell of a storm, huh?"

"Definitely," I replied.

"Where you headed?" he asked, his eyes searching the interior of my car.

His demeanor was not unfriendly, but it was oddly probing.

"Actually, I'm not sure," I answered. "West."

"Ah, the proverbial journey to find yourself?" he asked, grinning slyly.

"Yeah, I guess that's it," I said.

"Good, good," he said, staring at me fixedly. "I hope it happens for you."

It was still hailing, and the wind was ripping through his hair and beard. His stare was unnerving me quite a bit.

"Where are you guys headed?" I asked with a veneer of calm.

"You know, just tooling around. We do this every Friday."

He paused for a moment, still staring at me.

"You know why I'm interested in you, why I walked over here?" he asked. "It's because you look exactly like my son. Haven't seen him in ten years."

I searched for the proper response but couldn't find it.

"He's 37 now," he continued. "That's about your age, right?"

"Yes, I'm 38," I answered.

"I need to see him. It's time," he said wistfully, looking down at the ground. "It was some stupid shit, too. He got into a beef with my girlfriend at the time. Called her a bitch. I went ballistic on him and punched him a few times, knocked him down. He got embarrassed and took off."

He stopped to kick at something on the pavement.

"He wouldn't take my calls after that or anything. Then weeks and months went by, and I found out he moved to Philly with a few of his friends. Then years went by, seems like in a flash. I lived my life, thought about him a lot, but just never got in touch again. And of course he never got in touch with me, probably out of spite."

The hail had turned back to rain, and that was now slowing down a bit.

"Life's short," I said sympathetically, unsure of what else to offer.

"That's the god's honest truth," he replied softly. "It's short as fuck. I'd like to run through it again... Play it out differently..."

His voice trailed off for a moment, his eyes narrowing as he gazed down at his feet. After a few seconds, he snapped back to the present.

"Well goddammit..." he said gruffly. "Time to get movin'."

He reached his hand through the window and held it out for me to shake, which I did. It was solid and covered with callouses.

"Rain's done," he said, stepping back from the car and squinting up at the sky. "Catch you on the flip side brother, and thanks for listening."

With that, he sauntered back over to his bike, hopped on, and revved it up. He and his riding buddy both turned and nodded at me before driving off, and I watched as they disappeared into the light mist rising up off the pavement. The sun was coming out again and things were steaming up quickly.

The interaction had left me confused and slightly uneasy, but I was determined to follow my new law of letting it be, so I refocused on what was directly in front of me. It was now almost 2 PM and I hadn't had any lunch, but I wasn't particularly hungry. I had an old bag of Sheetz gas station cashews in my car, so I tossed a few of those in my mouth as I pulled out my map of Pennsylvania. I-70 veered up into PA in about an hour. From there, Pittsburgh was a little over two hours away. That seemed like as reasonable a place as any to grab dinner and stay for the night. I started up the car and drove off through the haze.

{ 15 }

Suicide

I HAD DECIDED TO STAY at the Hyatt, but on the way I stopped at a Target to pick up some clothes and toiletries. I picked out two pairs of pants, one pair of shorts, three t-shirts, a button-up shirt, three pairs of socks, three pairs of boxers, and a backpack. I also bought some deodorant, toothpaste, and a toothbrush. As I gathered my items at the register, I saw a little boy viciously kick his mother in the shin, after which she screamed at him and squeezed his arm until he started crying. On my way out, I saw a little old woman fruitlessly attempting to hoist a huge box out of her cart and into her trunk. As I passed by, I maneuvered the box in and shut the trunk for her. No words were exchanged, only brief waves and smiles.

When I got to the Hyatt, I checked in at the desk, threw my stuff in the room, and headed to the hotel restaurant for some food. After dinner, I made my way to the bar to have a quick drink. Most of the stools were occupied, and I ended up sitting between two women. The one on my left was turned away from me, immersed in a shrill, drunken conversation with a bearded man decked out in golf gear. The one on my right was wearing a glittering silver dress and seemed to be alone. She was clutching a glass of wine and staring down at a picture of a shaggy black dog on her phone.

I ordered a Manhattan and swiveled around to survey the bar. For what seemed like a full minute, the silver-dressed woman stared pensively down at the picture of the dog. Finally, she glanced over at me with a slight grin.

"Are you wondering why I'm looking at this dog?" she asked with a strange intensity.

"No," I answered, smiling. "Well, I guess a little."

"My mom just sent me this picture of my dog from when I was a kid. We had this dog for fifteen years. Her name was Nora."

"Fifteen years huh? She must have meant a lot to you."

"Well, most of the time she was a total bitch, honestly. But one time she saved my life."

"Well now you have to tell me about that," I said.

"Do you really want to hear about it?" she asked, grimacing. "It's a sad and depressing story."

"Sure I want to hear it," I replied.

She took a long sip of wine.

"I have no idea why I'm going to tell you this, but here it goes," she began, looking down at the ground, her dark blonde hair draping her face. "This was about ten years ago, and I was 21 and really depressed. I had dropped out of community college and was living at home in Virginia, doing nothing. And when I say doing nothing, I was really doing absolutely nothing. I would lie in bed staring at the ceiling, paralyzed with fear and anxiety. Sometimes I'd turn over and look at the wall. I was scared of life. There was no chance of me leaving the house or even my room most days. I'd only leave the bedroom to eat and go to the bathroom."

She sat up straight and looked over at me, and I saw that there was a deep, ethereal beauty in her face. Her eyes were dark brown and perfectly round, and her stare was both forceful and oddly comforting.

"I'm done with that fear now, but back then it was brutal. I don't know if you've ever experienced overwhelming fear that won't release you, but it's not fun. This was this dense black cloud that enveloped me nearly every minute of the day. I'd have some moments where it let up, mainly when I drank, but then it would come right back. I also deeply hated myself, so throw that in the mix."

She smiled and took another drink.

"I told you this was sad and depressing."

Ease

"You were right," I said, laughing. "But I want to hear about this Nora dog saving your life."

"I'm getting to it, I promise," she said, grinning before turning more serious. "I want to ask... have you ever experienced fear like what I'm talking about?"

"I think so," I answered. "Especially lately. I've been having these strange feelings of dread that abruptly come and go."

"Then you know a little of what I was feeling then. Anyway, one day just like all the others that bled together, I woke up from an afternoon nap perfectly certain that I needed to kill myself. I decided to do it with pills. I had an almost full bottle of Ambien that I decided to take that night, when everyone else was asleep. I made the decision around 3 PM, and from then into the evening I felt an incredible weight lifted off me. It was all going to end. No more of this dark, cursed, churning mind I'd been given. That would be gone forever."

She paused and took another quick sip of wine.

"My name's Samantha by the way."

"I'm Byron."

"Well, Byron, have you ever been suicidal?"

"No, not the way you're describing," I answered. "I've been depressed before, for sure. I never made *the* decision though."

"Good for you," Samantha replied. "Well that evening I waited until I knew my parents were asleep, around 11. I placed the bottle of pills in front of me on

{ 67 }

the covers of the bed. I remember sitting there meditating on what I was about to do. I had no doubt or hesitation. I closed my eyes to consider the end, how it would all fade to pure darkness and there would be no more sensation, no more anything at all. At that exact moment, Nora pushed the door to my room open—it had always had trouble fully latching. She jumped up on the bed and snatched the bottle of pills in her mouth. She was playing, and she ran off hoping I would go after her. This bitch was ruining my plan, so I got up and chased her angrily through the house. She ran into the kitchen and out the doggie door, of course. I was so mad I could barely think."

She stopped for a moment and gazed up at the ceiling with a soft, pensive smile.

"I grabbed a flashlight from under the sink and ran out the kitchen door, trying to find her. I could hear her panting and digging somewhere in the distance. My parents' house was backed up against the woods, so she could have been anywhere. I was shining the flashlight around frantically but I couldn't see her anywhere. After about ten minutes, I gave up and just sat down on the ground and cried. I hated that fucking dog so much in that moment. But then a strange thing happened... time just kind of stopped. It was a clear night in the early fall, and the moon was almost full. I just sat there staring up at it for God knows how long. After a while, I noticed that Nora was lying right in front of me, without the pill bottle. She and I had never really been close. She just did her own thing and I did mine. But that night, she lay there with me like she knew I needed a companion."

The couple next to us was laboriously getting up to go, and the woman accidentally backed into my elbow, spilling some of my drink.

"Oh, I'm sorry. So sorry. Fuck. I'm such a klutz when I'm drunk," she said, slurring all the words.

"Yes, yes you are," said her golf-geared companion, chuckling condescendingly. "You're a fucking mess. Let's get you out of here."

Samantha laughed as she watched them stumble away.

"Beautiful people."

"Finish the story please," I said, truly wanting to hear how it would wrap up.

"Really?" she said, laughing some more. "Well, you asked for it. So Nora sat with me for a while that night, and I began to notice something odd—my fear was gone. I felt peaceful for the first time in months. I lay back on the ground and looked up at the stars, feeling myself pressed back into the earth, substantial, but also light and floating on this tiny speck in space. It was a defining moment in my life, what you would call a mystical experience I guess. Since then I've definitely had some depression and anxiety, but never that crippling fear. In fact, over the past year or so, I've stopped feeling much fear at all. I'm not sure what that means."

She paused and looked over at me, her gaze flitting back and forth from my mouth to my eyes.

"Are you staying in the hotel?" she asked.

"Yes."

"So am I. I'm in sales, believe it or not. One of our main clients is in Pittsburgh and I have to stay through the weekend."

She put her hand on my knee.

"I'd like to sleep with you," she said abruptly. "Not necessarily have sex, but sleep with you, next to you. Would you want to do that?"

"Um... sure," I answered, in the spirit of my new law.

I trusted her, for whatever reason, and I was also attracted to her.

"OK then, let's go to my room," she said.

She insisted on paying for our drinks, and as we walked over to the elevators, she playfully linked her arm with mine.

{ 16 }

Here

"**W**HAT KIND OF PERSON ARE YOU?" she asked, reclining back on her elbows on the bed.

I stood leaning against the dresser next to the TV.

"What do you mean by that?"

"Just what I said. What kind of person are you? Are you kind? Sad? Insecure? Anxious? Funny?"

I pondered for a moment. Samantha started pulling her dress up little by little with her fingertips, which distracted me a good deal.

"OK then, I think I'm a kind person for the most part," I began, smiling awkwardly. "But I can be selfish. I tend to cling to my own personal comfort."

I paused, blushing a little.

"You feel embarrassed?" Samantha asked with a knowing grin. "Don't. Please go on."

"Well," I continued hesitantly. "I seem outwardly calm, but I internalize my anxiety, which is a habit passed down from my mom. I can be vain, but most of the time I don't think much about my appearance at all. People say I can be funny. I'm an introvert, and I was very shy when I was a kid. I'm less shy now, but I like being alone and I don't like talking to people in groups... How's that?"

Samantha was staring at me as she continued to pull her dress up toward her hips, very slowly. She wasn't wearing any underwear.

"Go on," she said after a few seconds, her eyes glinting mischievously. "More please."

"Really?"

"Yes, I want to hear all about what you think of yourself."

"OK," I said, chuckling at the absurdity of the situation. "What else? I do deal with deep fear. I always have. I've basically suppressed it in the past, but I just quit my job in Baltimore for no real reason and I have no idea what I'm doing now, so that fear is coming to the surface. But there's also this strange sense of peace, which is new."

"What else?" she asked, when I paused.

Her dress was now up above her hips, and she was casually caressing the lips of her vagina with the fingers of her right hand.

"I tend to think about how tiny and insignificant we are in the big show," I went on despite the distraction. "The big show that takes place over billions of years. And how each thing we do is just swallowed up in that insane stretch of time. No matter what it is, stupid or wise, it's just swallowed up."

"And does that feel liberating to you?" she asked.

She was now lying back with her legs spread open and her hands resting on her belly.

"Yes, and terrifying," I replied, forcing myself to look only at her face.

"When I was in that time of overwhelming fear, I thought a lot about all this," she said. "How actions and feelings mean nothing in the grand scheme of things. And how we're probably all just here being toyed with for someone or something's amusement. And how that someone or something that's toying with us is itself completely insignificant in the grand scheme. And so forth and so on."

She laughed incongruously and sat up a bit, resting her head against the headboard and extending her legs out flat.

"It was pure nihilism, I guess, but for me it wasn't liberating," she continued. "Nothing meant anything at all, which led to the obvious conclusion that I didn't mean anything at all. Nothing I could ever do, even in my wildest ambitions, could ever amount to anything at all, which scared the hell out of me. And depressed me. And paralyzed me..."

She trailed off for a moment, gazing up at the ceiling.

"But after that night under the moon, I slowly began to realize that however you choose to look at it, there's still a life to be lived, and we're all in the exact same fucking boat. No one really knows what to do here, and in a way that *is* liberating."

She stared at me and smiled.

"I'd like you to come over here, please," she said matter-of-factly.

I walked over to the bed and she gently pulled me down on top of her. She pressed her lips against my ear and whispered, "You can fuck me if you want, but no pressure. Either way, it's all swallowed up, right?"

I stared down into her eyes for a moment, and then kissed her on the mouth. Her fingers began to slowly unbutton my pants.

{ 17 }

Forward

I WOKE UP AROUND 6 THE NEXT MORNING, just before dawn. Samantha was asleep next to me, sprawled out naked on top of the dark blue bed covers. I pushed myself up and leaned back against the headboard. I had only slept about five hours, but I was not remotely tired. Energy was coursing through me. I sifted through images and sensations of the previous night... Samantha's dark eyes staring into mine, her voice quavering then steadying, her hand sliding between her thighs and down my pants, her legs opening and wrapping around me, her breasts shaking as her body moved on top of me, her warm breath seeping into my ear and my mouth.

I hoisted myself up from the bed, slowly and quietly put on my clothes, and then walked to the bathroom to pee. After throwing some cold water on my face, I went out and searched the nightstand by the bed for a pad of paper and pen, then returned to the bathroom to write a message.

"Samantha, Thanks for the connection. Despite your crippling nihilism, I'd like to know you better. Now I'll go resume my walkabout, wherever it leads, and prepare myself to be fully swallowed up. My cell number is below. Get in touch if you'd like. – Byron"

I left the note on my pillow and took one last glance at Samantha—stretched out and bare and peaceful—before walking out the door. I went straight to my room, gathered my meager possessions into my backpack on the untouched bed, and jumped in the shower.

Back in my car on the highway, I took a long sip of coffee as the elongated shadows of the trees slipped by in the early morning light. My destination was Terre Haute, Indiana. I'd chosen it at random the night before while I was eating dinner. I was cutting into a piece of asparagus and that name and the image of that particular dot on the map had popped into my head.

After savoring the memory of Samantha a bit more, I began to sift through flashes of my time in Baltimore, and my mind eventually fixed on one night in particular—the night I met Marion. Multiple lifetimes ago, seemingly. I was 23 at the time, and she was 21. We were at a house party a good friend of mine was throwing for his birthday, and she came with a mutual friend of ours. I had recently recovered from surgery for

Crohn's disease, so I was self-consciously adjusting to being back in society.

I was standing in a group talking about something, probably some dry recitation of my recent physical ills, when she and Shannon walked into the room. Marion had long black hair at the time, which she liked to smooth back from her ears every few minutes. Her eyes were unforgettable—dark green and deeply set—and she had a tendency to stare at people for long periods of time without a hint of self-consciousness. She would skin you with that stare, leaving you raw and exposed.

When she finally noticed me that night, she stared directly at me without once looking away. I could barely take it, and I kept looking down at my drink and pretending to listen to the group conversation. After a few minutes, she edged her way over to me.

"Do I know you?" she asked tranquilly.

"Ha," I said, trying to play it cool. "Is that a pickup line?"

"No," she said, smirking a little. "I really think we've met before. You're friends with Shannon, right?"

"Yes, but I don't think we've ever met," I said. "I'd remember."

"Would you?"

She was challenging me, which she would do every day for the rest of our time together.

"Yes. Do you know your stare is just a tad bit intimidating?"

"Ha!" she said, chuckling. "Yes, people tell me that. Does it bother you?"

"No, no. I'm just not used to it. People are usually scared to stare like that, especially in a party situation."

"True," she said simply.

She paused to sip her drink and scan the room. I thought she might be losing interest, but her attention quickly rotated back around.

"What about you?" she asked. "Are you scared?"

"Of what?"

"I don't know, of anything."

"Yeah, sure, of course."

"Is this conversation too intense for you?" she asked, smiling slyly.

"Not at all," I lied.

"So do you know John well?" she asked.

"Yeah, he's a good friend," I said. "We went to school together at UMBC."

"I've never met him," she said.

"Well, he likes to throw himself parties, as you can see."

"Is he interesting beyond that?"

"Yes, very. You'd like him."

She laughed strangely and pushed her hair back behind her ear. This was never in any way a bashful move for her—she did it with conviction, still staring directly at whoever she was talking to.

"I'm probably going to leave soon," she said. "Well, like right now. Do you want to come with me?"

"Where are you going?"

"Do you care?" she asked, again with a sly smile.

I chuckled nervously and downed the rest of my drink.

"No, I guess I don't," I said, tossing the cup in the trash.

She grabbed my hand and led me to the door. I didn't have a chance to say goodbye to anyone, but that was no longer a concern.

"We'll go to my place," she said when we got outside.

And so it began.

That Saturday morning on I-70, I was approaching Wheeling, West Virginia, just before the border of Ohio. It was almost 8 and I was getting hungry, so I pulled off and found a Bob Evans. I ordered a short stack, scrambled eggs, and bacon, and as I waited for the food I thought again of Samantha, naked and dreaming on the hotel bed. This led me back to an image of first real girlfriend, Liz, lying naked on top of her dark red sheets, her legs spread apart and her eyes riveted on mine. Finally, I saw Marion lying on her stomach in the bed at our first apartment, her chin resting in her open palms. She was staring up at me with her characteristic expression, simultaneously inviting and repelling.

{ 18 }

A Call from Dan

AFTER BREAKFAST I DECIDED to just drive straight to Terre Haute, which was about five and half hours away. This would put me in town around 2:30 or 3, and I could just grab a late lunch somewhere then. I had no idea where I was going to stay—I'd just choose a motel at random.

About an hour into the drive, I got a call from an unknown number. I put the phone on speaker and answered it.

"Byron, it's Dan," came the deep and familiar voice.

Dan was an old and difficult friend of mine who had moved out to Colorado a few years back. The rumor was that he had become part of some cult out there, and I hadn't talked to him since he left. He was originally a close friend of Marion's from childhood, and they'd stayed in touch as far as I knew.

"Dan... good lord. How long's it been?"

"I think at least a couple of years," he said. "Communication's a two-way street, as you know, so we're both at fault."

"I know," I said. "Sorry about that. I had no idea where you were, actually."

"It's not a problem now," he replied. "Anyway, I'll get straight to the point of why I'm calling. I talked to Marion yesterday and she told me you're on a road trip out west?"

"Yup. It's kind of a random thing. Started driving on 70 with no real destination in mind. I'm in Indiana at the moment."

"What's the point of this trip?" he asked, with his typical directness. "Are you just dicking around or are you trying to figure something out for yourself?"

"I have no idea," I replied. "It's just something I felt called to do."

I didn't want to get into any of the other stuff with Dan on the phone, for many reasons.

"Well, this is perfect. You have no destination and no purpose, so I think you should come and see me. I'm on a beautiful piece of land outside of Lyons, Colorado, just above Boulder."

"How'd you end up there?" I asked.

"I found a wonderful teacher, a pure soul named Laura Day. She owns the retreat center on this land. I think she has a lot to offer you. You sound like you're drifting."

"I'm not drifting, really. I'm just not sure what'll happen next. That's a realistic way to look at things, I think."

"I suppose on a certain level it's realistic," Dan said impatiently. "So are you going to come here? You're welcome to stay for a while. There are many, many interesting people living here and passing through. All types of spiritual seekers and thinkers."

I struggled to come up with a reason not to go, but I'd backed myself into a corner with all the talk about being aimless.

"OK, I'll stop there for a day or two," I said.

"Excellent," Dan replied excitedly. "Let's see, if you're in Indiana then you're probably about 15 or so hours away. Do you want to say the day after tomorrow? I'll prepare a bed for you."

"OK, that sounds good," I said. "Thanks for calling, and thanks for the invite."

"You're very welcome. But before you come, I want to ask you one other thing. Are you willing to leave all your judgments and preconceptions behind? Can you do that?"

Good lord, this version of Dan was even more intense than the previous one.

"I don't know, Dan. Don't you think a bit of rational judgment is a good thing?"

"I'm asking if you can leave that behind for your visit here," he said flatly.

"Rational judgment?"

"All judgments."

"I'll try."

"Good. There's a certain level of release required here, to really get the full effect."

"OK, got it," I said, ready to wrap up the conversation. "Well, thanks for inviting me, my friend."

"You're welcome," he replied. "I'll see you Monday evening. The place is called Beyond. Ask anyone in Lyons and they'll tell you how to get there."

And with that, he hung up. I shook my head and chuckled to myself, recalling some of my extensive dinner conversations with Dan over the years. He had always fancied himself a philosopher, and as long as I'd known him, he'd been assembling what he called the "ascendant life philosophy." It would encompass both Western and Eastern thought, as well as choice snippets from all the major religions, and it would provide people a step-by-step path to achieving unlimited freedom. He was very adamant that it was not a religion, just a new, systemized way of looking at the universe.

In the year or so before he left Baltimore, though, he had begun to grow disillusioned with the effort. He told me about his moments of "soul despair," when he questioned whether there could ever be any type of life philosophy that would not eventually become corrupted by human greed and ego. He also developed an ugly drinking habit during that period, and nearly every time I saw him he would drink himself to slurring incoherence.

He was one of the only people I'd ever known who had absolutely no natural sense of humor, but he had a basic innocence that made him tolerable to be around. I had no idea what he'd gotten himself into now, though. I had to admit I was intrigued, and I could always make a quick getaway if things got weird.

{ 19 }

Terre Haute

A ROUND 3 PM, I FOUND MYSELF at the tiny Woodridge Motel in Terre Haute. It was broiling at this point, without a hint of a breeze. As I parked the car, I watched the heat rise up in waves off the roof shingles. There was no one in sight—everything seemed asleep except for the insects. I walked inside to the front desk and rang the bell for service. Nothing moved, so I rang it again. This time I heard some rustling in the back. Eventually, after about two or three minutes, a young girl emerged from the back room. She was about 10 or so, wearing a bright green bikini and her hair up in a bun.

"Hi," she said, grinning welcomingly.

"Hi," I said, smiling back. "Are you the one to help me? I'd like to get a room for tonight if I can."

"OK, sure. Where are you from? I always wonder where people are from."

"I'm from back east. Baltimore."

"Wow, I've never been there. But I've heard of it."

"It's a fascinating place."

"Would I like it?"

"I'm not sure. I don't know you yet. What kind of stuff do you like?"

"Animals, jewelry, friends, sleepovers, pizza. That type of stuff."

"Well, there's a huge aquarium there."

"Oooh. I love aquariums!" she squealed. "There's one in Indianapolis, at the zoo. I like the fish that are all full of colors, the ones that swim in the reefs."

"Me too," I said. "Are your parents around? Could they help me check in to a room for tonight?"

"They're taking a quick nap," she replied.

"That sounds nice," I said.

"I'll go wake them up in a minute. A room is 55 dollars, I think."

"That's fine with me."

"I have 44 dollars in my little bank," she said.

"That's a lot."

"No it's not, silly."

She laughed and held out her right hand. There was a ring with a huge fake ruby on her index finger.

"See this ring? Isn't it beautiful?"

"Definitely," I answered.

"I'll be back," she said, turning around and sashaying off to the back room.

I waited for a few minutes, hearing no sound whatsoever. I rang the bell again. I soon heard someone softly rummaging around in the back, and out walked the same young girl. She smiled and placed an open lunchbox filled with gaudy plastic jewelry on the desk.

"There are so many beautiful things in here," she said. "I want to show them to you. Can you please watch it for me for a second?"

She surveyed the group of keys hanging on the wall next to her, then chose one and handed it to me.

"My mom said to just give you the key to room 7. She'll come by the room later to get the money from you. Is that OK?"

"Sure," I said, laughing. "She can come by whenever she wants. Tell her if I'm not there I just went out to get something to eat."

"How old are you and what's your name?" she asked.

"I'm 38 and my name is Byron."

"I'm 9 and my name is Bonnie."

"Well, it's good to meet you, Bonnie."

"I'm wondering... what are you doing here?" she asked, prominently displaying her ruby ring as she twirled a stray lock of hair with her finger.

"You mean here in town?" I replied.

"Yeah."

"I'm just exploring."

"I like to explore too," Bonnie said, grinning. "Whenever I walk around outside in a place I don't know, I look for bugs and worms."

"That sounds great," I replied. "Well Bonnie, it was good talking to you, but I'm gonna go to my room now."

"What's your hurry?" she asked, sounding hurt.

"I actually want to put my stuff in the room and go get something to eat," I said. "I'm hungry."

"OK, that makes sense," she said more gently. "There's a pizza place real close to here, that way. It's called Rollie's. You'll have to drive. It's good. I went there for my birthday this year."

She was pointing west.

"Thanks Bonnie," I said, chuckling. "You're super helpful. I'll probably check it out."

"I'll see you again... later," she replied.

With that, she turned and pranced off, her bouncing bun disappearing beyond the half-open door.

After gathering my belongings from the car, I made my way to room 7 in the stifling heat. I tossed my backpack on the bed and sat down at the small round table by the window to flip through the local business directory that was left there for guests. It did indeed list a Rollie's Pizza nearby, so I walked back to the car and drove the 10 minutes to get there.

There was one other customer sitting in a booth as I walked up to the counter over a floor set up like an airport runway. The entire restaurant had an aviation theme, and the white-bearded man at the counter was wearing aviator sunglasses. He stood patiently as I grabbed a menu and looked it over.

"I think I'll have a small Rollie's Special pizza," I said, stepping up to the counter.

The Rollie's Special apparently had a whole array of toppings.

"Good choice," he said. "Any drink?"

"Just water."

"That'll be $10.17 my friend."

I fished $11 out of my pocket and handed it to him.

"Never seen you in here before, and you don't seem like an Indianan," he said as he handed me my change. "No offense of course."

"None taken," I said. "And you're right, I'm a Marylander, from Baltimore."

"Ah, excellent. I have family in Maryland, on the eastern shore near Chestertown. What brings you here?"

"I'm headed to Lyons, Colorado, near Boulder, to visit a friend."

"Very nice. It's beautiful out there."

He walked off to bring the order to the kitchen, and a voice rang out behind me from the only occupied booth.

"Come here a second."

I wheeled around to look at the speaker, who was a pale, thin man about my age wearing a red t-shirt and cutoff jean shorts. His shirt was adorned with a very detailed drawing of an eagle with its wings spread wide, perched atop a military tank. His hair was pulled back in a ponytail, and he had extremely thick glasses with dark black frames. He motioned toward the empty seat across from him at his booth.

"Come here, I want to talk to you."

His voice was high-pitched and nasally. I walked over hesitantly.

"Have a seat," he said. "Come on now, let's not waste time."

I sat down across from him out of sheer curiosity.

"So I'm not a big believer in fate, as some people call it. I believe shit just happens. But you told Jim up there you come from Baltimore. It just so happens I had a dream about Baltimore last night, and I think you were in it."

He paused to observe my reaction.

"Oh yeah?" I said, a bit rattled but superficially projecting calm.

"Yes I did. I dreamt I flew into Baltimore, then took a cab downtown. I ended up at this weird fucking restaurant, eating octopus. The octopus tentacles were still squirming when I put them in my mouth. Sitting across from me at my table was someone who looked a hell of a lot like you."

A deep chill passed through me, moving almost instantaneously up my spine and out the crown of my head. My booth companion just stared at me, smirking.

"I don't remember what the person said to me, but he kept jabbering and I eventually told him to shut up, that I needed to concentrate on eating. Then he stood up looking really dizzy and fell over, flat on his stomach. I think the guy died—well, I think you died—but the scene changed and suddenly I was in my old girlfriend's place and we were fucking. I'll spare you the details on that."

He paused to take a huge bite of a half-eaten slice of pizza. I leaned back in my seat, at a loss for words.

"What's your name, partner?" he asked as he chewed.

"Byron," I answered softly.

"I'm Tommy. I'm not telling you this to freak you out, I swear. I had to tell you, right? Like I said, I don't believe in weird spiritual shit—I have no interest in it. I've never had something like this happen before."

"Yeah, you had to tell me," I said. "I would have told you if the roles were reversed, no doubt."

"Glad you understand. Let's just chuckle about it and move on, right?"

"Right," I replied hesitantly.

"Now I gotta go, though," he said abruptly. "Picking up the new girlfriend from work. Can't be late."

He stood up, wiped his fingers on a napkin, and held out his hand.

"Good to meet you, Byron," he said as we shook hands firmly.

"Good to meet you, Tommy," I said.

I watched as he walked briskly out the door, his ponytail swaying back and forth.

"Your pizza's ready my friend," Jim called from the counter. "Want me to bring it to you?"

{ 20 }

Tired

BONNIE WAS STANDING OUTSIDE my room when I returned to the motel. She was clutching her lunchbox full of jewelry, and she grinned and waved when she saw me. I was still reeling a bit from my encounter with Tommy.

"Hi Byron," she said, approaching me as I got out of the car. "Do you need to go lie down and rest?"

"Do I look that bad?" I asked, laughing.

"You look tired and scared," she answered sympathetically.

"Well, I guess I should go rest then, just for a little bit," I said.

"The pizza wasn't any good?" she asked, wrinkling her nose.

"The pizza was great," I said. "Thanks so much for recommending it."

"OK good," she replied, smiling and walking away. "Go rest now. I'll bring you some lemonade later."

Suddenly overcome by the desire to sleep, I made my way into the room, cleared off the bed, and flopped down on my stomach. When I became fully conscious again, there was a gentle but persistent knocking on the door, and the light through the window had faded to a dull grey. The digital clock by the bed read 8:15. With a tremendous effort, I got to my feet and opened the door. Bonnie was standing there grinning and holding up a glass of lemonade with ice.

"Here's your lemonade. Doesn't it look good?"

"For sure, thank you Bonnie. This is perfect right now. I'm so thirsty."

I took the glass and drank it nearly to the bottom.

"You were sleepy," she said. "I'm glad you got some rest. Did you have a dream?"

"No. No dreams at all, sadly," I replied.

"I usually have dreams. Sometimes I have nightmares, which I don't like that much. They teach me things though, like how to not be scared."

"That's a great thing to learn—how to not be scared. I'm still learning that."

"Are you scared now?" she asked me.

"Yes, a little."

"Why?"

"It's hard to explain. Just thinking about what might be coming next for me."

"I want you not to worry," she said.

"Talking to you makes me very relaxed," I replied. "You're fun to talk to."

"Thanks!" she said happily, and then started digging around in her lunchbox.

Eventually she pulled out an adult-sized ring with a fake green emerald.

"Hold out your hand," she said.

She gently placed the ring in my open palm.

"Here is something quite beautiful for you. When you wear it, you don't need to worry."

"Thanks Bonnie. I love it," I said, surveying the ring for a moment before dropping it in my pocket.

"Oh, my mom said could you please give me the money for the room?"

"Sure, of course," I said, pulling out my wallet and handing her three 20s. "Don't worry about change."

She stuffed the bills in her lunchbox, then closed and latched it.

"Goodnight Byron. It's my bedtime."

"Goodnight Bonnie."

She turned and walked off toward the office, swinging her lunchbox. Every ten steps or so she'd look back and wave, and I'd wave back. I suddenly felt sleep consume me again, so I shut the door and collapsed back down into the bed.

{ 21 }

The Second Dream that Teaches

I WOKE UP FROM A DEAD SLEEP at 5 AM the next morning, dragged abruptly from a vivid and somewhat disquieting dream. The room was completely dark except for the digital blue glare from the numbers on the alarm clock. My body felt reinvigorated, coursing with a deep and pulsating energy. My mind was focused on recovering every detail of the dream that it could.

It began as an accurate memory from childhood, on a playground when I was in first grade. My school was small then, and part of our playground was the parking lot of a church, which is where we were playing that day. My classmates and I were involved in some sort of vague chase game, with a few of us handing a rolled-up magazine off to one another and the rest of the group trying to chase down the one holding it. I was standing upstream from the center of the chase, observing intently from the outside as I always did. Unexpectedly, my friend Mike broke away from the core group and ran straight toward me, stretching the magazine out in front of him. I froze, and he ran up beside me and forced it into my hand.

"Run!" he shouted.

I remained frozen for another split second, and then started sprinting as fast as I could away from the rest of the group. I quickly neared the edge of the parking lot, which in the dream jutted out over a deep abyss. I couldn't stop myself in time and I toppled off the edge and began free-falling through a massive bank of clouds. As my body picked up speed to a terrifying degree, random bursts of sunlight came streaming through the gloom. Soon the clouds and light faded away and I was left in absolute blackness. I felt as if my body was continually thrusting downward through space, but it was impossible to tell—there was no way to get any sort of bearing. For what seemed like hours, I saw nothing, heard nothing, and felt nothing except sheer panic and dread.

Finally there was a respite, as my speed began to abate and I approached what appeared to be a small cube of light. The edges of the cube were perfectly distinct, and the light was warm gold, producing a sense of incredible energy and peace. The light allowed me to realize that I no longer had a body. I wasn't "me"—I was simply awareness. I hovered next to the cube of light, separate from it but somehow also partially merging with it. There was no struggle here. All the terror that had led me here was erased.

Suddenly the scene changed and I was in my body again, floating just above my childhood home. I was watching my father dangle by one arm from a roof gutter, his fallen ladder lying sideways on the ground beneath him. Blood was pouring down his arm, onto his face, and into his mouth until he finally began to choke on it. My father then transformed into a construction worker in a hard hat who'd just fallen four stories onto his back. He was lying on a sidewalk gagging on the blood filling his lungs. The scene then shifted again, and I was projecting forward through the air about to smack my head on the bottom of a stone staircase. As my nose struck the stone with a sickening thud, my body was suddenly suspended a few hundred feet above a field during what appeared to be the U.S. Civil War. Both sides were charging and retreating with wave after wave of soldiers. Cannonballs and bullets from muskets were mowing men down by the hundreds, with skin and limbs and brains flying through the air and covering the grass. I felt no fear as I gazed down, but instead a surprising sense of peace. What I was witnessing felt inevitable and part of something infinitely vaster than anything I could comprehend with my limited senses. At that point, I woke up.

After mentally recounting all the dream details I could and still seething with energy, I switched on the lamp by the bed, pulled my U.S. map out of my bag, and traced the path of I-70 with my finger. It looked like Topeka, Kansas was close to the exact midpoint between Terre Haute and Lyons, so maybe that was where I should stay. It was about seven hours away, and it was currently 5:30 AM. If I left right then, which I definitely felt like doing, I'd make it to Topeka in the early afternoon with too much time to kill. I looked down at the map again and found the town of Hays, Kansas. That was almost ten hours away, and would get me that much closer to Lyons. Hays it was.

The mundane activity of perusing the map helped settle my mind, and I was beginning to feel somewhat normal again, if a little wired. I was definitely well-rested. Counting my nap, I'd slept for nearly twelve hours. I started assembling my things on the bed, and then headed to the bathroom to take a quick cold shower.

Before driving off in the pre-dawn darkness, I wrote out a note for Bonnie and pushed it under the office door along with my room key.

"Dear Bonnie, Thanks so much for the beautiful ring you gave me and for being so nice to me. I will put the ring on when I feel sad or nervous. Tell your parents I liked staying in their motel. I hope you always have great dreams, or at least dreams you learn from. Your friend, Byron."

{ 22 }

Onward Again

A ROUND 7:15 I REALIZED I was getting hungry, so I pulled off at a Denny's in Effingham, Illinois. I sat down next to a small group of elderly men who'd likely been having coffee there together for years.

"These younger generations are just out there without any base," one of them was opining as he cradled his coffee mug. "They just want to float out there with nothing tying them down, but then they've got nothing to hold onto. No church, no community, no nothing. But you've got to have *something*."

The rest of the group mumbled their assent.

"There are things that don't change and won't ever change," the same man continued. "Those are the things to hold onto. Not sure what happens when those get abandoned, but it can't be good."

The same general theme was then restated by each of member of the group in succession, with slight alterations of detail. Essentially, they were all worried.

As I walked back to my car after paying the check, my cell phone rang. It was a North Carolina number I didn't recognize.

"Hello?" I said as I sat down in the driver's seat.

"Hi Byron," came a familiar voice.

"It's you."

"Yes, it's me," said Samantha. "Are you wondering why I'm calling?"

"Yes, but it doesn't really matter. I'm glad to hear from you regardless."

"I'm calling because I was lying in bed thinking about you. Where are you?"

"Effingham, Illinois. Where are you?"

"Still in Pittsburgh, in the same bed. I'm here through Tuesday. I wanted to call to say goodbye in case we don't see each other again."

"What are you planning?" I asked, only half joking.

"Nothing like that," she replied, chuckling. "It's just a feeling. But it would be OK if we don't see each other again. I have pure memories of you."

"Same here. Not that I'd mind seeing you again, of course."

"Do you want to keep it like that?" she asked. "Should we stop talking now?"

"Not necessarily," I responded.

"OK, one more minute on the phone, but we won't talk."

She started breathing in and out, slowly, about one full breath every ten seconds. She stopped after a minute or so.

"Now you'll remember that sound when you think of me," she said.

"Yes, I will."

"What do you see in front of you?" she asked.

"A thin little tree with only a few leaves on it, and behind that a Rite Aid. I'm in a parking lot."

"OK, I have it."

She was silent for a few seconds, and then the call dropped. I decided to let her call me back, but she never did. After a few minutes, I started up the car and drove back toward the highway.

I had a fleeting, eerie sense that I'd done all of this before—the early wake-up at the motel, the breakfast at Denny's, the call with Samantha in the parking lot, the drive west on 70. This soon passed and I was left with a vague feeling of nostalgia. I scanned through the radio stations before settling on an Elton John song I couldn't remember the name of.

I sat back and relaxed into the long journey ahead. Hays was about nine hours away.

{ 23 }

Hays

I PULLED THE CURTAINS CLOSED in my room at the Hays Motel 6. It was almost 6:30 PM, and I'd just returned from eating a fried chicken dinner at Al's Chickenette in town. I was suddenly brutally tired again, as I had been the evening before in Terre Haute, so I decided to lie down for a brief nap.

I was awoken out of a deep sleep by a loud knock on the door. I sat bolt upright, unsure of when or where I was. I wiped the drool from my chin and tottered unsteadily over to the door.

"Who is it?" I asked suspiciously.

"Next door neighbor person. Name's Alex," came a gruff but cheery voice.

I opened the door cautiously, leaving the chain attached. It was still quite light out, so I couldn't have slept that long. A grinning, bearded face appeared in the gap.

"Hey there friend, I'm inviting you to come out and join us for a drink."

I hesitated for a moment, then surrendered.

"OK, give me a sec. Just woke up from a quick nap."

"Sure, sure," Alex said. "We'll be right out here."

I shut the door and opened the curtains. Alex was standing with his back to me, conversing somewhat heatedly with someone who was just out of view. He was wearing a black leather vest and jeans, with a cigarette behind one ear. I went to the bathroom to splash some water on my face, then threw on my shoes and walked outside. Alex grinned when he saw me and motioned for me to have a seat. His companion was a very young girl with bleached blonde hair, dressed in a pink track suit and white sneakers. She couldn't have been more than 18 or 19, while Alex was probably about my age. The girl smiled at me apathetically as I sat down on the dusty white plastic chair in front of my room and took in our surroundings.

A bare dirt field was spread out in front of us until it ran up against I-70, with a small park and nature area extending out a bit past the highway. Beyond that, a series of flat fields stretched out as far as the eye could see.

"What's your name?" asked Alex, pouring some Jim Beam into a clear plastic cup and handing it to me.

"Byron," I replied, hoisting the cup in thanks and then taking a sip.

"Like I said before, I'm Alex. She's Deb."

He waved his arm half-heartedly in the direction of his companion, who was now staring blankly down at the ground.

"Deb doesn't like to talk to new people. She's scared."

Deb just shook her head and said nothing.

"What are you doing here in Hays, friend?" Alex asked, plopping down in the chair next to me.

"Passing through on my way to Colorado, actually," I replied.

"Passing through. Passing through. Always passing through," said Alex, suddenly seeming aggravated. "Motherfuckers always just passing through."

He stared out over the dirt field toward the highway, grinding his teeth. I shifted uneasily in my chair and took another sip of whiskey.

"Whatever," he said, smirking. "Who gives a fuck, right?"

"What do you do in Hays?" I ventured to ask.

"Whatever I need to do," he replied. "I'm between houses right now, which is why I'm here drinking with you outside a motel room. Don't get me wrong, I'm grateful to be alive, you know. Almost died a few times this year, so I'll take drinking outside a motel room. No fucking doubt."

He took a huge swig of whiskey straight from the bottle.

"What do you do here, Deb?" I asked, looking over at her.

She was sitting on her hands, still staring down at the pavement.

"I just hang out, I guess," she said softly.

"She doesn't do jackshit," said Alex loudly. "She gets to cruise by on her looks."

"I pull my weight when I have to," she replied, glaring over at him with obvious irritation.

Alex scoffed and leaned back in his seat.

"I call bullshit on that right there," he said almost reflectively.

He took the cigarette from behind his ear and lit it, then looked over at me.

"Byron, let me ask you something. What would you do if you suspected some bitch was cheating on you, but you couldn't exactly prove it? You haven't caught her in the act or anything, but you just know... you know?"

The conversation was going places I wasn't prepared to follow. Alex sensed my hesitation.

"I get it, I get it. You think I'm talking about Deb right in front of her but I swear I'm not. This bitch ain't the one cheating on me, or at least she better not be. I'm talking about another bitch I just kicked to the curb a few days ago. So now that one's saying I'm being unfair, that I have no proof, but I've always just followed my gut on most shit, and my gut is telling me she's fucking around."

"Well, I'd probably ask her point blank what's going on," I began hesitantly. "I'd ask her to be perfectly honest, and if she seemed like she was telling the truth, I'd accept it, assuming there was no real evidence she cheated."

"So you're saying give her one more chance to tell me the full truth? Look her straight in the eye and ask her?"

"Sure, why not?"

"OK, that sounds reasonable," Alex replied, taking a long drag of his cigarette and exhaling the smoke through his nose. "I'll try it."

"Well what about me then?" Deb suddenly snarled, scowling at Alex.

"What *about* you?" he said dismissively.

"You told me you and Donna were done."

"And I told you the goddamn truth. We were done, and we're probably still done, but I'm gonna take this man's advice and give her one last chance to tell me the truth."

"Well fuck you then!" Deb screamed.

She tossed her empty plastic cup at Alex, barely grazing his shoulder. Alex stood up and punched her square in the left temple as hard as he could, knocking her sideways off her chair onto the pavement. She lay there sprawled out for a few seconds, moaning and twitching slightly, only partially conscious. Alex spun around and glared at me.

"Don't even think about reporting me on this. It would not end well for you."

I stood completely still, trying to remain calm. As he bent down to check on Deb, I looked around frantically to see if anyone had seen what happened. It was now late evening and the sun was setting behind us, forming elongated shadows that spilled across the parking lot. There was no one else on our side of the motel, unfortunately. Deb was now sitting up and rubbing the side of her head.

Alex suddenly turned around and bounded over to me. He stood directly in front of me for a few seconds, staring me down, then pulled a knife from somewhere inside his jeans and held it up to my throat.

"Go back to your room, shut the door, and don't you fucking dare call anyone," he hissed in my ear.

I did what he said. As I sat on the bed, I heard some loud rustling in the room next door, followed by two car doors slamming, an engine starting, and a car backing up and speeding off. After a minute or so, I left the room and nervously surveyed the scene. There was still no one on our side of the motel, and the only sound was the steady stream of cars on I-70. The door to their room was partially open, and I could see beer cans, liquor bottles, and empty food containers strewn everywhere.

Ease

I returned to my room, packed up my things, and headed to the motel office to let them know what happened. The manager called the cops, and I gave a statement over the phone. Then it was back to the highway for a few hours, or at least until I got too tired to drive anymore.

{ 24 }

The Third Dream that Teaches

I WAS BEGINNING TO FADE A BIT as I approached Goodland, Kansas around 10 PM, so I pulled off at a Super 8. When I got to my room, I pulled out my map and plotted the time I'd have to drive the next day. Not long at all—maybe three and a half hours. After completing my bathroom behavior, I turned off the light and let my body sink into the bed, releasing the adrenaline and fear churned up by my encounter with Alex and Deb. I wondered where they were at that moment. Were they fighting? Making up? Sleeping? In jail? Driving around to avoid the cops?

Sleep began to descend, and with it came a vague memory of my father picking me up off the sidewalk after a fall from my bike. My knee was bleeding, and he was assuring me there was nothing to worry about.

We'd clean it up when we got inside the house. My father abruptly transformed into Alex grinning down at me, and Alex then transformed into what I can only describe as a dark clump of matter in the shape of a human. This dark matter was cradling me in its "arms" outside of my parents' house, and I felt only a strange sense of calm. Soon the clump of matter grew and morphed to cover most of my vision. The only thing left that was not this blackness was a small strip of backyard where a baby resembling my old neighbor Jason was crawling in the grass. Soon even this was overtaken and I was encased in the darkness. All was silent here, with no sensation whatsoever. I let the peace of nothingness overtake me, but I soon heard something breathing in my ear. Whatever it was started to hum softly, which then turned into a sort of song, which then turned into an ear-piercing scream.

When I came to, the glowing blue clock digits said 11:15, so I'd been in this half-sleep state for about 20 minutes. I sat up in bed and realized that my mind was totally empty, as if it had been wiped clean. I tried to reach out and grasp a thought, any thought, but there was nothing there. It was off-putting at first, but then I stopped resisting and just let myself ease into this new territory. It was neither pleasant nor unpleasant—it just was. It felt like I sat there in that state for hours, but when I looked back over at the clock, it was only 11:25. The thoughts then came rushing back in suddenly, flooding the brain at first, but then gently rippling around and coming to rest in a kind of tenuous equilibrium, like a bucket of water poured into a bathtub. Sleep felt like the natural next step, so I dropped my head back down on the pillow and shut my eyes.

It was morning when I woke, and the sun was streaming in through a narrow gap in the curtains. I sat up and stretched, feeling reasonably refreshed. No dreams this time. I got up and started brewing the shitty one-serving motel coffee, and then hopped in the shower. There was no hot water whatsoever, which eliminated any lingering grogginess. I wrapped myself in the bath towel and sat down on the end of the bed, sipping the wretched coffee and thinking about the retreat center and Laura Day. Where had I heard that name before?

{ 25 }

Beyond

I T WAS A LITTLE PAST NOON when I pulled onto the narrow dirt road outside of Lyons. Every few hundred feet or so, there was another wooden sign painted with dark green letters—Beyond. Above the name was an arrow pointing upward. The road wound back and forth, skirting the side of mountain for a bit and then veering off through a fairly dense forest. The farther I drove down the road, the more uneasy I became, despite the undeniable beauty of my surroundings. Where was I going anyway? How isolated was this place? Who was I going to meet there? Would it be easy for me to leave? All I really knew about it was that Dan had been happily staying there, completely cut off from his family and friends.

Eventually the forest ended and a grassy hillside appeared about a quarter mile ahead, dotted with a variety of tents, teepees, and buildings. There were about fifty or so people milling around—hanging laundry, gardening, lying down on blankets, or just walking in the grass. A sign appeared that said Visitor Parking Lot, with an arrow pointing to a little patch of grass with two other cars parked on it. I pulled up next to a white Toyota Prius and stepped out into Beyond.

It was a beautiful afternoon, with a few billowing white clouds spread out overhead and a soft breeze stirring the branches of the nearby pines. I saw a figure exit one of the buildings and start hurrying over to meet me. It was Dan, dressed in a loose white shirt, baggy green pants, and an elaborate beaded necklace. His black hair was long and flowing, and he was grinning from ear to ear.

"Welcome, Byron," came his deep and booming voice. "Welcome. I'm so glad you're here."

He came up and gave me a long hug, leaning his tall frame over to rest his head tenderly on my shoulder. The moment lasted long enough that I had to gently but firmly nudge him away. He took a step back, put his hands on my shoulders, and looked me deeply in the eyes.

"It's OK to relax now, Byron. You've arrived."

"Thanks for inviting me, Dan."

"Of course I invited you. I felt like you needed it, and Laura Day told me you needed it too."

"Laura Day told you?" I asked incredulously.

"Yes, she felt it. I told her what you told me, about your aimless journey. But don't worry about any of that right now. You'll meet her soon and she'll tell you. Now go get your stuff together and follow me. You'll be sleeping in the bunk below me."

I grabbed my backpack from the car and followed Dan as we made our way toward the group of buildings. After passing and greeting a wide variety of retreaters, we entered a long bunkhouse just past the building Dan had originally emerged from. Inside there were about twenty bunk beds, with backpacks, bags, clothes, books, and spiritual trinkets strewn everywhere. Dan led me to the far side of the room and motioned to a clean bottom bunk.

"Here you are, right below me," he said, smiling and patting me on the back.

I tossed my backpack on the bed, and then leaned down to test the mattress with my hands. It was unexpectedly firm, likely a decent quality foam.

"Things here are high quality," Dan said. "That's part of the experience."

He gazed up at the ceiling and smiled wistfully, seemingly reliving a memory. After a few seconds, he looked back over at me with a gleam in his eye.

"Come on, let's go sit outside in the grass and catch up."

"OK, lead the way," I replied.

He led me outside to a spot on the hill just behind the bunkhouse.

"Why don't you lie back on the grass and look up at the sky?" he said. "Just lie back and relax and don't think about anything at all if you don't want to."

I leaned back with my hands behind my head, reclining flat against the sloped hillside. The clouds floated slowly by from left to right, outlined with particular clarity on the deep blue Colorado sky.

"In there I said we should catch up, but I didn't necessarily mean that," Dan said. "The past can become irrelevant if that's what you'd like."

He was sitting cross-legged, watching me with a slight smile.

"No, let's catch up," I said. "I want to hear more about how you ended up here."

"Hmm, where to start," Dan replied, running his hand through his hair. "Well, I think you remember my dark time in Baltimore a few years back. I felt completely lost and disillusioned, and I was drinking myself into a stupor every night. My life philosophy project began to seem unrealistic to me, a naïve pipe dream. One night I decided I would either kill myself, or I'd leave town and go searching for something meaningful outside of all my previous experience. Something that would hopefully allow me to escape my rational mind in some way."

He paused for a few seconds to greet someone passing by.

"Don't worry, I'll introduce you to everyone later. Anyway, I drove out west on 70, just like you, and eventually ended up in Boulder. This was almost exactly two years ago. I rented an apartment there, started working in a recycling plant, and lived a pretty simple existence for a few months. I was drinking, but not as much, and I stopped obsessing every day about the life philosophy. In fact, I dropped it completely. I still felt empty though, and aimless. Nothing really interested me, and I didn't socialize with anyone outside of work."

Someone whistled loudly off in the distance, likely for a dog.

"So one evening I was drinking a beer at a bar in town and an older woman dressed entirely in white came and sat next to me. Before even saying hello, she told me to relax and that I could say whatever I wanted to her. Very quickly I started telling her all about myself, how I got there and how my life felt aimless and pointless, and she told me that I was lucky. 'Stop whining and start seeing the blank slate in front of you,' she told me."

"And this was Laura Day?" I asked.

"Yes. She was there for a book signing."

A book signing! That was how I knew the name—Marion had a few of her books in our old apartment. I recalled one in particular that she'd left in the bathroom for months, called *Destroying the Fortress*. I think I picked it up a few times to read the back cover, but I never opened it.

"She told me about Beyond, and I came here that weekend," Dan continued. "Then I moved out of my apartment a few weeks later and have been here ever since."

"What made you want to live here?"

"Many different things. The main reason is that it feels consistently new. It's peaceful here, but something or someone is always popping up to overturn your expectations. There is challenge."

The way Dan said the word "challenge" made me vaguely uncomfortable. I sat up and stroked a stray piece of grass between my index finger and thumb.

"You're worried about something," Dan said. "I see it in the way you bunch up your eyebrows. Don't start with that."

I chuckled awkwardly and stood up, brushing the grass off my back.

"OK, I'll stop," I said, smirking. "I swear."

{ 26 }

Laura Day

A FEW MINUTES LATER, Dan was leading me downhill along a winding path through a dense pine forest. We'd left everyone else behind on the hill clearing, and now all was silent, with the sunlight streaming through the trees and glinting off the bed of pine needles under our feet. The smell of the clean forest air was exhilarating, as was the prospect of getting to meet the famous Laura Day.

"Just a few more minutes," said Dan. "You're going to love her house. Everyone is welcome there at any time."

The path took a hard turn to the left and started heading slightly uphill, with a building eventually becoming partially visible through the trees. Soon we passed through a huge, elaborately carved wooden gateway in the form of an oval. The bottom of the oval was buried beneath the ground, and there was an antique brass lantern hanging from its top. In front of us loomed an imposing wooden house with green shutters and a massive portico overhanging the doorway. New pine trees had been planted in straight rows on either side of the pathway leading to the front steps, with Tibetan prayer flags strewn throughout their branches. We walked up to the deep red front door and knocked. After about thirty seconds, we heard a female voice bellow out from inside.

"Yes? Who is it?"

"Laura, it's Dan."

The door opened a crack.

"What the fuck are you doing here, Dan?" the voice asked irritably.

He hesitated for a moment, then pressed on.

"We're here for a quick visit. My friend Byron is here. I told you about him."

"I'm trying to write here, Dan. No one is visiting today. I thought I put the word out."

"Oh," Dan stuttered, embarrassed. "I hadn't heard that. I'm sorry Laura, we'll come back tomorrow then."

He looked over at me and shrugged his shoulders, his face flushed red.

"Wait," said the voice. "Let me ask Byron a question. Byron, are you out there?"

"Yes," I answered hesitantly.

"What do you think goes on here? Be honest with me. You probably think this is a standard issue cult we're running here, right?"

"Yes, I do," I said flatly, surprising myself a bit with my own candor.

The door then abruptly swung open to reveal a grey-haired woman of indeterminate age—she could have been anywhere from 45 to 65—dressed in a billowing white shirt and jeans. She smiled broadly when she saw me, her blue eyes gleaming.

"I like honesty," she said warmly. "I apologize for being a bitch just now. I'm just testing the situation, looking for cracks."

She held out her hand for me to shake.

"Do you like to shake hands or hug?" she asked. "I can do either."

I took her hand and shook it with a sly smile. She laughed loudly and executed a slight bow in my direction. She then turned to Dan, gave him a brief hug and kiss on the cheek, and placed her hands on his shoulders.

"Dan, can you leave us alone now? I'm sure Byron can find his way back if he needs to."

Dan flushed red again, smiling awkwardly.

"Sure I can. Byron, I'll see you later this evening."

He turned and walked quickly away down the pine tree path and through the oval gateway. We watched him silently until he disappeared into the forest.

"Shall we?" Laura said, gesturing toward the open doorway.

I followed her through a large foyer, down a hallway, and out into a bright, open living room area with a soaring, slanted wood-beam ceiling. There was a massive fireplace facing us as we entered, with long white couches along all the walls. In the center of the room was one of the most bizarre and spectacular rugs I had ever seen. It was a huge circle decorated in the center with a vivid depiction of a jungle scene, with the ruins of a pyramid jutting out from beneath a mass of vines. Around the edges of the rug were rings of crude symbols I didn't recognize, almost like hieroglyphs. They repeated in layer after layer, forming about twenty concentric circles around the central scene.

"You like the rug?" Laura asked, sitting down on one of the couches and watching me intently.

"Yes," I replied. "I've never seen anything like it."

"I had it made for me. When you're done looking, come sit over here and talk to me. Actually, never mind, let's sit on the rug."

She stood up and walked over to me, grabbing my hand to lead me to the center of the pyramid. We sat down cross-legged facing each other.

"Ask me anything," she said, staring at me.

"OK. What is it you're doing here?" I asked, determined not to be intimidated.

"Doing where?"

"Here, with Beyond... bringing all these people to this place."

"I've set up an experiment. I have a lot of money and supposed influence, and I want to use it to wake people up, over and over. Because once you 'wake up,'" she said, using air quotes, "you typically need to continue to wake up every single day."

"What do you mean by wake up?" I asked.

"Do you think you're awake?" she asked instead of answering the question.

"I have no idea, but something's definitely happening with me," I replied.

"Like what?" she asked matter-of-factly.

"Well, back in Baltimore, I kept having feelings—or intuitions, really—that got so strong that I just up and quit my job and headed out this way. And now a lot of other things have started mixing in... odd health issues and coincidences and dreams and memories. Basically, everything I thought I knew is being overturned and I don't know what the fuck to do next."

"OK, you're definitely waking up," she said, chuckling, "but you're thinking about it too hard, which is understandable but unfortunate. Do you feel like you want to stay here for a bit, to figure it out? Because you're welcome to. You can stay in the house with me. Bunks are for suckers."

I laughed uneasily.

"Well, I'm not sure I want to stay here yet."

"That's only natural. You don't know me."

"My ex-wife had a few of your books," I replied.

"Did you read any of them? Hell, it doesn't matter," she said. "I write them as an exercise."

"What's the point of the exercise?"

"I guess it's to keep track of the shit that comes through me. People can just take whatever they can use and discard the rest. If you choose to discard every-thing, I don't care. No offense taken."

"Well I didn't even open the books, to be honest. I think Marion and I were fighting so much during that time that I didn't want anything to do with what she was reading. She probably spouted off some of your quotes to me when we were arguing."

"If she did, I'm sorry," said Laura, laughing.

"Not your fault," I replied. "She loved to pull out all sorts of spiritual quotes as part of her ongoing mission to show me all my weaknesses."

I paused to gaze through the enormous windows on either side of the fireplace. The tall pines outside were swaying gently in the late afternoon light.

"Let me ask you, why do you think you're here right now?" Laura asked, staring over at me intently.

"I'm trying to stop thinking about things like that," I answered.

"Meaning what?"

"Meaning, I could speculate on why I'm here talking to you right now, but what's the point? If there's one

thing I've learned over the past few weeks, it's that I
have no idea what's going on."

"You don't know shit about shit," she said, chuckling. "I'm there every day."

"Right," I replied, laughing.

"I'm done feeling like I need to know more," she
said. "I'd like to know more, sure, but only because it's
fun. I don't need it like I did when I was younger. I can
take in knowledge like it's food, digest it, let it nourish
me a little, then shit it out. And once I shit it out, it's
gone. Knowledge and learning are different though.
Knowledge is acquisitional, learning is not. You learn
every moment of every day if you let yourself, even if all
you're learning is that you don't know shit about shit.
Or you could learn to stop following a certain pattern
of thought, or to stop dwelling on specific things that
happened to you in the past. As you get older, learning
is mostly about paring away all the uselessness."

She paused and looked down at the rug.

"So do you want to stay in the house for a few days?"
she asked.

"Who do you let stay in the house?"

"I invite someone whenever the mood strikes me,"
she replied. "Why?"

"Is anyone staying here now?"

"No, you're special."

"Dan told me everyone is welcome in your house at
any time."

"True and not true, like everything. Anyone can feel free to come knock on the door to see if I'm good with people coming in that day. Sometimes I let people come in, sometimes I don't. Honestly, a lot of the people here are insufferable."

"So then I'll ask again, what are you doing here? Why did you set this place up?"

"I told you, it's an experiment," she replied. "I want to continuously wake people up, including myself. Unfortunately most people are not ready to be woken up over and over. It's too uncomfortable. This especially applies to quote-unquote spiritual people."

"Do you like people?" I asked.

"If you're ready to be honest with me, I love you. Otherwise no, I don't really like people. Which leads to me staying alone in this big quiet house, separate from all the spiritual campers out there."

"Why are you asking me to stay here?"

"Why do you think?" she asked. "You're honest, and I love you for it. Plus I recognize something in you, something familiar."

"OK then, I'll stay, at least for tonight. As an experiment."

"Good. You should stay as long as you want, and then get on your way and allow this shift that's coming to destroy and rebuild you. You're really just delaying it by staying here, but that's OK. It's probably either death or near death, I hate to tell you."

My breath caught in my throat and I sat bolt upright.

"Why do you say that?" I asked, my voice quavering.

Laura put her hand on my knee to steady its shaking.

"Don't be scared of it. It's going to happen no matter what... whatever it is."

I stood up and walked a few steps toward the fireplace, my brain churning. She was right—something inevitable had been put into motion.

"Don't worry," she said. "Go get your stuff from the bunkhouse and bring it back. Tell Dan you're sleeping here for a few nights."

I sat down on the edge of one of the couches and tried to focus. OK, I'd stay for a bit. Two or three days max. What the hell? I was definitely in it now.

{ 27 }

What Do You Think You're Supposed to Be?

W HEN I EMERGED FROM THE WOODS, I saw that Dan was anxiously waiting for me out-side the bunkhouse. He waved and ran over when he spotted me.

"So how did that go?" he asked breathlessly. "Laura can be pretty challenging when she wants to be, but it's all for the good."

"It went fine," I answered. "Actually, I'm going to grab my stuff now and head back to the house. She in-vited me to stay there."

"Really?" he asked with obvious surprise.

At that point, a shirtless man with long dirty-blonde dreadlocks and baggy tan pants walked up to us, grin-ning and holding out his arms to Dan for a hug. When this first hug was over, he approached me for a hug as well. I complied somewhat reluctantly.

"Welcome," he said warmly as we embraced. "What's your name brother?"

"I'm Byron, an old friend of Dan's."

"Very cool. I'm Colin."

He stood back to take a full survey of me.

"So how do you like our little place so far?" he asked.

"I think it's beautiful," I replied.

"That's it? Just beautiful?"

"You were expecting something more?"

"Well, yeah. Can you feel the energy in this place? Intense, isn't it?"

"Yes, very," I answered to appease him.

"Laura built on this spot for a reason. She sensed it. The dreams I have here, good god. They are incredible."

He smiled broadly, then threw his head back and held out his arms.

"You gotta drink in the sun here," he said blissfully.

"How did you end up here?" I asked him.

"It just called to me. I ended up here about three years ago and never looked back. I can barely remember what came before. Pain, confusion, narcotics. I was drifting."

"And this place has resolved all of that for you?"

"Being here has allowed me to resolve things for myself."

"So you've been here three years? You don't feel like you want to go back to regular society?"

Colin smiled and scratched his scraggly beard.

"You like to ask questions, huh? I'm here because I want to be here more than anywhere else. This place allows me to become what I'm supposed to be."

"What do you think you're supposed to be?" I asked.

Colin folded his arms over his chest and sighed.

"And now, gentlemen, I'm off," he said, ignoring my question. "Gotta go prep dinner for the crew. Great to meet you, Byron. Great to see you, Dan."

With that, he bounded off toward a building on the upper end of the clearing.

"Colin's a good guy," Dan said, smiling. "Now, you need to go get your stuff, right?"

He turned and led the way toward the bunkhouse. When we entered, there was a young girl meditating cross-legged in the center of the floor between the bunks. After a few seconds, she bowed to the ground with her hands flat against the floor, then sat up and looked at us. She had curly blonde hair and huge round eyes, and couldn't have been more than 10 or 11 years old.

"Hi Dan," she said calmly. "Who's your friend?"

"Carly, this is Byron," Dan replied. "Byron, meet Carly."

Ease

Carly nodded in my direction with a slight smile. I nodded back.

"What are you doing here?" she asked me dispassionately.

"I came to visit Dan," I answered, a bit taken aback by her tone. "And also to check out what's going on here."

"Do you like it?"

"Yes I do, so far."

"Are you confused about it?"

"What do you mean?"

"I mean, are you confused about what we're doing here?"

"What *are* you doing here?" I asked, prying as usual.

"Well, I'm here because my parents came here five years ago. But that's not what you're asking."

"No, not really," I replied.

"We're here to learn how to live without fear."

"And Laura teaches you how to do that?"

"Yes," Carly answered, standing up. "You should come and hear one of her talks."

"Do you ever go to her house?" I asked.

"No, I'd never do that," Carly said, shaking her head and frowning.

"Why not?"

"I don't think she'd want me to."

"But Dan told me everyone is welcome there at any time," I said, glancing over at Dan with mock surprise.

"It's true, everyone is always welcome at her house," he said confidently.

Without saying anything more, Carly abruptly strode past us out the door, and then briefly turned to look back through the screen after the door had slammed shut.

"Bye now," she said almost tauntingly.

Dan chuckled as she walked off.

"Carly is an interesting one," he said. "Wise beyond her years, I think."

"Indeed," I replied, smiling but even more confused about the place than ever.

{ 28 }

Further Beyond

W HEN I RETURNED TO LAURA'S HOUSE around
6 PM, she had dinner ready. She'd cooked
up a vegetable stir fry—mushrooms, broccoli, spinach, and tofu seasoned with ginger and soy
sauce and served over brown rice. We sat down to eat
in the kitchen, which was on the opposite side of the
house from the living room. The kitchen had a similar-
ly soaring ceiling, with a massive skylight that caused
the white floor and walls to radiate brightly.

Laura had been relatively quiet since I'd returned to
the house, and she kept her eyes fixed on me as we
slowly chewed her food. I finished my meal and leaned
back in my chair, gazing up through the skylight at the
evening sky above, where the clouds now
stretched out into long, thin wisps. The house was
completely silent other than the soft ticking of a clock

on the wall behind me, and I was lulled into a sort of trance as the lines of clouds drifted by.

"So here we are," Laura said suddenly, her voice echoing off the bare walls of the room. "Is it again? It feels like again."

"You mean we've done this before?" I asked.

"Maybe," she replied. "What do you think?"

"I've had that feeling a few times lately," I admitted.

"Might have been in a dream."

"True."

We both went quiet again, staring up at the sky, and I felt a deep sense of peace descend on me. We were floating freely through space, completely unmoored. If we had done all this before, it was perfectly fine, and if this was the very first occasion, it was equally fine. All the circumstances that had led us here—or had led anyone to where they were in this moment—were condensed into a microscopic particle of collective memory that could be flicked away like ash from a cigarette.

"Do you feel that?" Laura asked softly, almost whispering.

"Yes," I answered.

I felt entirely unencumbered, as if the last of what had come before had been chiseled away. I became aware of my consciousness spreading out broadly through space and time, while simultaneously resting within my body in that kitchen, utterly content. As the minutes passed, unheeded by us, the color of the evening sky overhead began to subtly shift from light blue to pink.

Eventually I began to feel my body again, and the fairly urgent need to urinate. Across the table, Laura was sitting upright with her eyes closed, meditating. I stood up unsteadily and made my way out of the kitchen and down the hall to the bathroom we'd passed on the way in. When I returned to the kitchen, Laura was still sitting motionless in her chair. I gathered the dishes and glasses from the table and brought them to the sink, trying to remain as quiet as possible.

"Don't worry about the dishes," Laura said softly without moving or opening her eyes.

I left everything in the sink and returned to my chair. It was now almost 8:30 according to the wall clock, and the kitchen was growing darker by the minute. Laura suddenly glanced over at me and smiled.

"I'm back," she said.

"Where'd you go?" I asked.

"Same place you were."

"I'm not sure where I was."

"You've been there before, no?" she asked.

"I have no idea. It felt somewhat familiar, if you could even use a word like that to describe what it was."

Laura yawned loudly and stood up, stretching her arms up toward the ceiling.

Stephen Intlekofer

"Let's go have an after-dinner drink," she said, grabbing my hand and leading me off through the dark hallway toward the living room.

{ 29 }

A Conversation

"SO ARE YOU COMFORTABLE YET?" Laura asked me as we lounged on one of the long white couches, sipping Laphroaig scotch neat.

The only light in the room came from a floor lamp to my right and the nearly full moon shining beyond the tall windows bordering the fireplace. The far corners of the room were completely submerged in shadow.

"No," I answered, chuckling. "Not yet. Plus, don't you thrive on making people uncomfortable?"

"Oh that's right, I do," she replied, smirking.

"Honestly, I'm not sure what you want from me," I said. "Why have you singled me out?"

"You have a problem with the attention?" she asked.

"No, I'm just curious what you see in me."

"Don't question it," she replied. "Let it go."

"That's easy to say."

I took a sip of scotch and gazed out at the moon. I could feel Laura staring at me.

"You can stop your analyzing and speculating," she said gently. "It's not worth it. You were there in the kitchen just now. What more do you need?"

"You don't think some analysis is natural, and necessary?" I responded. "I also think it's natural to be a little skeptical, especially in a place like this."

"Sure, just don't make it your default."

"This whole place looks and feels like a cult to me," I said. "But being here in this house with you feels familiar, and I have no idea why. I guess that's why I'm uncomfortable... I'm confused."

"Confusion is our natural state at this stage. I'm confused every day, and then I get little moments of clarity that I try to string together."

"Your people out there don't feel like you're confused. They seem to think you've got all the answers for them."

"I can communicate my direct experience to them, and I can ever-so-lovingly undermine whatever they feel certain about. If they're into that process, they stick around. If not, they leave."

"Do you consider this a cult?"

"I don't even really know what that means, but I'm not as scared of the term as everyone else seems to be. It's a label. In any case, I doubt I fit anyone's tradition-

al definition of a cult leader. And I promise I don't re-
cruit anyone... they just show up here."

"Do you have any tenets? Any core beliefs?" I asked.

"Not really. All is paradox. That's one. A few more
too that are slipping my mind at the moment."

"Can the people here leave whenever they want?"

"No, of course not. They're here forever," she said,
laughing. "It's almost like you really want this to be
some crazy Jonestown cult thing. Would that make
things easier for you, to just call bullshit on the whole
thing and never look back? What are you so scared of?"

"I'm not scared."

"Yes you are, and it's fine to admit it."

"Well, you seem to know me, and that scares me a
little."

"We know each other," she said, abruptly standing
up and walking to the center of the jungle rug. "You
know me just as well as I know you. Look just beneath
the surface of all that conventional fear and you'll see
it."

She stood facing me in the center of the rug with
her arms crossed and her legs spread shoulder-width.

"I've stood here before in this exact position, looking
at you on that couch," she said. "You told me about a
dream you had when you were a kid."

"Shit. I don't think I'm ready for this discussion," I
replied, smiling awkwardly and shifting in my seat.

"Can we talk about something mundane, like the plan for tomorrow?"

"Sure," she answered, laughing and softening her stance. "I'm giving a talk at 9 AM in the dining hall. You should come for shits and giggles."

"What's the topic?"

"Don't know yet."

She glided over to the fireplace and adjusted a small Buddha statue on the mantle. I took another long sip of scotch and leaned back against the couch cushion.

"Fortunately there's nowhere else we can be except here," she said cryptically while stroking the statue.

She turned around and gazed at me almost lovingly.

"I see you very clearly," she said. "Very clearly. And I can tell you there's absolutely nothing to worry about."

I stared back at her without blinking, testing the moment.

"And now," she said without taking her eyes off me, "I'm off to bed."

She grinned and walked out of the room without another word, apparently forgetting that she'd never told me where I was supposed to sleep. I suppose it was a subtle invitation to follow her, but I decided to lie down right there on the couch. I grabbed a stray cushion and a colorful South American blanket covered with geometrical patterns, and then switched off the lamp and watched as the moonlight bathed the room. Very quickly my eyes grew heavy...

{ 30 }

The Talk

I WOKE UP just after dawn. Through the towering windows abutting the fireplace, the pine trees were silhouetted against the brightening sky. I stood up and stretched my arms up to the ceiling and then down to the ground. I felt surprisingly light and refreshed. The house was completely silent, and my empty glass of scotch was overturned at the foot of the couch. I folded up my blanket and replaced it on the back cushion, and then picked up my glass and made my way to the kitchen. When I got there, I found a note on the counter next to the sink:

"Good morning Byron, Grab some yogurt from the fridge and have some coffee and juice or whatever else you want. Then come join us at the dining hall at 9. It's the building directly behind the bunkhouse. Love, Laura"

The clock said 7:00, so I had some time to kill. I opened the fridge and pulled out some yogurt, then poured myself a juice. I felt called to read something with my meal, so I wandered out into the hallway. There were some bookshelves there on the way to the living room, and the first book that caught my eye was, naturally, *Destroying the Fortress* by Laura Day. I grabbed it and headed back to the kitchen.

I made it through 20 pages while slowly eating. According to the author, it is necessary to destroy certain, if not most, structural supports of the personal "fortress" you have built over the course of your life. The purpose of the fortress—the persona—is to protect you and to provide you with a solid identity, but it also prevents you from flowing with the moment and living with awareness. So the author suggests ways to set up uncomfortable "triggers" for yourself that will allow you to subtly undercut the key structural supports of your fortress. This way, it eventually ceases to be a solid, confining structure and becomes more of a helpful set of guidelines for navigating conventional reality. As I read, I distinctly recalled one particular fight where Marion screamed that I needed to find some "triggers" to snap me out of my complacency.

After 20 pages, I started skimming through the rest of the book, which seemed to just restate most of what I'd already read. So this was the famous Laura Day? I had to admit the writing wasn't bad, and the ideas were fairly challenging. I was surprised that a self-help book encouraging personal discomfort was able to sell so well.

I changed my clothes and washed up in the bathroom, and then left the house around 8:45 and headed through the woods to the dining hall. When I arrived at the clearing, there was no one in sight, so I walked straight to the building behind the bunkhouse. I opened the door to find about 40 or so people from across the age spectrum sprawled out on the floor in the middle of the room. All the tables and chairs had been pushed toward the walls, and Laura was sitting on a low stool in the front of the room holding a notebook. Everyone turned around to look at me as I entered from the back. Most smiled welcomingly—including Dan and Colin, who were sitting together—and a few of the children waved. Laura motioned for me to come and sit at the front to her left. As I sat down, I noticed Carly glaring at me suspiciously on the far side of the room. Her faced softened somewhat when I caught her eye.

"OK everyone, it's nine o'clock," Laura began. "I feel so formal up here, starting ever-so-precisely on time, like a professor."

There was scattered chuckling in the audience, most of whom appeared somewhat nervous and almost over-attentive.

Ease

"Today I want to talk about complacency, and I'm going to pick on a few people, as usual. First, though, I want to let you all know how complacent I myself am, nearly every day. Just sitting over there in that big house, doing nothing for days on end. Well, I write, and I think about what to write next, and I send emails and take phone calls, etcetera and so on. But there is no movement, no flow, no progression. I fall into cycles and patterns, becoming self-satisfied and stagnant, until I am able to calm my mind long enough to step outside myself and bear witness to it all. But then after those fleeting bursts of clarity, it's typically right back into the swamp. So I am up here not as an example to you of non-complacency—I am simply a flawed medium for this message."

She paused and smiled, turning the page in her notebook.

"Before we go any further, I want to talk about peace. Peace is the essential state of the universe, encompassing everything that has ever happened and could ever happen. For humans, it is the understanding that no matter what, everything is, always has been, and always will be fine. It is the cushion of support we always have, if we would only allow ourselves to identify with it, become one with it. Peace is naturally present inside of every moment. But watch out for the intermingling of peace and complacency. Complacency is often hidden inside peace, especially when everything seems to be going well, but complacency will ultimately pull you away from peace."

She paused to take a sip of water from a glass on the floor next to her.

"Now let's ask an important question: Can you be content but not complacent? Yes, but it's a very thin line. To be content is to be happy in the moment and grateful for what you have. To be complacent is to be mindlessly caught up in a pattern or cycle or comfort bubble—positive or negative. You cannot be both complacent and fully present at the same time. You cannot be both complacent and truly at peace at the same time."

Laura scanned the crowd, her gaze eventually settling on an older woman in the back.

"Julia, please stand up for a minute."

The woman hesitantly rose to her feet. She had long black hair flecked with grey, and was wearing a flowing white dress bordered with brightly colored stitching. She flicked her fingers nervously as she stood waiting for Laura to address her.

"Hi Julia," said Laura, smiling.

"Hello," Julia replied softly.

"Tell me, how are you doing?" asked Laura.

"I'm good."

"What does that mean?"

"Well, things have been good here."

"How long have you been here now?"

"A little over a year."

"And have you changed at all during that time?"

"Yes, I think I have."

"How?"

"Well, for one thing, I've learned to identify when I'm falling into self-destructive patterns."

"What's a self-destructive pattern for you? Name one."

"Dwelling on my son's death, and then drinking to cover up that pain."

Julia looked down at the floor, tears welling in her eyes.

"And do you see how even that could be called complacency?" Laura asked after a long pause. "You rely on that pain, and then you rely on the method you use to cover up that pain."

"Yes, it's definitely a form of complacency," Julia admitted. "But being here has allowed me to see that particular pattern very clearly. I haven't stopped it yet, but I'm getting there."

"What does *getting there* mean?"

"I have the urge to drink and I don't."

"That's a start. The deeper pattern is your complacency around this feeling of pain. In a way, the pain is comfortable for you. It holds you in a familiar space. Does that make sense?"

"Yes, that makes some sense, but I would never call this feeling comfortable."

"Not in any traditional sense, but the familiarity is comfort. Your body is addicted to the familiarity and scared of what lies outside of that familiarity."

"I can see that," said Julia softly. "Or at least I'm beginning to see that."

"Beyond that personal familiarity is freedom. It's the open sky, with no past or future. Once it's all released, you discover the deep familiarity that all the little personal familiarities imitate, but never touch. It's the return to your true nature. But damn, it seems impossible to get there sometimes, and even when you glimpse it, you fall right back. Such is life. You are on the path, though, Julia. How does it feel?"

"Hard," she replied with a slight smile. "But necessary."

"Good, good." said Laura, grinning. "OK, you're released. And the rest of you are released as well. I'm going to end here and we'll pick up at the next talk, whenever that is. I love you all very much, even if I don't always act like it. Amen and so be it."

With that, she stood up and walked over to me as the attendees started conversing amongst themselves.

"That was fairly typical," she said. "What did you think?"

"They're scared of you," I replied.

"Oh, only during these talks. It's just because I single people out."

"Do you ever ease up?"

"No," she said, grinning.

I noticed that Julia had ventured up behind Laura and was patiently waiting to speak with her.

"I think Julia wants to talk to you," I said softly. "Why don't you try being nice to her?"

Laura leaned over and whispered "Fuck you" in my ear, then kissed me on the cheek. She then turned around and embraced Julia warmly, and I quickly escaped out the front door to get some air.

{ 31 }

A Walk

I LEFT THE BUNKHOUSE and randomly started walking to the north end of the clearing. To provide some spatial perspective, the path to Laura's house was on the east end of the clearing, and I was parked on the southwest end, where the dirt road connected in.

I spotted a trail at the edge of the woods that seemed to lead in the general direction of the nearby mountain, so I started along it. I felt intensely agitated for some reason, but as I walked, the essence of the air and the trees began to seep into my body and calm me down.

After about ten minutes, I spotted a man in the distance peeing on a log on the side of the trail. When he saw me, he zipped up his pants and started walking briskly in my direction. He was reed thin and dressed in a very dirty pale yellow shirt and dark brown pants, with long black hair nearly down to his waist. He looked to be somewhere in his early 30s, but it was nearly impossible to tell.

"Hey there," he said loudly in a high-pitched voice as he drew near. "My name's Richard. I'd like to know yours."

He stopped in front of me with his hands on his hips, blocking my way. His light blue eyes flashed with a disconcerting, unrestrained energy.

"I'm Byron, good to meet you," I said as calmly as possible, extending my hand.

He looked down at my hand and then back up at my face.

"Do I know you?" he asked agitatedly. "I think I know you."

"I don't think so," I replied. "I've never seen you before."

"I'm not going to shake your hand," he said almost apologetically. "I don't do that. I assume you're coming from Beyond?"

"Yes," I answered.

"Then why haven't I seen you yet?" he asked.

"I just got here yesterday."

"Did you go to Laura's talk this morning?"

"I did."

"I wasn't there," he said. "I'm still figuring out whether I buy any of this."

"Me too," I replied truthfully.

"I'm here with my brother Colin. Have you met him yet?"

"Actually, yes," I said. "Nice guy."

"Well he begged me to come here. I was having some issues. Fucked some stuff up in my life. So he kept asking me over and over to come join him here. So finally I did about a week ago, and I'm just about ready to get the fuck out of here now."

"You seem angry."

"Know-it-alls piss me off," he said. "Laura seems like a know-it-all to me. And I don't trust all these people just staying here for years and buying into everything she says."

"I get it," I replied. "That kind of thing typically turns me off, too."

"It's a fucking cult," he said bitterly. "And Colin has bought in all the way."

He started pacing back and forth across the trail, clapping his hands together and muttering something incoherently.

"I've had breakdowns before," he said, turning back to me after completing several circuits. "I don't want to have one again, but I think I'm close if I stay in this place."

"You don't think there's anything here to help you?" I asked.

"I don't know," he replied, staring down at the ground. "I bought a bus ticket out of Boulder next

Monday to take me back home to Phoenix. I have to get Colin to drive me to Boulder though, which he won't."

He started pacing and clapping his hands again.

"Why don't you walk with me for a bit?" I ventured.

"Why?"

"Walking helps me calm down, and it might help you calm down."

Richard stopped pacing and stared at me suspiciously. His face, even when agitated, had a disarming innocence.

"OK," he said after a few seconds, his body loosening up a bit.

I began walking down the trail at a leisurely pace, and he eventually started following about 20 feet behind me. We continued like this in silence for about 10 minutes, until he finally decided to catch up and start walking next to me. He kept subtly glancing over at me as if for approval, his gaze quickly darting back down to the ground each time I caught his eye.

"We should probably turn around soon," I said, breaking the silence. "That mountain doesn't seem to be getting any closer, and I don't have any water, do you?"

"Nope," he answered. "But I am getting a little calmer. It feels good."

"Do you want to turn around?" I asked.

"I don't care," he answered.

I made my way over to a huge fallen pine and plopped down. Richard started pacing again, but a little more gently.

"What are you pondering over there?" I asked.

"I feel like there's this big secret I'm not in on," he said, kicking a stick along the ground. "It's been driving me crazy since I was a kid. This place makes me feel it even stronger than usual."

"What kind of secret?" I asked.

"The secret of how to live in this world."

"You think other people know the secret and are keeping it from you?"

"Yes."

"It's not true," I replied. "No one really knows what the fuck they're doing."

"I watch people real closely, and most of them seem to know what they're doing all the time. I never do."

"Why do you think people come here?" I asked. "It's because they don't know what they're doing in life. They're lost and drifting."

"Well they sure hide it. I look around and everyone acts like this is the only place they want to be, like they planned to be here all along."

"I promise you it's not true. They still don't know."

"I think that's what being sane is then," he said. "Figuring out how to fake like you know what you're doing. The people they call mentally ill don't know how to fake it. They can never figure it out."

"And you think that's you?" I asked.

"Definitely. I've been called crazy my whole life. That's an easy way out for people. It's a box to put me in. Oh, Richard's just crazy. He's disturbed. I know that's what they're saying behind my back. And then doctors put a name on it and give me pills that just make me fucking tired and braindead."

He stopped pacing for a moment, then shuffled slowly over and sat down next to me on the tree. We stayed silent for a minute or so, listening to the breeze rustle the pine branches. Richard shut his eyes and breathed deeply.

"I'm trying to meditate," he said. "I can never do it right."

"I wouldn't worry about getting it right," I replied. "Just sit quietly and concentrate on your breath. At least that's what they tell me."

"I know all about that. I just can't concentrate. Never been able to. My mind's always moving so fast and I'm always imagining all sorts of shit."

He sighed loudly and looked up at the sky.

"There really is a secret, isn't there?" he asked plaintively.

"I swear to God there's not," I said.

"I don't believe you," he replied softly.

He then abruptly stood up and clapped his hands together as hard as he could. The sound ricocheted like a gunshot around the forest, startling the birds and squirrels on the branches above us. Richard paced a few lengths back and forth, then started marching back the way we came. I watched until his swaying hair disappeared from view.

I sat forward on the fallen tree, my elbows on my knees and my head in my hands. The forest sounds were lulling me into a sort of reverie, and I suddenly longed for a place to lie down. I remembered passing by a large bed of moss a few hundred yards back on the trail, so I headed back to find it. My head was unbearably heavy all of a sudden, so as soon as I reached the moss I collapsed down on my back and closed my eyes. Why was I so tired?

{ 32 }

Joanna

I WAS AWOKEN FROM A DEAD SLEEP by someone repeatedly kicking my leg. I rolled over to find a young girl grinning down at me and giggling. She was no more than 8 or 9 years old, with a dirty white dress and long blonde hair.

"Ha! You're up!" she screeched, giggling almost uncontrollably.

I sat up slowly and tried to get my bearings.

"It's you!" she yelled. "I saw you up front when Laura was talking."

"And who are you?" I asked, groggy but amused.

"I'm Joanna!" she yelled, laughing. "What are you doing out here? This is where I walk by myself!"

"I was out here hiking and I got really tired, so I fell asleep on this moss."

"What? That's crazy!" she said, her eyes widening. "Did you have a dream?"

"No, I don't think so," I replied, getting to my feet. "What time is it now?"

"I don't know," she said. "It's after lunch."

I started wiping the stray dirt and branches off my clothes and hair.

"You got dirty," Joanna said, staring at me with a huge grin.

"It's true."

"How old are you?" she asked.

"38. How old are you?"

"8. I've been here since I was really tiny. My mom is here. I don't know what happened to my dad."

"Well I've only been here since yesterday," I replied.

"If you want to know where things are, you can ask me," Joanna said merrily.

"Thanks very much."

"You're welcome. I try to help everyone. If I ever saw my dad, I'd even try to help him, even though my mom says she hates him."

"That's a great way to live," I said, smiling. "Can I ask you a question? Do you go to school here?"

"My mom teaches me things, and I learn from other people here too, like Miss Laura," she replied. "I learn something new every day. I would never want to go to regular school where you sit at desks. That sounds awful."

"I can understand that."

"Why are you here?" she asked, suddenly growing serious.

"You mean at Beyond? My friend Dan invited me. But I really don't know why I'm here, honestly. I just kind of ended up here."

"It's important to know why you're doing something," she said sternly.

"I guess that's true."

"I want you to think hard about it," she continued in a lecturing tone. "What are you really doing here?"

"Wow," I said, chuckling. "You got really serious."

Her face brightened again instantly.

"I know! I can do that whenever I want."

"Well, to answer your question, I'm here because I don't really know what else to do with myself."

"Is that sad for you?" she asked with concern.

"No," I said, laughing. "Does it sound sad?"

"Kind of," she replied. "You don't have a job or a wife or a kid? Or anything else you want to do like draw or read or something?"

"Hmm. Well I don't have a wife. I used to, but I don't anymore. I don't have any kids. I quit my job a few days ago. I do have things I like to do, like read and take walks, but I guess I needed something else to do that would distract me from thinking too much about myself."

Joanna nodded knowingly as she took in everything I was saying, like she'd heard it all before.

"OK, I get it," she said after a brief silence. "You don't know what you're doing. Would you like me to lead you back now?"

"That would be great," I replied. "I'm incredibly thirsty."

"You should have brought some water," she yelled over her shoulder as she started running back down the trail.

I started half-heartedly jogging after her, but soon realized she was running at full speed, daring me to keep up. Her peals of laughter floated back to me as I ran faster and faster behind her. Her hair was glowing bright against the dark green of the pines, disappearing around turns and then reappearing out of the midst of the branches. Her enthusiasm was infecting me, and I began to feel the euphoria of running aimlessly that adults tend to lose as they age.

By the time we reached the clearing, I was completely winded, and I stood bent over with my hands on my knees while Joanna giggled loudly at me. She flitted off somewhere for a minute or so, and then returned with a cup of water, which she handed to me with a grin. I drained the water in one gulp and handed the empty cup back to her.

"Did that taste good?" she asked, beaming proudly.

"Yes, thank you," I replied. "Very good."

"You're a pretty good runner."

"You're much better than me."

"I know, but you're old," she said, laughing. "And you're going to die soon, right?"

My breath caught in my throat for a moment. I couldn't tell whether she was serious or not—she just smiled up at me calmly.

"Why do you say that?" I asked, trying not to appear alarmed.

"No reason. I just said it without thinking about it."

"Is it a joke?"

"I guess so, yeah," she said, smiling. "It just came out. That happens to me a lot."

I let it go, mainly because I suddenly realized how hungry I was. I'd had nothing to eat since that yogurt in the morning, and it was now well after lunch. Joanna must have sensed something, because she abruptly waved goodbye and ran off without a word in the general direction of the dining hall. I thought about following, but decided to just head back to Laura's to see what she might have in the kitchen.

As I started on the path to her house, I thought I spotted someone on my left. I turned to see Richard standing about 30 feet off with his feet wide apart and his arms folded across his chest. His pose felt vaguely threatening, and his stare didn't waver when I caught his eye. I began to lift my arm to wave, but thought better of it and continued on my way, slightly unsettled.

{ 33 }

Prep

W HEN I GOT TO THE HOUSE, Laura was sitting on the front steps smoking a joint. She grinned and motioned for me to come and sit next to her, which I did. She handed me the joint without a word and I took a long drag. We sat in silence for a few minutes, watching the smoke waft up to the treetops. Laura closed her eyes and leaned back on her elbows, inhaling the late afternoon air.

"So you're back from your sojourn?" she asked.

"Yup," I replied. "I walked on the trail toward the mountain, then stopped and fell asleep, and now I'm back here."

"Did you eat lunch?"

"Nope."

"Are you hungry?"

"Yes, very."

"Then I'll make us dinner."

"That sounds great, thanks."

Laura nodded but didn't budge. After a minute or so there was some rustling on the trail, and suddenly Richard materialized at the far end of the pathway of pines leading to the house. He stood with his arms folded, glaring at me with his mouth pursed in a scowl. Laura either didn't notice him or didn't care—she just continued to recline peacefully. I decided to just sit tight and let the moment unfold. We stared at each other in silence for an inordinately long stretch of time, with Richard never shifting his position or averting his gaze.

"I followed you here," Richard said finally, and loudly.

"Why don't you come over here and talk?" I replied. "You're too far away."

He hesitated for a moment, then began nervously ambling down the path toward us. His stance and his scowls were just a show of course, and here again was the unalloyed innocence I'd sensed earlier in the day. When he reached the foot of the steps, he paused and looked down at the ground, waiting for one of us to address him. Laura had finally deigned to sit up, and she was gazing at him sedately.

"Why did you follow me?" I asked.

"I wanted to see if we could talk again," he replied softly. "I have some things to tell you."

"Yes, of course we can talk again," I said.

"You two know each other?" Laura asked.

"Yeah, we met on the trail today," I said, smiling.

"Well then you must join us for dinner," Laura said to Richard. "I'm going to whip something up in a few minutes here. You're name's Richard, right? Colin's brother?"

"Yes, that's right," he answered, his leg shaking anxiously.

"Good, good," she said. "You can let go of some of that nervous energy, by the way. Nothing to be afraid of here."

"I can't help it," Richard replied, blushing and looking down at the ground.

Laura slowly rose to her feet, then reached out her hand to pull me up.

"Let's go inside, shall we?" she said, pushing the front door open wide and gesturing for us to enter.

{ 34 }

Dinner and After

L AURA COOKED US A SIMPLE DINNER of pasta with mushroom sauce and asparagus. She and I had wine, but Richard refused and stuck with water. The conversation while we ate was mundane, with Richard remaining nearly silent, but as soon as Laura took the plates away, he stood up and started pacing back and forth in his familiar pattern.

"You can relax, Richard," Laura said, leaning back and sipping her wine. "Or maybe there's something you want to say?"

"Well, I feel like I need to tell Byron about some of the things I've seen," he began hesitantly. "Some of the really dark shit."

I was intrigued, needless to say.

"You can tell me," I said.

"Can I listen too?" Laura asked.

"Yeah, you can listen too," he replied.

Stephen Intlekofer

He stopped pacing for a moment and stared at me.

"I think it will disgust you. It might make you sick," he said softly. "I'm sorry."

"It's fine," I said. "Really."

"OK," he began, resuming his pacing. "Since I was a kid I've had nightmares almost every night. Some keep coming up over and over, like a few where I see myself die. In one of these, I'm in some other country—for some reason I think it's Germany. I'm at a gas station talking to someone, and I step backwards and trip over something on the ground and fall flat on my back. At that moment, I look over and see a dump truck that's shot off out of traffic, completely out of control, coming straight for my head. I don't have time to move, and the truck runs right over my skull and I feel a split second of agonizing pain, and then everything goes to black and I wake up, usually with my heart racing like crazy."

He paused to take a breath before continuing.

"In another dream I always have, I'm standing on the shore of a sort of endless lake of flesh and guts and blood. It's kind of writhing around, twisting and turning, and there are flashes of light coming from inside it like it's got all this energy in it. Sometimes a figure rises up out of it for a little bit, like a section of a human, but then it usually just falls apart again back into the collection of skin and intestines and veins and blood in the lake. I used to be a lot more scared of this dream than I am now. Now it just seems like some sort of creation is going on. Nothing bad, just kind of a basic creation of bodies, almost peaceful. Does this sound crazy?"

"No," said Laura.

"Not at all," I seconded. "Trust me, I can identify."

Richard suddenly paused and stood stock still, his gaze fixated on something in the imaginary distance. As he watched whatever it was unfold, his face steadily sank into an expression of deep sadness, until he collapsed back into his chair with tears in his eyes.

"I see a lot of things when I'm awake too," he said softly, his voice quavering.

"Why do you think you've been chosen to see these things?" Laura asked gently.

"What do you mean, chosen?" he asked with a trace of irritation. "Who would have chosen me?"

"You tell me," she replied calmly.

"I don't know what the fuck you're talking about," he said agitatedly, sitting up in his chair. "No one chose me, I've just got a lot of shit wrong with my brain."

"I think this stuff has been given to you because you can handle it," Laura said. "You just don't believe you can. Think about what you said earlier, about how you now see that lake of blood and guts as a place of peaceful creation. Only an advanced soul would come to that conclusion."

"Really?" he asked incredulously, his face softening.

"Yes," Laura replied with a gentle smile.

"Why were you so keen to talk to me about all of this?" I asked, after a pause.

"Do you really want to know?" he replied.

"Sure, why not?"

"It will make you uncomfortable," he said, staring at me fixedly across the table.

"That's OK," I replied, attempting to remain outwardly unruffled. "I want to hear it."

"Well, the last time I had the lake dream was about a week ago," he began. "This time there was a mountain in the distance behind the lake, and at the top of the mountain was this huge cube of light. I don't know how else to describe it. It was a cube of blinding light, so bright that I could barely see the edges of it. A beam of light was shooting out of the cube and hitting the surface of the lake right in front of me, and I could see all the blood and intestines and limbs begin to swirl around, creating something. A figure began to be assembled and I could see legs and arms forming, and a head, and then eyes. I definitely remember the eyes. So after I saw you in the forest today, it took me a while to figure out where I knew you from, but then I remembered."

He paused and gazed up at evening sky through the skylight, his index finger tapping softly on the tabletop.

"It was definitely you," he said wistfully.

I suddenly felt a surge of heat in my chest, not altogether unpleasant. I shifted uneasily in my chair and glanced over at Laura, who seemed transfixed.

"Light began to flow out of your eyes and mouth, and then out of your chest. The same blinding light coming from the cube was coming out of you. It was being shot through you. After a few seconds all your skin and organs and muscles fell back down into the lake—they kind of melted off of you—and this body made out of light was standing right in front of me."

He paused again and leaned forward in his chair, his elbows on the table.

"And then I woke up."

I sat silently for a few moments, unsure of how to respond. My mouth was bone dry, and my underarms and back had begun to sweat profusely. I leaned forward in my chair and tried to detach the damp shirt from my skin. Laura was just sitting there calmly, watching me squirm.

"Sorry," said Richard. "I told you it would make you uncomfortable."

"No, no... I'm glad you told me."

"It was just a dream," he said. "I wouldn't worry too much about it if I were you."

"But you felt compelled to tell me about it," I replied, still fiddling with my shirt.

"Yes, in case maybe it had some deeper meaning for you. And it *was* kind of beautiful in a way. Who knows what the fuck it means..."

"You said you've had dreams like this your whole life?" asked Laura.

"Yeah," said Richard. "I drew pictures of them when I was a kid and freaked out all my teachers."

"Of course you did," she replied, chuckling knowingly. "I actually experienced something very similar when I was a kid. From when I was around 8 until I was 19, I had nightmares pretty much every night. Very gory, very intense. Recurring images of me dying, my parents dying, my sister dying, my friends dying. Bloody war battles, executions, human sacrifices. Also apocalyptic images of the Earth being destroyed, sometimes from a sort of God's-eye view from space."

"Yup, I've had most of those," said Richard, nodding.

"The event that caused them to stop for me was pretty interesting," she continued. "It was about a week after my 19th birthday. My friends and I were at a park outside Charlotte, North Carolina, where I grew up. I was lying on my back in a field looking up at the clouds, trying to relax—unsuccessfully as usual—when this massive Great Dane sauntered over and started gazing calmly down at me. We stared at each other for what had to be a full minute, and I swear to God this animal looked at me with such love, probably the deepest love I'd ever felt. There was an incredible purity to the moment—no subtext, no before or after, no fear, no distraction. Everything was completely silent and still. Eventually someone whistled from across the field, which broke the spell, and the dog just bolted off. From that day on, things started to shift."

"I think I need something like that," Richard said softly.

"See, I think you're much further along than I am," Laura replied. "You take the so-called horror and transform it. You instinctively know how to do it."

"Do you really think so?" he asked, his eyes glistening.

"Yes," she said warmly. "I admire you."

Richard buried his head in his hands and sobbed as we looked on in silence. By then, all my agitation had passed, and that blessed, all-consuming peace was beginning to flow through me again.

After a minute or so, Richard gathered himself and rose to his feet. He looked at both of us and bowed, then abruptly walked out of the kitchen, down the hallway, and out the front door. Through the kitchen window, we watched his hair sway down the pathway of pines until it finally disappeared through the oval gateway and into the dusk.

{ 35 }

Nighttime

L ATER THAT EVENING, Laura and I were again reclining in the living room, gazing down at the vine-covered jungle pyramid. We hadn't said a word for about five minutes, and were both seemingly content with our respective silent contemplations. I was reflecting on how, aside from an extended detour into the world of sickness in college, I'd essentially coasted through life before unaccountably veering off and arriving in this place.

"So what now for you?" asked Laura finally, seemingly reading my thoughts.

"I have no idea," I answered. "I was just thinking about it."

"I don't have any advice for you," Laura said, smiling.

"None?"

"Let everything that came before go. Do it now, and then keep on doing it. How about that?"

"Is that even possible? Isn't that really just denial of all the shit you have to deal with?"

"Maybe. I guess it's a delicate combination of looking at what comes up, accepting it, and then letting it go. Can that be balanced so it doesn't lean too far in one direction? Ultimately, though, the past is gone. It's liberating to know that."

"But it all affects you regardless," I said. "It's all part of you, wrapped up inside your body and mind. You can pretend you're beyond it, whatever it is, but you never really are. You're continually fucked up by what came before."

"Yes and no," Laura replied. "The truth is paradox, above all. You are made up of the aggregates, as the Tibetans would say—everything you've accumulated over the course of your life, both from the outside world and inside yourself. But all that can be thrown off in any given moment. Yes, it tends to come back, sometimes with a vengeance. But with some level of awareness, the past can be continually falling away."

"Continually, huh?" I asked skeptically.

"It's all a big experiment," said Laura with a knowing grin. "If you can understand that, you're never hemmed in."

I got up from the couch and began to stroll around the room.

"I think I'm leaving tomorrow," I said.

"Where are you going?"

"South."

"Why south?"

"Why not?"

"You're welcome to stay here as long as you want. I like having you here."

"Thank you, but I need to leave. Like you said, I need to let whatever's going to happen, happen."

I paused in front of a large hanging tapestry I hadn't noticed before, probably because it was immersed in shadow in the corner of the room. On it, a four-armed Kali was standing on top of a pile of dead bodies. Her hair was flowing wild, her eyes were wide and frenetic, and there was blood streaming from her bared teeth and protruding tongue. In her upper right hand she was grasping a bloody scimitar, and in both of her left hands she held severed human heads. Her body was blue, and around her neck was the familiar necklace of skulls. Her dress was made out of severed arms and legs tied together with a long, twisting lock of black hair.

"You like it?" Laura asked with a mischievous smile.

"Not sure yet," I answered, chuckling.

I'd seen similar images of Kali before, but this one transfixed me. It projected both eerie calm and frenzied violence—the energy of destruction. I recalled my dream a few nights before when I was floating over the Civil War battlefield.

"Appropriate for you right now, no?" said Laura.

"Yes."

I stood silently in front of the tapestry for a few minutes, gazing into the eyes and mouth. I had no real thoughts, just an overwhelming feeling of spaciousness. No memories, no concerns for the future—simply open space.

"It feels good, doesn't it?" asked Laura.

"Yeah," I replied, turning back toward her. "Although I'm not sure what I'm even feeling, really. It feels almost like nothing."

"Let it be nothing then. It's whatever remains when everything constructed is destroyed. In any case, you're on the verge of going further than I ever have, so whatever I have to say is about to become meaningless for you."

She walked slowly over to me and wrapped her arms around me in a deep embrace, her head resting on my shoulder. I hugged her back, my arms tight around her waist. The moment felt deeply familiar to me.

"You'll be back to see me," she said, stepping back and putting her hands on my shoulders.

She stared at me tenderly for a couple of seconds, and then walked out of the room without another word. I slept on one of the white couches again that night, watching the moon ascend as I drifted off with surprising ease. I woke up around dawn the next morning after a dreamless sleep, gathered my things, and left Beyond without saying any goodbyes.

{ 36 }

Rhoda

I LEFT BEYOND AND LYONS BEHIND ME and headed southeast on Route 36 through Boulder, then down past Denver on I-25 toward Colorado Springs. By the time I cleared Denver, it was about 7:30, and I pulled off at a Dunkin Donuts to grab a bagel and a coffee. As I waited in line, I gazed around at all the people on their way to work on a Wednesday morning. The woman in front of me was scanning the donut selection with her wallet in hand, ready and anxious to step up to the counter as soon as the man in front of her was finished paying.

"My turn to feed the office," she offered by way of explanation as she ordered two dozen in business-like fashion.

As I sat at the counter eating my bagel and sipping my coffee, everything seemed light, almost insubstantial. I felt a sense of relief to be back in the "real" world after the alternate universe of Beyond, but then this didn't feel all that real either. The edges of things were blurring and combining, and I was trying not to think too deeply about any of it.

Where was I headed? South, all the way down the bottom of the country—Big Bend National Park in Texas. And on the way, I was going to walk through the desert for a while. I had no endgame—I'd figure out what to do next when I got to Big Bend.

Next to me at the counter, an elderly man in a cowboy hat was staring blankly into his cup of coffee. He had a long, droopy white moustache and massive bags beneath his eyes. Every so often he would silently mouth a couple of words, and then blow gently into his cup. He seemed to be deep in thought, stuck inside some cycle of memories.

"Rhoda," he said suddenly, without taking his eyes off his coffee.

I hesitated, unsure of whether or how to respond.

"Rhoda came by a bunch of times that summer," he said, glancing over at me briefly.

"She did?" I asked.

"Yes. She taught me a few tunes on the piano. Then we'd go walking on the dirt road behind my house, and she'd show me all the different types of flowers. She seemed to know them all."

He paused to blow on his coffee again.

"We'd sit on the porch drinking tea as the evening wore on into twilight, as the crickets and katydids started to sing. We talked about everything you could ever want to talk about. Then in the fall she moved away."

He took a long sip of his coffee and gently placed the cup back down.

"I think she's dead now, but I'm not rightly sure. I hope she's alive. Rhoda was her name. She was beautiful all the way through. She looked at me like she was in love with me, even though we really barely knew each other. But she left and I never got to talk to her again."

"You still think about her a lot?" I asked.

"No, just occasionally. This morning she popped into my head. I only knew her for a few months. Only a few months one summer, then it was done. I never found her again."

"Maybe one summer was enough," I said.

"Maybe," he replied. "Whichever way you want to look at it, that's how it happened."

He resumed blowing on his coffee, apparently finished talking. After a few minutes, I stood up and stretched my arms over my head. It was time to get moving again.

{ 37 }

Descending

ROUND 2 PM, I STOPPED for lunch at a Mexican place near Santa Fe. As I was leaving, I picked up a brochure for a spa called Ten Thousand Waves. I knew the name—Marion had gone there for a friend's bachelorette party when we were still together. She had raved about it, so I decided to go check the place out for a bit.

I bought a day pass for the main spa area and proceeded to cycle through the hot tub, the dry sauna, and the cold plunge, over and over. The place was fairly empty except for a few quiet older folks who seemed to be staying put in the hot tub. After several cycles through, I felt deeply relaxed. The setting was beautiful, perched on a hill with pine trees surrounding and the wide-open southwestern sky stretching out overhead.

Ease

At the end of about my fifth cycle through, as I climbed out of the cold plunge, something abruptly shifted. My pulse started racing, objects blurred and wavered in front of my eyes, and the now-familiar sense of dread and impending disaster overtook me. I sank down heavily on the wooden bench near the sauna and tried to breathe through it, but this one was burrowing deep. The muscles in my chest clenched up and shot waves of anxiety out through my arms and down into my guts. I was intensely nauseous, and my forehead felt like it was about to burst open. Was this a panic attack? Some weird detox reaction? Was I dying?

I leaned back as best I could on the bench and looked up at the sky, desperately searching for something to calm me. I tried to focus on a distant flock of birds flying in a scattered V formation, but then the entire sky suddenly separated into thin, blue, glass-like shards that started collapsing and plummeting toward me. I closed my eyes tight, then opened them, and there was nothing there, only blackness. I yelled out involuntarily and sat up rod-straight on the bench, my body now in a full-on panic. I felt someone next to me, and then a warm hand on my shoulder.

"Are you OK?" asked an alarmed male voice.

"I don't know," I heard myself saying.

Very slowly, light and form began to reappear.

"Should I call an ambulance?" the voice asked.

"No, no," I said. "I think I'll be OK. Just need a minute."

The person attached to the voice placed a cup of cold water in my hand, which I drained in one gulp. I could now make out distinct shapes and colors, and my heart rate was steadily decreasing.

"You're probably dehydrated," said the voice. "Crazy shit can happen when you're dehydrated."

"Yeah, maybe I am," I replied. "Thanks for the water."

"Of course my friend," the voice said gently.

I focused only on breathing deeply through my mouth, in and out, but the sense of impending doom was barely dissipating at all. I stared down at the knobby knees protruding from beneath my towel. They were shaking uncontrollably.

"Steady yourself now," said the voice.

I glanced over to see a heavyset, balding older man with a thick gray beard. He smiled at me kindly and patted my shoulder.

"You're coming out of it now... you'll be fine," he said.

I attempted to smile at him, but it likely came across as a pained grimace.

"You don't need to say anything," he went on in his deep southern drawl. "Just lean back and relax as much as you can. I'm here to take care of you for as long as you need it. Do you need more water?"

I nodded my head, incredulous at the kindness he was showing me. He stood up, naked, and strode off purposefully with my cup. As I surveyed the scene, I noticed that nearly everyone else there was staring at me nervously. I waved awkwardly and again attempted to smile.

"I'm OK," I said as loudly as I could.

This did nothing to placate them, and they continued to stare and whisper amongst themselves. Mercifully, my friend soon returned with the refilled cup of water. I took it from him and started slowly sipping on it. I felt incredibly fragile, like any slight surprise or jolt would destroy me. Fortunately, my designated helper was projecting only a profound gentleness. He sat silently beside me for about a minute or so, breathing along with me.

"I've been where you are, but worse," he said, finally. "A few years ago I passed out at a spa. Fell completely forward onto my stomach, my bare-naked ass shining up to the sky. I can only imagine the view."

He paused, chuckling softly to himself. I noticed that the other spa-goers had seemingly lost interest now that I was apparently not going to pass out or die.

"So my point is, don't worry about it," he continued, smiling. "It happens."

"I want to thank you for helping me," I said weakly, my voice cracking.

"It's my pleasure and duty," he replied.

"Well, it's much appreciated," I said, suppressing my ongoing terror as best I could.

A deep, involuntary shiver passed through my body, which he didn't seem to notice.

"The name's Sheldon," he said. "Sheldon White."

"I'm Byron," I replied.

"It's a pleasure to meet you, Byron. I will not soon forget this meeting, I'll tell you that."

"Me neither," I said with a sad laugh. "The humiliation will live on."

"Ah, no need to dwell on that, my friend. Life gives us what it will, and there's nothing to be done but accept it. My wife died five years ago this week—had a heart attack on the toilet at a 7-11. I'm still not over it by a damn stretch, but I'm done asking why. It's a pointless question."

"I hear that," I replied, my voice still shaky.

My head was pounding uncontrollably, and the air felt dank and oppressive. I was in a slightly lesser state of panic than a few minutes before, but that was hardly a consolation. Sheldon was truly the only thing keeping me from descending into full-on incapacitation. He placed his hand on my shoulder, firmly but with deep kindness.

"You may feel weak right now, but you're not," he said. "You're very strong, so you hang in there."

"I definitely feel weak."

"I know you do. Like I said, I've been there, and I'm here with you for as long as you need me. Hell, I'm retired. I've got nowhere to go, nowhere to be."

He chuckled and squeezed my shoulder almost playfully.

"I've got no one left. Wife's gone. Never had kids. Parents are long dead. But I'll tell you, I'm enjoying myself. I just open myself to conversations, everywhere I go. I've learned to listen to people. They seem to love it."

"Of course they do," I said.

I was beginning to stabilize just a bit.

"You saved me just now," I went on. "That's no exaggeration."

"Nonsense. It was no sweat at all. You'd have done the same for me."

I gazed up at the spacious blue expanse of the late afternoon sky, willing my body to release into it. Sheldon gazed up with me, sighing contentedly.

{ 38 }

Life Is but a Dream

ABOUT AN HOUR LATER, Sheldon and I were having a quiet dinner together at the Japanese iza-kaya in the spa. I had almost completely recovered from my unfortunate episode, and as I savored my cucumber salad bite by bite, I listened to Sheldon describe for me what he did with his days now that he was retired.

"I like to get outside and just walk," he said. "Aimlessly. No rhyme or reason, you know? I spent so much time in my career just sitting on a chair."

"I hear you on that," I replied, staring into the colorful depths of the intricate spa-provided kimono he was wearing.

"I take walks into the desert when I can, to take it all in. Can't go too far without a bunch of water, with my physique. But I do OK."

He paused to take a quick sip of his green tea.

"I'm originally from the Dallas area, lived in Albuquerque for the last 20 years, but I'm here in Santa Fe all the time," he continued. "I love it here... But I want to hear something about you, if you're up for it. Give me the lowdown. Where are you from? I can tell you're not from here."

"It's that obvious?" I said, smiling. "I'm from Baltimore. I just up and quit my job a week ago and now I'm out wandering. I have no idea why I'm here in particular. I don't know anything for sure anymore, to be honest. I do know I'm enjoying sitting here having dinner with you."

"Interesting," replied Sheldon. "I like it, I like it. We need to enjoy ourselves as much as we can, I say. We could keel over any time, especially a fat fool like me."

"Agreed," I said, taking a bite of my salad.

"Agreed that I'm a fat fool?" he asked, laughing.

"No, Sheldon, you're neither of those. In fact, you're pretty much my new favorite person."

"Shut up, I'm fat as hell," he said, blushing slightly.

"You're downright svelte," I replied, smiling.

"You're a bald-faced liar, but I'll take it. I'm 69 years old, fat, alone..."

"And free," I said.

"Yes, I am free," he said, grinning. "I am completely free. I could die tomorrow... hell, I could die right now, and it would be perfectly fine. But here I am, alive and kicking."

"With that in mind, and now that I'm fully recovered, let's order some drinks."

"Yes, yes, indeed we must. It's time," Sheldon said gleefully.

Three Japanese scotches later, we were somehow gearing up to sing Row, Row, Row Your Boat with our waiter.

"Sing it with us," I pleaded tipsily. "I swear it sums up the whole fucking game."

"If you say so," the waiter replied, grinning and shrugging his shoulders. "I'm ready when you are."

"Well then, here we go," Sheldon said, raising his arms like a conductor.

"Row, row, row your boat..." we all began, shakily at first, then steadier, "...gently down the stream. Merrily, merrily, merrily, life is but a dream."

We sang it three more times, louder and louder, with almost everyone in the place staring at us bemusedly.

{ 39 }

Farther South

I WOKE UP AROUND 8 THE NEXT MORNING with a splitting headache. I was lying on the couch in Sheldon's room with my kimono hanging open and drool on my pillow. Sheldon was collapsed on the bed face-down, his slippers still on his feet. I got to my feet and staggered to the bathroom to pee and drink some water from the faucet.

When I came out, I got dressed and wrote a note for Sheldon:

"Dear Sheldon, You are my hero. We will meet again. I love you. – Byron"

On the way to my car, I stopped at the front desk for some aspirin. The painting on the wall behind the desk showed an empty field with a massive golden sun filling the sky.

"Is that sunrise or sunset?" I asked the woman at the desk.

"Pardon?"

"In the painting."

"Oh," she said, turning around to look. "I'm not sure. I've never thought about it."

"Let's say sunset," I said.

"OK," she replied, smiling. "Sunset it is."

Back in the car, I pulled out the map and plotted my way south. I decided to take I-25 to Truth or Consequences, which was about three hours away, and from there I'd take Route 51 into the desert as far as I could go.

I stopped at a gas station in Bernalillo to fuel up and grab a coffee and a bite to eat. When I returned to my car, there was a note wedged under my windshield wiper, scrawled on the back of a flyer for a strip club in Albuquerque:

"God said to Moses, I AM WHO I AM. – Exodus 3:14"

I stood contemplating that for a few moments before getting back in the car.

I pulled into Truth or Consequences around noon and quickly honed in on the A&B Drive In for lunch. I ordered the green chili cheeseburger and an iced tea, then sat down at a picnic table in the covered seating area to wait for the food to arrive. A young couple with a sleeping baby in a stroller was sitting at the table next to mine, arguing quietly but vehemently above the remnants of their meal. Apparently the man was at fault, as the woman seemed to be dominating the argument with an air of self-satisfied assurance.

"Why are we right here again arguing about this?" she asked icily, her blonde ponytail bobbing up and down with each word. "Seems like every other day you're pulling this type of shit."

"What do you want me to say? I fucked up. I forgot. It happens."

"But it happens all the time. I wouldn't be mad if it just happened once, or twice, or three times, but it happens constantly."

"And you're always right there to jump on it and blow it up into a huge issue," he said, his tone growing more biting. "I think you love this role, with all your righteous anger."

"Don't you dare blame any of this on me."

"The only thing I blame you for is pulling out this bitchy judgmental tone all the time. You talk down to me like I'm a fucking idiot."

"What about Monday night, when we had this exact same discussion? Or last Friday, or the weekend before? I ask you to remember to do one thing and you can't handle it. Bring the check to the bank. That's all I asked, but you couldn't handle it, and now the check I wrote to Becky will fucking bounce. And don't talk to me about night shift. I've pulled night shifts before and I still remember to do what I need to do."

"I said I'm sorry. Can we please move on for the love of God?"

At this point my food arrived, providing a blessed distraction. The burger was outstanding, with just a bit of a kick—exactly what I was craving. The couple left within a few minutes, and as I ate in glorious silence, I decided I'd stay in town that night and then head into the desert first thing in the morning.

As I wiped my fingers on my napkin after finishing the last of my food, I watched an older man wearing a disheveled beige linen suit and wraparound sunglasses place an order at the window. He paused to scratch his head as if considering something, and then pulled out his wallet to pay. Two teenage boys stood behind him in line, patiently studying the posted menu. One leaned over to say something to the other and they both grinned conspiratorially. These were probably their final days of summer before school began again. I felt grateful for this moment, which everything had led up to.

As I stood up from the table to head to my car, I suddenly felt so tired I could barely keep my eyes open. While slapping myself awake in the driver's seat, I spotted a pink building and a sign reading "Pelican Spa," so I decided to drive the necessary 200 feet or so down the road to see if they had a room. I didn't consider the potential causes of my fatigue too deeply—I just wanted to sleep.

{ 40 }

Nothingness (The Final Dream that Teaches)

I PULLED THE CURTAINS CLOSED in my room to shut out the bright afternoon sunlight, slid off my shoes and socks, and flopped down on the bed. The next 18 or so hours were a bizarre amalgam of deep dream sleep and half-awake stupor. In the dream, I was walking endlessly around a huge old house, through a series of nearly empty rooms with elaborately patterned rugs on the floors. Everything inside the house felt stuck, stagnant, cyclical. I left and reentered the same rooms again and again, and the house seemed like it was rotating on its axis to match the speed I was walking, preventing me from ever really moving forward. I repeatedly awoke in a daze and then fell back into this same dream sequence, over and over.

Eventually Marion arrived in the dream and convinced me that I could leave the house and go outside into the yard. I followed her out onto a vast lawn underneath the moon and stars. We sat down cross-legged in the grass, facing each other, and had a long conversation about our lives before we knew each other, recounting memories from far back in early childhood. We then talked candidly about our life together, forgiving each other again and again for specific times we'd been cruel or thoughtless. After a while, we realized we had the ability to replay our memories as holograms in the air between us, and we watched ourselves scream at each other during arguments, have sex, hike through the woods, eat breakfast in silence, read in bed, and so on, ad infinitum. We then went further back and showed each other moments from our respective childhoods, including each of us being born— emerging covered in blood and amniotic fluid, shrieking and gasping in terror as our bodies realized they suddenly had to breathe on their own. This memory of my birth felt surprisingly familiar to me, almost comforting, and it was beautiful to be able to share it with Marion.

At this point, I woke up briefly in a complete daze. The clock by the bed said 10:15 PM. I stood up unsteadily and stumbled to the bathroom to pee. I felt extremely dizzy, but I just attributed that to waking up from a dead sleep. As soon as fell back into bed, I was in the midst of another dream.

I was strolling slowly across a desert landscape at twilight, a soft breeze rustling the brush at my feet. Ahead in the distance, the last red vestiges of the sunset were receding just above the horizon. My body felt heavy at first, as if it was being pressed on from all sides. As I walked, though, layer after layer of some indefinable substance began to peel off me, starting from the bottom of my feet, slipping all the way up my chest and over my head, and then sliding off my back. Each time a new layer fell away, I turned around and watched the ground open up and swallow it. The layers were amorphous and glowed a sickening green, and I felt a strange sense of loss as each one disappeared into the earth. Eventually, after what seemed like hours, the layers stopped sliding off, and I realized there were no more left.

I stopped walking and looked down at my body, which was now nearly translucent. When I looked up again, I saw an identical version of me staring back from about 10 feet away. He (or I) was smiling cryptically and spreading his arms out like wings. My awareness began to shift from one version of me to the other, back and forth, every few seconds or so. A tiny but blindingly bright white light appeared in the center of our chests. The light expanded and shot out solid beams that intertwined in the space between us, twisting together into a single woven strand of gleaming rope. The rope began to shorten, pulling our bodies inexorably toward one another.

As the bodies touched, my awareness floated just above them, calmly observing. The bodies began to compress together, becoming thinner and thinner until they merged and exploded into light. I watched as the light swiftly dissipated beneath me, emitting a soft crackling sound as it vanished into the night air. I was left hovering there alone, as simple awareness.

I had nothing. I needed nothing. I wanted nothing. I was peace—the essence of the universe.

But that lifetime was not done with me yet. There was something yet to be done, and so I woke up at 5 AM the next morning, embodied and panicking.

{ 41 }

Death

T HE SECOND I OPENED MY EYES, I knew something was horribly wrong with my body. I was drenched in sweat and my heart was racing and beating in my ears. Another panic attack? No, this was something much worse. I switched on the light by my bed and stood up, then almost immediately passed out from dizziness. Was I having a heart attack? A stroke? As I steadied myself against the wall, I suddenly had the overwhelming urge to shit. During the first few steps toward the bathroom, my bowels began to release, and I felt the sickening sensation of warm liquid streaming down my legs. I reached the toilet, yanked down my pants, and out poured what felt and looked like an entire bucket of blood and clots.

"What the fuck? What the fuck? What the fuck?" was all I could think to say, over and over, as I looked down in horror at the rapidly filling bowl.

I knew I was losing dangerous amounts of blood, but I had no control over what was happening. Had I ruptured an organ? Was it a Crohn's relapse? No, it couldn't be—that had been under control for years. I gazed at the trail of red drops leading to the toilet, and then over at the neatly folded bathmat on the side of the tub. My vision started to spin and I realized I was about to pass out.

I was going to die. Here it was. I tried to grasp for the moment to try to solidify it in some way, but it resisted. It felt trite, insubstantial, unsatisfying. I thought of people finding me like this, keeled over with my pants at my ankles, covered in blood and feces. All the hours and minutes and seconds of my life had led me here, to this bathroom in New Mexico, to this moment on the morning of August 24. I almost laughed at the sheer absurdity... the utter pointlessness.

Suddenly I felt a surge of warmth and peace. I searched around to find the last thing I'd see, but I couldn't seem to focus. There was a cracked tile on the bathroom floor rising up to meet me, and a veil of light. Then my mother's voice singing softly in my ear. And then it was over.

Part II

{ 1 }

Absorption

NOW BEGINS A DIFFERENT STAGE of the story. I will by necessity have to refer to myself as "I" in this stage, but this "I" has nothing to do with Byron, the human being. It is, for lack of a better phrase, sheer awareness within desired limits. It is my identity now, in the present. By desired limits, I mean this—it is simple for me to deliberately confine my awareness to something as small as the interior of an atom, or something as large as the entire boundary of the visible universe.

With that established, we can return briefly to that hideous scene in the bathroom in New Mexico, with my inert body in a heap on the floor next to the toilet. I had passed out into the shallow, comatose outer void, still barely alive. This nothingness lasted approximately 90 seconds. At the precise moment of death, a blinding white light blew apart the void and "I" felt a sense of explosive expansion outward in all directions. All of my memories and individual patterns of thought were instantly obliterated, as well as any ideas, comparisons, or categorizations. My human purpose was removed, and all was open.

At some point, the light departed and I entered the dense blackness of the true void. The only presence here was a deep, constant hum that seemed to contain all possible sounds inside it. There was no more expansion—on the contrary, I felt contracted into an infinitesimal point. I didn't feel any fear. In fact, the very notion of fear was impossible here and had never entered this place.

Eventually my vision opened up again, and I was gazing down on an enormous field of unfolding light formations. Points of light began in tight spirals and then unfolded at unfathomable speed to form defined streams, all flowing onward together toward some undefined horizon. I soon became part of one of the spirals, building up unfathomable levels of energy before abruptly hurtling forward in a light stream parallel to all the others.

Up ahead, the streams began to converge at a specific point, spinning around and then diving into what appeared to be a massive black hole. As my stream drew inexorably closer, I watched the streams closest to the hole spin around one final time, dispersing outward in a momentary burst of intensity before being swallowed up entirely. Soon the hole's orbit took hold of my stream, and I whirled around the periphery countless times, in wide arcs at first and then tighter and tighter, uniting with a seemingly infinite number of other streams that had joined up from alternate planes and directions. In the few moments before the hole pulled us in, all the united streams burst forth in blinding glory, bathing everything in light and searing heat. All was simultaneously created and destroyed.

Then there was darkness, but only for a moment. Silence and void, and then an abrupt, incomprehensibly intense explosion of sound and light, and my awareness expanded across the entire breadth of a newly birthed universe.

{ 2 }

Understanding

AFTER WHAT MIGHT HAVE BEEN minutes or years, I arrived at a strange kind of equilibrium. In this state, I alternated seemingly randomly between expansion and contraction. At times I witnessed and comprehended everything happening in a given moment across all universes, galaxies, stars, solar systems, planets. At times I rested inside a molecule in a rock or a blade of grass, contemplating the steady, continuous motion of the atoms there.

Over this period, certain core truths were shown to me. I will try to convey the essence of a few of them here, very briefly.

All is energy. Energy is unlimited and infinitely "intelligent." All energy is equal.

When energy takes on form, it is a sacred act. Form is a limitation that makes energy temporarily visible and tangible.

Life is the most sacred form that energy takes on. Energy without life is incomplete.

Across all universes, life is experienced through a set of limited (yet expanding) senses. This is by necessity.

Time is a tool for life. It is infinitely malleable, and can be accelerated, compressed, repeated, created, or destroyed at will.

Life is consciousness. Consciousness evolves to join with and become "God." God is both energy and non-energy (void) simultaneously, which is unity. The human concept of love is an aspect of this unity.

I was also given a very clear message specific to my role on Earth. I was destined to live my life as Byron over again, born into precisely the same circumstances. I would remember nothing of any previous lives and nothing of these experiences after death, except occasionally in dreams and other random moments of intersection. To question the purpose of this rebirth was useless and didn't even occur to me. It was simply what would happen, what had always been bound to happen.

{ 3 }

Peace

I WAS THEN GIVEN THE CAPACITY to move and act of my own accord. Following some unknown impulse, I began to glide around through time and space to witness a seemingly limitless display of greed, violence, and destruction. Across myriad galaxies and planets, in a perpetual cycle, I observed acts of systematic torture and indiscriminate murder, as well as an endless parade of slavery and oppression. Billions of beings were forced into permanent bondage to serve the selfish, dominant classes. Civilizations claimed random territory as their own and destroyed everything that stood in their way, including nature itself. Entire races and societies were eliminated in methodical, holocaust-like slaughters.

I witnessed wars fought from a distance with energy weapons not yet encountered by humans in my era. Others were fought hand to hand, with flesh being ripped off and eyes gouged out. I saw human villages pillaged after an attack, with women raped and children run through with spears. Occasionally planets were evaporated in an instant, and other times wave after wave of combatants surged forward only to be brutally mowed down by gunfire or blown apart by bombs. I could enter the fray whenever I wanted, and I inhabited hundreds of beings in the moments before death, directly experiencing their anger, fear, pain, and release. I sometimes stayed on after death, observing from inside a mangled shred of skin, a stopped heart, or the brain in a severed head.

I also witnessed enduring civilizations that had transcended this brutality, living in harmony with their fellow beings, their planet, and their universe. For these civilizations, the true united consciousness had nearly arrived, and life was a joyful process of mutual discovery and expansion. There was death, but it was not feared—it was simply seen as one gateway among many others. Each individual mind was joined to and nourished by the collective mind, and every being inherently understood the glory that was to come—complete union with the source. It was not only possible for any given long-lived civilization to reach this point; it appeared as if the vast majority did.

Eventually this period of observation ended, and I willed myself to come to rest inside a clover leaf in a field somewhere on Earth. The mid-afternoon sun was streaming down, bathing me in warmth and light, and the occasional breeze rustled me gently. There was nothing to do here but simply be still and witness the cyclical motion of atoms, the leisurely growth of the plant cells, and the meandering flow of the vast external world. The days passed by—some with rain, some with sun, some with wind. Occasionally I heard human voices, but I didn't feel the need to decipher their words. Finally, after what might have been weeks or months, my leaf began to slowly shrivel and die. I stayed with it to the very end, when the last bit of life departed, and then I stayed on as it began to decay. Day by day it grew more brittle, until finally a stiff wind blew it completely apart. I stayed with one tiny piece as it spiraled up into the air, briefly cavorted above the treetops, and finally settled down inside a soft green bed of moss. In here was perfect silence. In the morning, the rays of the sun illuminated the air and filled me with life, and at night, the moon stilled the world and lulled me into a perfect state of rest. All was at peace in this sliver of the universe, and I longed to remain here forever.

But then, suddenly, I knew it was time to return to the human form.

{ 4 }

Reconstitution

I WILL PREFACE WHAT COMES NEXT with the disclaimer that I am now able to recall every moment of my lives as Byron with perfect clarity. While I was in the midst of this subsequent go-round on Earth, however, my memory was essentially normal. I grew up and experienced life as most humans do, remembering and forgetting things seemingly haphazardly, with only hazy memories from very early childhood. There were some variations, however, that altered the course of this particular life, but alas not the date or manner of my death.

As I did when writing about the final ten days of my previous life, I will mostly revert to a writing style that reflects how Byron the human would write, with a few exceptions. I will focus on specific moments and realizations—an expressionistic portrait—rather than providing any type of comprehensive account. No need to get bogged down.

Proceed again.

All was dark, and I was floating in a comfortable sea of warmth. I saw nothing, but I could hear two distinct, repeating sounds—one loud and fast, the other slower and softer. The sounds occasionally varied in speed, sometimes even commingling into one deep, unified rhythm before separating again. This was the extent of my world. There were no concerns here—no thoughts, no discomfort, no wants, no needs, no time—only pure sensation. How long this went on, I had no way of knowing.

Eventually a shift occurred, and I began to notice that there was a kind of soft barrier surrounding me. This barrier seemed to be tightening against me, very slowly. This intrigued me, and I started pushing outward with my hands and feet to try to regain my space. Soon I even began kicking the barrier, but it would only bend slightly and then resume its normal, shrinking shape. After one particular kick, though, I felt something push back against me, gently but firmly. Could there be something outside the barrier? The idea of this (if you could call it an idea) was my first human worry. The barrier kept tightening, and I kept pushing and kicking against it. More and more often, whatever was on the other side would push right back.

Then, abruptly, the critical sequence arrived. Intense pressure suddenly enveloped my body, cutting off all movement. This compression released as quickly as it began, but it soon returned even stronger. After many cycles of this compression and release, I began to slide headfirst—toward what, I had no idea. I was being slowly rammed through some sort of tunnel, propelled by some mysterious, tightly constricting force. Over the course of this agonizing journey, my progress would occasionally halt, leaving me confined and alone. I had no reassurance here except the familiar rhythmic sound in my ears—one sound now, rather than two.

This incapacitation ended with one final, brutal push, and I was ejected out into the open world. The contrast with my familiar warm sea was absurd and cruel. Everything here was overwhelmingly bright, loud, and cold, and I felt immensely lonely. I shivered violently and let out a long, terrified wail.

Part III

{ Age 0 }

THERE WAS A PARTICULAR TREE I saw nearly every time my mother took me on a journey outside the house. It was much larger than all the other trees, and its branches reached up farther than I could see. Squirrels clambered up and down its trunk, and there was one red bird that always seemed to be gazing over at us as we passed by. This bird became my first friend, and I waved to him every time we saw each other.

"There's that little bird again," my mom would say. "You love that silly red bird, don't you?"

The tree and the bird entered my dreams, along with my mother's voice and the milk she fed me from her body, my father's bearded face, the billowing clouds in the sky, the green grass in our yard, the bright sun on my bedroom ceiling in the morning, and a multitude of other details that comprised my life. The boundary between my dreams and waking life was tenuous, and the two states blended together as one continuous flow. I was barely aware of this, though, and I was happy whenever and however the red bird came to me.

Occasionally the bird took on the voice of my mother or father, telling me how cute I was and asking me if I was happy. I would laugh and answer back in my babbling syllables. Sometimes the bird hovered above my crib and soothed my fear as I screamed for my mother at night. Sometimes he even let me magically peer through the roof of the house up into the night sky, where the moon shimmered calmly down.

Ease

{ Age 1 }

I T WAS A SUMMER EVENING, nearing twilight. I had just learned to run fast, and I was weaving dizzily around the backyard chasing lightning bugs. My mother was watching me from the porch steps, laughing with someone on the phone. I tripped and fell harmlessly into the grass face-first, then turned over on my back and looked up at the sky, where the first stars were just beginning to materialize. My mother's voice mingled with the soft din of the crickets rising up all around me, and my eyes began to grow heavy. Suddenly I saw a white flash of light streak down from the top of the sky.

"Byron, did you see that?" my mother yelled from the porch. "That was a shooting star!"

I knew that word, "star." My mind whirled as I sensed something much grander than the house, the yard, or even the moon. I became giddy and started rolling around on the ground, grabbing handfuls of grass and tossing them in the air. I heard my mother laughing, and soon she was standing over me and grinning down, her white teeth glowing in the light from the porch. She picked me up and spun me around and then pulled me into her, hugging me tight enough against her chest that I could hear her heartbeat in my ear.

Later that night, I was roused from a deep sleep by a noise in the house. I pulled myself up in my crib and stared at the sliver of hallway light shining under the door. I called out for my mother a few times, testing to see if she was there, but there was no reply. I shut my eyes and tried to conjure my tree, my bird, or the shooting star, but nothing came, so I started to cry. Was I alone in the world now? For a few endless moments, I felt true confusion and despair. I called out over and over for my mother, with tears streaming into my mouth.

Finally, the bedroom door opened and my mother rushed in and took me in her arms. She whispered calming things I didn't fully understand, and I soon forgot about everything that had come before. My heartbeat slowed, and my eyes began to flutter and close...

{ Age 2 }

MEANDERING THROUGH THE WOODS one fall afternoon, I paused, as I usually did, to inspect every leaf that caught my eye. My parents were up ahead on the trail chatting about something dull and adult, and my six-year-old cousin Isla was wandering behind me, busily gathering acorns and stuffing them into her pockets.

"Do you like acorns, Byron?" she asked happily.

"Yes."

"You like leaves the most though, right?"

"Yes."

"I think I like them both the same."

"Look," I said, holding out a leaf to Isla.

"There's a caterpillar on that leaf!" she exclaimed, grinning and clapping her hands.

Her excitement infected me and I started giggling uncontrollably. Isla took the fuzzy black caterpillar between her fingers and held it up in front of her eyes.

"Look at it wriggling around," she said, laughing.

We watched it squirm for a few moments until Isla accidentally dropped it on the ground, where it disappeared beneath the top layer of the bed of leaves. Isla knelt down and began frantically searching for it, her eyes scanning every leaf. I stepped forward to help and immediately felt something squish beneath my foot. I bent down and turned over the leaf I'd stepped on, instinctively terrified of what I'd find. There was the flattened body of the caterpillar, its guts spread out along the leaf. My lip quivered and I began to cry softly.

"It's dead," said Isla, now standing over me. "When you stepped on it you killed it, but that's OK."

"Dead?" I asked.

"Yes, dead. It's gone forever. Everything has to die though, so it's OK."

I plopped down on the ground and started sobbing loudly. My parents soon appeared, and my father put his hand on my head and asked me what was wrong.

"He killed a caterpillar, but it's OK," said Isla cheerfully. "He stepped on it. See?"

Through my tears I could see the mangled caterpillar still clinging to the leaf as Isla held it up for my parents. I thought about *forever* and what that could possibly mean. The caterpillar would never wake up.

"Byron, don't be sad," my father said. "You didn't mean to step on it."

I wiped my eyes and stood up unsteadily. Isla wrapped her arm around my shoulder and led me carefully up the trail.

"The caterpillar is in heaven, I think," she said, somewhat reassuringly.

{ Age 3 }

I WAS TOSSING AND TURNING on the sofa, sweaty and miserable with a fever. My mouth was bone dry and I couldn't get enough water, so I just lay there panting like a dog and occasionally whimpering for my mother. *Sesame Street* was on TV—Oscar the Grouch was scowling in his trash can—but I was barely watching. Every inch of my body ached, and no position on the couch gave me any relief. The disgusting sensation brewing in the pit of my stomach suddenly pushed up into my throat, and I projectile vomited on my lap and all over the couch.

"Mommy!" I screamed after I caught my breath. "Something happened!"

The liquid on my lower half was beginning to turn cold as my mother rushed in.

"Oh, poor baby," she said, remaining calm. "You threw up. It's no big deal. Everybody does it. I'll go get a towel from the kitchen and be right back to get you all cleaned up."

When she'd sopped up all the vomit she could, she put her hand on my forehead.

"You're burning up! Let's go upstairs and get you into a cool bath."

Up in the bathroom, she gently peeled off my wet, fetid clothes and deposited me in the tepid bathwater. For some reason, instead of abating, my fever quickly spiked and I went into convulsions. I assume (well, I know) my mother was panicking, but I crossed into a curiously peaceful dream state.

I was floating through our house, with my feet just a few inches above the floor. I entered my room and floated to the foot of my bed, where I passed through the wall and into a hidden corridor. The walls of the corridor were bare, and there was a closed door at the end. As I drew near, the door opened to reveal a vast staircase leading down to seemingly infinite depths. Earth vanished, and I appeared to be out in space underneath the stars. As I began to float down the staircase, I heard a deep, calming voice.

"Are you Byron?"

"Yes."

"Are you sure?"

"Yes, I think so."

"We want you to remember that no matter what, you are fine."

On hearing this, I felt a deep sense of joy and exhilaration. The voice went silent, and I kept peacefully descending the endless staircase, floating down into space. Finally, after what seemed like hours, I heard my mother anxiously calling my name.

"Byron, can you hear me? Byron! Please, please wake up!"

I opened my eyes and I was back in the bathtub, staring down at my body in the water. It took me a few seconds to adjust to having weight again. I felt happy.

"Hi mommy," I said, smiling up at her.

{ Age 4 }

"**Y**OU HAVE TO RUN LIKE THIS!" yelled Jeremy, his long blonde hair flowing behind him as he held his arms out like wings and sprinted down the hill.

I ran after him with my arms held out and my head thrown back, taking in the wide open spring sky. Up ahead, Jeremy suddenly stopped dead and pointed into the distance.

"See those birds there," he said. "They just came up from the south. My dad told me how that happens."

We stood and watched the V formation ripple peacefully across the sky. I turned and saw that our mothers were also watching the birds from the top of the hill. They waved to me and I waved back. Jeremy started running again, barreling forward at full speed while still looking up at the birds.

Suddenly, his foot caught in an indentation in the dirt and his body projected forward through the air. He put his arms out to break his fall, and there was a sickening crack as both hands hit the ground. Next came a moment of horrible silence, followed by a blood-curdling scream and loud sobbing. I stood over him in a panic as he held up his arms to show me his limply hanging wrists.

Later that day, in the midst of a seemingly endless session in the waiting room of the ER, I sat eating a bag of peanuts from the vending machine. My mother was sipping a coffee while skimming through a magazine with a fancy blonde woman on the cover.

"What's that magazine?" I asked.

"People," she replied, smiling. "It's about famous people."

"Oh," I said flatly.

I ate another peanut and simultaneously had a terrifying thought.

"Do you think Jeremy will have to get his hands cut off?" I asked nervously, sitting up straight.

"No, no, of course he won't," my mother answered, lowering the magazine to her lap. "Why would you think that?"

"When something gets hurt real bad, sometimes they cut it off. It was in dad's show."

"Listen, I promise you they are not going to cut his hands off."

"OK," I said, relaxing a bit.

After a few more peanuts, Jeremy's mother emerged through the sliding glass doors. Her face seemed tight and anxious.

"What's happening now?" my mother asked. "How's Jeremy?"

"Well, two broken wrists, basically. Bad breaks. He's got pins in both and they're putting the casts on now."

"Good lord," my mother replied. "Is he in pain?"

"They gave him something for that. He's actually more fascinated by it all than anything."

That evening, we had dinner together at the Friendly's restaurant near the hospital. Jeremy got a clown cone sundae as a reward for being brave, and my mother had no choice but to order me one as well. Jeremy chattered away as his mother fed him bites of ice cream.

"It was scary, a little, but I was brave," he said, hot fudge dripping off his chin. "They put metal in my hands."

He held up both his casts for us to see.

"Whoah," I said, impressed.

I thought about how Jeremy would now need help to turn doorknobs, eat, pee, wipe himself, and on and on. He just sat there grinning—perhaps obliviously, perhaps in spite of it all.

{ Age 5 }

WITH MY FEET HANGING off the kitchen counter and the plastic bowl in my lap, I whisked the eggs as fast as I could. The yolks merged with the whites and the mixture started turning the familiar light yellow. My mother came over to inspect.

"Great job, honey!" she said, smiling. "You're the best helper."

I whisked until my arm got tired, and then handed her the bowl.

"Are eggs little chickens?" I asked.

"Not yet," she answered, pouring the eggs out onto the hot pan. "They would become chickens if you kept them warm and cared for them. But the eggs we're eating are not chickens."

"Was I ever in an egg?"

"Well, sort of," she said, chuckling. "In a way, you started out as an egg inside me, but you never hatched out of an egg like a chicken. You formed inside my belly—getting bigger and bigger—and then when you were ready, you came out."

"On the day I was born?"

"Right, on the day you were born."

Stephen Intlekofer

"Are you only born once?"

"Yes, only once," she answered, looking at me quizzically.

"And do you only die once?"

"Yes, you only die once."

She pulled a cooked waffle out of the waffle maker and tossed it on a plate. The eggs had begun to solidify, and she started pushing at them with the spatula.

"Why are you asking me about this?" she asked, turning to me. "Did you hear something different?"

"I don't know," I replied. "I think it would be weird to live more than once. But it would also be weird to just live once."

"Well, you know, if you just live once, you need to enjoy every moment because that moment will never happen again."

"It'll never happen again, ever?"

"No, just that one time."

"But what if it's not exactly the same?"

"What do you mean?"

"I mean if you live again. What if everything is kind of the same, but also a little different?"

"Byron, you're a nut," she said, laughing. "How are you even thinking about this stuff? You're five years old."

"I don't know," I answered with a sly smile. "I think I dreamed about it."

"I see. Well, dreams aren't real. You know that, right?"

The eggs were all scrambled, so she turned off the burner to let them cool.

"But what if a little part of them is real?" I asked.

"Dreams are just things your brain makes up while you sleep. That's all they are."

No part of me really believed this, but I decided to humor her.

"OK, mommy."

"Why don't you just think about playing and having fun?" she asked, smiling. "That's the beauty of being five."

She picked me up off the counter and swung me playfully in the air before lowering me to the floor. I giggled and wrapped myself around her leg so she'd have to drag me around as she walked.

"Go sit at the table, silly. Breakfast is almost ready."

{ Age 6 }

RECESS HAD JUST BEGUN, and I was hovering shyly on the periphery of a group of boys, observing the proceedings as they set out the "rules" for some sort of chase game. My classmate Patrick waved a rolled-up magazine in the air.

"This is a baton, like they have in the Olympic races," he yelled. "We can pass it to each other and whoever gets it has to run away from everyone."

With that, he started sprinting up the sidewalk that cut through the parking lot section of our playground. The others ran wildly after him, with me cautiously bringing up the rear. I drifted on the edges of the group, darting in and out of the melee where I could to keep up appearances. Eventually my friend Mike got the magazine, and he started running directly toward me from the top of the sidewalk, with the others trailing in his wake. His eyes grew wide as he stretched out the "baton" to me.

"Run!" he screamed.

As I grabbed the magazine, I felt a shiver pass through me. There was a distinct and unsettling familiarity to the moment—the angle of the sun, the smell of the cool spring air, Mike's breathless yell, the small crowd of boys stampeding toward us. I had no time to dwell, though, and I started sprinting away as fast as I could.

As I ran, I could sense the distance between me and the rest of the group increasing. I veered to the right when I reached the fence at the bottom of the playground, and then looped around the back of the kindergarten building. When I reached the main building back at the top of the parking lot, I paused briefly to catch my breath. I was in the heart of the action for once, and it was exhilarating.

"I'm right behind you!" Patrick yelled.

Suddenly his hand was on my shoulder, and I spun around to catch a brief glimpse of his grinning face.

"You're fast!" he said admiringly, grabbing the magazine from me and sprinting off.

The others soon migrated in his direction, screaming and laughing and flailing their arms. I took a deep breath and raced down to join the group.

{ Age 7 }

A
S THE MID-MORNING LIGHT streamed in through the window, our Sunday school teacher stood gazing out over the group of kids sitting cross-legged on the carpet. He smiled for a moment and then grew serious.

"The Bible does say that those who don't accept the truth of Christianity will go to hell. This is what I like to call a harsh truth. Now you may say 'What about my grandmother? She isn't a Christian. Is she going to hell? And what about people in Africa who've never heard about Jesus?' Well, the Bible clearly says in the book of Romans, 'For since the creation of the world God's invisible qualities—his eternal power and divine nature—have been clearly seen, being understood from what has been made, so that men are without excuse.' This means that everyone has been shown the truth of Christianity in one way or another. Everyone is able to see that God is powerful and holy, and everyone is also able to see how beautiful the Earth that he created is. A lot of people just choose to reject all this, which means they say it isn't true."

He paused and took note of our demeanor, which was mostly bored. A few of the listeners though, including me, were completely engrossed. This was an adult saying this, and he seemed completely sure of it.

"What do you think of this, Byron?" he asked, sensing my interest.

"I don't know," I replied softly. "It sounds kind of scary."

"I know it might be hard to think about all this, but it's important. It seems unfair in a way, doesn't it, that people would be sent to hell? But the fact is Jesus came to Earth to show us the truth, and now it's up to us to accept it. John 3:16 says, 'For God so loved the world that He gave his one and only Son, that whoever believes in Him shall not perish, but have eternal life.' This is great news! You are being offered heaven, which is eternal life with God. What could be better than that?"

He paused again to take stock. More ears were perked up now, it seemed.

"The Bible also says that 'all have sinned and fall short of the glory of God.' Since the very beginning, when Adam and Eve chose to eat from the Tree of the Knowledge of Good and Evil, humans have been sinful. To sin means to go against God and what he says is good and true. All humans are sinful, even all of you. Everyone actually deserves to go to hell, believe it or not, but Jesus came to offer a way for us to be saved from what we deserve. God sent Jesus because he loves us and wants us to be saved."

He smiled and sat down cross-legged on the floor.

"So, today, I am offering you all the opportunity to accept Jesus into your heart. All you have to do is say a prayer I will lead you through. Then you are saved forever. You will spend eternity in heaven with God. Isn't that amazing? So now, please raise your hand if you'd like to come and pray with me to take Jesus into your heart. Each of you will come up one at a time and I'll lead you through."

All hands went up except mine. As I glanced around the room, my face went beet red, and I finally raised my hand as well. One by one, everyone was called up, and eventually my turn arrived. The teacher led me through the prayer with his hand on the top of my head. I repeated the words after him, trembling with anxiety. What if it didn't work? How would I know if I was really saved? How could a bunch of words give me eternal life in heaven?

When I stood up afterward, I felt relieved. It was done. There was no joy though, no exhilaration. I felt no different than I had a few minutes before.

At lunch that afternoon, I decided to tell my father what had happened. He was overjoyed, as happy as I'd ever seen him.

"This is a huge moment for you, Byron," he said, his eyes beaming. "The biggest. I'm so happy."

The level of pride he felt overwhelmed me and made me squirm a little.

"Do you have any questions for me?" he asked. "I wanted you to come to Christ on your own, and now you have, but I know it can bring up a lot of questions."

I had many questions.

"Did God create hell?" I began.

"Well, yes, I suppose he did. He created everything."

"Why did he create it?"

My father shifted a bit in his seat.

"It's part of his bigger plan, I think. We humans can't really understand that plan. It's too big for us."

This felt deeply unsatisfying to me, but I continued on.

"Is Grandmom going to hell?"

My father began to speak, paused uncertainly, and then began again.

"Well, I believe your grandmom is in a very good position to accept Jesus, so I have faith that she will be in heaven when she dies."

"But if she dies now, will she go to hell?"

"First, she's not going to die now. She's got a lot more time to live. Second, I'd like to think she'll go to heaven, but I have to admit I'm not sure."

I hated this answer, but I moved on.

"When God created humans, why did he make them sin?"

"He didn't make them sin, he just gave them the choice whether to sin or not, and they picked sin."

"Didn't he know they would pick sin? Doesn't he know everything?"

"Hmm. That's a good question. I'm sure he did know. But his mind is so much bigger than ours. He knows things we can't know, like the reason things have to be the way they are."

I hated this answer too, but I moved on.

"What about the people who lived before Jesus? And what about little babies who die? Are they all in hell?"

"That I'm not sure about, but I do think God shows mercy," my poor father answered with a feeble smile. "Boy, you have some tough questions, don't you?"

"Why doesn't God just let everyone go to heaven when they die?" I asked, not relenting.

"I think because we are given the choice on Earth whether to accept Jesus or not. We are free to decide, and we then have to deal with the results of what we decide."

"I don't understand why God would send anyone to hell. Doesn't he love us?"

"Yes, he definitely loves us. There are just some things we'll probably never understand, I think."

I decided right then that I didn't believe in hell or any type of god who'd create such a place. If I was saved, I certainly wasn't yet a proper Christian.

{ Age 8 }

DOZING UNDER THE UMBRELLA on a broiling hot mid-July afternoon at Rehoboth Beach, my parents had apparently forgotten about lunch. I nudged my father with a sand-covered foot.

"Dad, wake up. I need to eat."

He slowly turned to look at me, and then began fishing around in the beach bag for his wallet. He pulled out a ten-dollar bill and handed it to me.

"Go on up to the boardwalk and get whatever you want," he mumbled. "I trust you."

I felt a surge of excitement. Going up to the boardwalk alone? This was new.

"OK dad, thanks. I'll probably just get a hotdog and fries and a lemonade. Or maybe a piece of pizza. I'll have to see what looks really good when I get there."

"Whatever you want," he replied sleepily, turning back over on his stomach.

I tucked the money in my swimsuit pocket and started plodding across the hot sand in my flip-flops. When I reached the boardwalk, I stomped my feet to shed the loose sand and scanned the storefronts to see if anything caught my eye. I spotted a Grotto Pizza down to the right, so I started off in that direction. As I walked, I relished the novel feeling of being on my own in the world. There was a subtle undercurrent of anxiety, of course, but it was easily quelled by the wonder of all the details I was taking in—the screaming children, the teenage couples holding hands, the parents hoisting beach chairs and umbrellas, the blaring of the video games at the arcade, the intermingled smells of taffy and popcorn and cotton candy.

When I reached Grotto, I strode up to the counter and ordered a slice of cheese pizza and a lemonade. The cashier took my ten-dollar bill with a smile.

"OK sweetie, here's your change."

She handed me 6 ones and small pile of coins. When my order was ready, I took it over to an open bench in the shade. As I blew on my pizza to cool it down, I noticed a tiny woman laboring toward me from the beach side of the boardwalk. She was walking with fitted metal crutches, and one of her shoes had a massive sole on it to account for the fact that one leg was much shorter than the other. It was apparent she was eyeing the open spot next to me on the bench.

"Hello there," she said when she reached me.

She smiled and blew a stray lock of hair away from her mouth.

"Hi," I answered shyly.

"May I sit next to you?"

"OK," I said, smiling awkwardly.

She swiveled around on ends of her crutches and carefully placed herself down next to me. I was too fascinated to eat, so I nervously sipped my lemonade and stared at her out of the corner of my eye.

"What's your name?" she asked. "Not that names matter, but still..."

"Byron," I replied softly.

"I like that name."

She detached her crutches and rested them against the side of the bench. I took a bite of pizza and continued to observe her as unobtrusively as possible.

"Are you here in Rehoboth by yourself?" she asked with a sly smile.

"No," I said, grinning. "My parents are on the beach sleeping."

"Oh, I see."

She leaned back on the bench, her deep blue eyes scanning the horizon intently. She looked to be about my parents' age, but it was hard to say for sure.

"I was here alone, but now I'm not alone," she said. "I saw you from the other side of the boardwalk when I was walking and I said to myself, now there's a person I need to talk to."

"Oh," I answered with a nervous chuckle.

"I said, I need to talk to him because I sense he's perfectly positioned on the same path as me," she continued in a deliberate tone, staring at a lit cigarette butt someone had just flicked close to our feet.

I had no idea what this meant, so I just gazed down at the crust bubbles on my pizza and said nothing.

"OK, enough of that," she said, smiling again. "How's the water? Have you gone in yet?"

"Yeah," I replied. "It's cold, but you get used to it."

"Ah yes, you do get used to it. And then it feels so good when you get out and lay in the sun. So warm, with the water just steaming up off your body. It feels perfect, doesn't it?"

"Yeah, I love that."

"You know, I've been on a journey, and it feels good to be sitting here with you. It's peaceful. The bustle of the crowd, the smell of the food and the ocean, the sound of the waves, the relief of the breeze. All the various details to dip in and out of. There's such beauty in all of it, don't you agree?"

"Yeah," I agreed, my mouth full of pizza crust.

She smiled and slowly ran both hands through her hair.

"It feels good to let bitterness go," she said, almost to herself. "Don't resist."

After a few moments of silence, she turned to face me, her eyes gleaming.

"You can leave if you want. I know you probably want to get back to the beach and your parents."

"OK," I said, relieved.

I grabbed my lemonade and my empty plate and got to my feet.

"Can you remember one thing for me?" she asked.

"Sure," I said, glancing back at her.

"The key is to just release into the experience of it all."

"OK, thanks," I said, smiling nervously and not really comprehending.

As I turned and made my way back across the teeming boardwalk, I could hear her lilting voice above the din of the crowd.

"Great to see you."

{ Age 9 }

MY GRANDMOTHER WAS STANDING over the hot griddle smoking a cigarette and flipping pancakes with a spatula. She was wearing her familiar blue terrycloth bathrobe, and her short grey hair was full of curlers. Isla was sitting next to me at the kitchen table immersed a Judy Blume novel, and I was listening to my grandmother pontificate about a shopping experience she'd had at some point in the recent past.

"So when I found the dress, I went up to the register to buy it. This was Macy's so there was a register right in that section. Anyway, in front of me in line was this lady who was screaming at the poor saleslady. 'This dress is half off! I pulled it from a sales rack that said 50% off!' she yells. The saleslady was very calm actually, and just told her, 'Now ma'am, I scanned the dress and it's 10% off. All these dresses are in the same place, on the same racks, and they all say 10% off. It might have been placed on the wrong rack. If that's true, I'm sorry about that.' So she was very reasonable I thought."

She paused to pour more batter on the griddle and take a drag from her cigarette. She held the smoke in her lungs as she talked.

"So then the woman yells some more, starts cursing and waving her hands around. So eventually the security people had to come and escort this bitch out of the store. We were all clapping as they took her away."

She turned toward the table, exhaling a large plume of smoke in our direction.

"So then I went up to buy my dress, and I congratulated the saleslady on how she handled the situation. She was a darkie, but very smart and together."

Isla looked up from her book with a frown.

"No one says that anymore, Grandmom."

"No one says what?"

"Darkie."

"Why not? That's how everyone talked in North Carolina when I was growing up. It's not a rude name. It's not like saying nigger."

"Grandmom!" Isla exclaimed, horrified, as I fidgeted uncomfortably in my chair.

"What? I said she was smart. I liked her."

"It doesn't matter, Grandmom, you shouldn't call people things like darkie."

"Well, I know what I mean by it. I'm old now, and I ain't changing."

She grinned at us, took a drag from her cigarette, and turned back around to tend to the griddle.

Later that day, after lunch, Isla and I made our customary trip to the drawer in the dining room where the York peppermint patties were "hidden." Ostensibly these were not meant for us, but we took them during every visit and the supply was mysteriously replenished every time we returned. We each grabbed a few patties and headed upstairs to the secret rooms for some exploration.

The top floor of my grandmother's house was for the most part no longer used, and the rooms were dark and dusty and full of enigmatic knick-knacks. We entered one of the bedrooms and started opening the drawers of an old dresser. In one of the small drawers at the top, I found a silver cigarette case filled with stale cigarettes. Yielding to an irresistible impulse, I took one out and placed it between my lips. Isla's eyes widened as she watched me.

"What are you doing?" she asked, chuckling.

I said nothing and walked over to the closet door next to the bed to view myself in the full-length mirror. I stood with my arms crossed and the cigarette dangling from my lips. Isla was standing behind me on the opposite side of the bed, observing me with amusement. Suddenly the reflected image multiplied and receded backward in a seemingly infinite regress, like a funhouse hall of mirrors. I felt profoundly disoriented and dizzy, but I was frozen to my spot on the floor. For what seemed like minutes, I could see nothing but the limitless repeating images extending out to an infinitesimal point in the distance. Finally, I heard Isla's voice calling me.

"Byron, what's going on? Can you hear me?"

She materialized next to me, her green eyes wide and frightened. I just stood there dazed, the cigarette still between my lips.

"What happened to you? I was calling you so many times. It looked like you zoned out or something."

"I don't know," I said softly, pulling the cigarette out of my mouth. "It was weird. The reflection in the mirror was repeating over and over as far as I could see."

"That's crazy!" said Isla excitedly. "Like in a hall of mirrors? I've been in one of those before."

"Yeah, just like that," I replied, sitting down on the very edge of the bed.

I was sweating, and a tight ball of anxiety had formed in the center of my ribs.

"I think you were in a trance or something. You weren't answering for like 30 seconds."

I glanced around the room to verify its reality. All was stable and in its place. Isla sat down next to me and held out a peppermint patty.

"Here, eat one of these. It'll make you feel better."

{ Age 10 }

I
T WAS A FRIGID EVENING in late November, and I was hopping from foot to foot and clapping my hands together to keep warm as I scanned the field from my perch in the mouth of the goal. The action was all on the other end, as it had been for most of the first half. My soccer team was good, which meant the games could be fairly boring for the goalie, but I was consumed with anxiety.

What if the ball just went right through my hands? What if I accidentally kicked it into my own goal? What if I accidentally kicked it to one of their players right in front of the goal? What if my mom was trying to wave to me as usual and she distracted me and the ball went through my legs?

Already, my brain thrived on inventing random, worrisome possibilities that could perhaps occur—one of the truly pointless human pastimes.

"Pay attention!" came a familiar taunting voice from behind the goal.

"Shut up, Ally," I replied flatly without turning around.

She was the coach's daughter, and for whatever reason she had an ongoing interest in tormenting me, especially when I was trapped in goal like this with nowhere to go.

"What!? Just some friendly advice."

I stayed silent, ruminating. The ball was still well beyond midfield, and there was no imminent threat of it crossing back over.

"Are you worried about them kicking it to you?" she continued. "You should be."

"I'm not worried," I answered through my teeth.

"I can tell you are. You're scared. But it's OK, even if you make the team lose, your mommy will still love you."

"Shut up," was all I could think to say.

"No, I don't think I will," she replied.

I seethed and searched for a clever comeback, but the action suddenly, unexpectedly spilled over the midfield line and barreled my way. My fullbacks seemed bewildered as one of the opponent's forwards bore down on goal with the ball. He reared back to kick and unleashed a sad, looping shot that I had no trouble corralling. As I shielded the ball, the other forwards closed in around me and tried to kick it out of my hands until the ref finally blew the whistle to call them off.

After I took my free kick and the action pushed back across midfield, I noticed the side of my right hand was bleeding through my white goalie glove. Even though it was just a tiny spot, this gave me immense satisfaction.

"Think I'm scared now?" I said loudly, holding up my hand without turning around. "My hand's bleeding and it doesn't even hurt."

"You didn't even get kicked that hard," came the bored response.

{ Age 11 }

A S I LAY IN BED, I tried to sift through the contents of the day. Why did Laurie grab my hand like that? What made her so interested in me? She looked like she was at least fourteen, and I looked like I was nine. All the boys made fun of me for it, calling me Bitty Byron and hoisting me up off the ground to show how light and weak I was. All the girls said I was funny and made them laugh, but that was the end of it. They treated me like their little brother. Laurie looked at me differently, though, which made me squirm and twisted my stomach into knots. Then today she'd grabbed my hand at lunch, which had left me both confused and thrilled.

My mind churned on the Laurie conundrum for a while until sleep slowly started to overtake me. I entered the twilight world between waking and sleeping, and I found myself in an empty room with white walls and no doors. I was sitting on a metal folding chair with my hands resting on my knees. Everything was utterly silent.

After what seemed like a few minutes of me simply staring at the wall in front of me, I stood and stretched my arms over my head. I looked up and saw that there was no ceiling on the room. The walls extended up nearly as far as my eyes could see before eventually melting into the starry night sky.

As I gazed up, I noticed a point of warm golden light begin to form in the center of the sky. It descended toward me, its form solidifying as it grew nearer. Eventually, it settled in the room as a small cube about the size of my head, hovering just above the floor about ten feet away from me and emitting a low, intense hum. As I sat down in the chair to observe it, I felt no fear, just curiosity. A deep and soothing female voice echoed around the walls.

"You have passed through the central axis point and can now see things from the perpendicular plane."

As the words faded away, the light cube just continued to gently pulsate and hum.

"What's the central axis point?" I asked softly, almost unconsciously.

"The point around which all human experience revolves."

I couldn't think of any response to this.

"Do not focus on any one aspect," continued the echoing voice. "Simply let yourself observe."

"OK," I replied prosaically.

The contrast between her voice and mine was disconcerting. Mine was so small and insignificant, sucked up immediately into the ether.

"Enjoy this form and its limitations," the voice went on after a pause. "Enjoy the process of living and dying. There is no before. There is no after."

At this point the floor and the walls began to fade, leaving me alone in darkness with the cube. I felt at home, as if there was nothing else I could ever need. The hum soon dropped me into a deeper sleep state, and oblivion took over.

{ Age 12 }

"**B**YRON AND TARA, for the love of God, can you please stop your aimless chattering and pay attention?"

Mrs. Gonsall had paused in the process of writing out an equation on the board and was staring at us with obvious irritation.

"OK, sure," I answered with a smirk, showing off for Tara.

"See, that right there," she said, pointing at me. "That attitude's not working for me. Either you cut the snark, or you go to Principal Miller's office."

"Fine, I'm sorry," I replied, suppressing a giggle as Tara nudged my leg beneath the desk.

"OK then, we continue," said Mrs. Gonsall, turning back to the board.

After a few minutes, Tara opened my fingers and placed a note in my hand. I unfolded it in my lap.

"Byron, Byron, Byron. You are quite bad. But I like you anyway..."

I blushed and glanced over at her. She was scribbling away in her notebook, pretending to pay attention to the teacher. Her dark red hair fell down over her face and brushed against her arm as she leaned forward.

Later that evening, I began pitching books violently across my bedroom. One by one, they fluttered through the air and crashed to the floor in a heap next to the dresser. I was pissed off about something I couldn't really identify, which only compounded my anger. Maybe it was Tara ignoring me as we were walking out of school, or my mother telling me to stop sulking around the house. I was swinging wildly between emotions these days—elated and euphoric some of the time, but mostly just confused and frustrated. Above all, I felt unbearably confined.

There was a loud knock on my door.

"Byron, what's going on?" came my mother's agitated voice.

"Nothing!" I yelled.

She swung the door open and strode into the room.

"What's this?" she said, gesturing toward the scattered pile of books in the corner.

"Books I threw over there."

"Why?" she asked, exasperated.

"I don't know. I guess I was mad."

"About what?"

"Not sure."

"That's not an answer."

"Well, what do you want me to say?"

"I don't know, Byron. Why don't you tell me something substantial? What's really going on?"

"I told you I don't know. You want me to make something up?" I asked irritably.

"I cannot wait until this stage is over," she muttered under her breath.

"Sorry I'm ruining your life."

"I didn't say that."

"You're thinking it."

"This is pointless," she replied despondently. "I give up. Stop throwing books or you're grounded."

She slammed the door behind her as she left. I immediately grabbed my tattered copy of *The Phantom Tollbooth* and whipped it into the corner with all the others.

{ Age 13 }

A S WE PULLED UP to the nursing home, I wondered what exactly my grandmother would ramble on about this time, between coughing fits. Her mind had been going downhill along with her lungs, and her latest pastime was providing us a running commentary of all the conspiracy theories in her head about the nurses, the food workers, and the other residents. As we signed in at the desk, I accidentally locked eyes with the senile old woman who seemed to believe I was her son John. I was hoping she'd be in her room, which was right next to my grandmother's, but she always seemed to be lingering out in the hallway.

"John, John, come talk to your mother for a bit," she said, holding out her arms to me as we passed by.

"Mrs. Donaldson, this is my son Byron," my mother said patiently, taking hold of one of her hands.

"It's not John?" Mrs. Donaldson asked plaintively.

"No, it's Byron, my son."

"Oh, but I prayed for John to come, so I think he's coming."

No one at the nursing home knew anything about her son John. Her daughter Karen had put her in the home and was the only one who came to visit.

"OK, well hopefully you see him soon," my mother said, patting her on the shoulder.

"Oh, I know I will," Mrs. Donaldson answered, smiling faintly.

When we entered my grandmother's room, she was lying on the bed staring up at the ceiling. She turned her head as she heard us enter.

"Well hello there," she said softly, grinning and trying to catch her breath. "What a pleasant surprise."

The rattle in her chest was even more pronounced today, and every breath was labored.

"I told you we were coming, mom," my mother said gently. "I called to tell you."

"Did you? They probably told you they'd tell me and never did. That's how it is here."

"No, I spoke to you. I told you myself."

"Ah, well, I don't recall that. Byron, come here and give me a hug."

I leaned down and wrapped my arms around her neck. The faint scent of her familiar perfume briefly transported me back to her old house—the kitchen, the screened-in porch, the den with the ancient TV.

"This may be the last time you see me alive," she said mournfully.

"Nonsense, mom," my mother scolded.

"The nurses are stealing most of my food. They just give me scraps. I'm starving here."

"I promise they're not stealing your food, mom."

"They are!" she yelled before collapsing into a brutal coughing fit.

My mother helped her sit up as she hacked and gasped for air, her eyes protruding grotesquely and the skin on her face turning dark blue.

"Should we call the nurse?" I asked, horrified.

"No, not yet," my mother said, gently rubbing her back. "It usually calms down on its own."

Eventually the attack subsided, and my grandmother eased herself back down on the bed with a grimace.

"This goddamn emphysema," she said softly. "Byron, if you start smoking I'll strangle you from the other side."

"I won't, Grandmom," I said to soothe her.

I'd just tried smoking for the first time a few days before, outside the mall.

"Last night I saw myself dead on this bed," she continued. "I guess I was dreaming... I don't know. I saw my body lying here, and then it kind of just crumbled into dust."

"Mom, can you tone the death talk down a bit?" my mother implored.

"Why? It's the reality we're dealing with. Anyway, I'm OK with it. I just want to stop coughing and choking all the time. It's miserable."

"How are things otherwise?" my mother asked. "Are you reading at all? Watching TV?"

"I've had a pretty good life, I think," she went on, ignoring my mother. "Treated people well for the most part. Hopefully God will take mercy on me."

The next morning, a Sunday, my mother got an early phone call and rushed out the door to the nursing home. When she came back home in the afternoon, wan and downcast, she rested her head on my father's shoulder and sobbed. My grandmother was dead. When I tearfully asked her why she didn't let me know so I could say goodbye, my mother visibly shuddered.

"It was horrible, Byron," she said bluntly. "She just slowly choked to death."

{ Age 14 }

I T WAS A SATURDAY MORNING in November and I was alone in the house, eating Frosted Flakes at the dining room table. Through the window, I could see my father positioning the ladder so he could climb up and clean out another gutter. With his gloved hands, he fished out handful after handful of damp leaves and tossed them to the ground.

I was bringing my empty cereal bowl to the kitchen sink when there was a loud clatter and a yell. I rushed back to the dining room and saw my father hanging by one arm from the gutter, suspended about ten feet above the ground. I ran outside to find that the ladder had fallen sideways into a bush.

"Can you grab the ladder and put it back up next to me?" my father asked with a veneer of calm.

He was now hanging by both arms and gazing down at me. I grabbed the ladder and hoisted it up against the gutter as close to him as I could get it. He edged over to it and started climbing quickly down.

"I think I cut my finger pretty badly," he said when he reached the ground. "Sliced it on the gutter when I grabbed it to keep myself from falling."

He yanked off his glove to reveal a deep cut at the base of his index finger. Blood was beginning to flow profusely, streaming down his arm and onto the ground.

"Can you go grab me a bunch of paper towels?" he asked.

When I returned, he used the paper towels to sop up the blood on his hand and compress the cut. He then made his way inside to the kitchen sink, where I watched in dismay as he rinsed the cut as best he could. The blood continued to pour out relentlessly.

"It's down to the bone, I think," he said. "We'll have to go to the hospital. Run upstairs and get me a few of the older looking washcloths and I'll wrap this with them."

The ride to the hospital was harrowing for us both. My father drove with his left hand while continually rewrapping his injured right hand in fresh washcloths and paper towels that I handed to him. I threw the used bloody ones in a plastic bag at my feet.

"Fun, huh?" he said with a smile as we turned into the hospital parking lot.

In the emergency room, I was allowed to watch the doctor stitch up the finger and then set up a splint. My father seemed to relish my fascination with the whole process.

"You kind of enjoyed that, didn't you?" he asked, amused, as we walked back to the car.

"Yeah, it was interesting," I answered in my typical monotone.

"I've liked spending this time with you, as weird as the reason is," he said as we pulled onto the highway. "Thanks for helping me."

"No problem."

"You know you can talk to me about anything you want to, right?" he asked cautiously.

"Yeah, I know."

"I know I can be a little strict sometimes."

"You're strict a lot of the time," I replied, recalling his recent confiscation of a stack of my 'secular' music CDs.

"Not compared to my father, I'm not."

"You always say that."

"It's true, though. You have it pretty good... you really do."

I folded my arms and stared out the window, retreating back into my habitual sullenness.

"You'll learn, eventually," he said. "Nothing's as bad as you think it is right now."

{ Age 15 }

GROUPS OF TEENAGERS congregated in tight groups outside the mall entrance, alternately laughing affectedly and glancing around to see who might be looking at them. I was off to the side with my friend Scott, observing. He wasn't afraid of smoking out in public like I was, so he lit up and let his cigarette dangle from his bottom lip as we talked. Scott was physically massive, towering over me and everyone else we knew, so hanging out with him gave me a distinct level of comfort and verification.

"There she is," I said under my breath. "Don't look over yet."

I was referring to Sarah, who was throwing looks our way every ten seconds or so from the midst of a huddled group of girls. She and I had a mild ongoing flirtation that began way back in sixth grade, but nothing had ever really come of it. At this particular moment, I was again interested in her.

"I remember her," Scott said. "Sarah, right?"

Scott had been kicked out of our small private school two years back for general insubordination.

"Yeah," I replied, trying to seem nonchalant.

"She's pretty hot."

"Yeah, she is."

"You gonna go talk to her?"

"No way. Well, not right now. I'll see if she comes over here. She keeps looking over."

"That's true, she does. But she may just be shocked and fascinated to see me here smoking."

"True," I said, laughing.

When I subtly glanced over again, Sarah broke off from the group and started walking over to us with her friend Ruth.

"Shit man, here they come," said Scott excitedly, tapping the ash off his cigarette.

"So impressive Scott, smoking outside the mall," Ruth said with a wry grin as they walked up.

"Thank you," he replied, flicking more ash. "I live to impress you."

"What are you guys talking about over here?" Ruth asked. "Or are you just looking at girls?"

"We're chatting about all sort of things," said Scott. "Things we'd never tell you."

"Ha!" said Ruth. "Like we'd wanna know."

Sarah and I just kept smiling and glancing at each other warily, gauging interest. I was grateful for Scott's audacity at times like this.

"How about you, Sarah?" Scott continued, poking my shoulder. "How are you these days? Byron here wants to know."

I blushed deep red and chuckled awkwardly.

"Oh does he?" Sarah asked, grinning at me.

"Oh yes," said Scott. "It's all he can talk about."

"Well, I'm great," she replied. "Just talking about stereotypical girl stuff and watching all these people walk out with their big bags of junk."

"Yeah, all the consumers doing what they're told," I ventured, sensing a pathway into the conversation.

"All part of the big show," said Sarah.

"People suck," said Scott, tossing his cigarette to the ground.

"Well, most of them do," Sarah replied, glancing at me and smiling.

I blushed again and looked down at my feet.

"Sheep, I tell ya!" Scott pronounced loudly, pointing in the general direction of the mall. "All you people are sheep!"

Ruth, Sarah, and I cringed and laughed.

"They know it's the truth," Scott muttered, pulling out another cigarette.

Sarah suddenly leaned in close to me.

"We should hang out sometime," she whispered in my ear.

I smiled and nodded nonchalantly, suppressing my exhilaration.

"And now," she said louder, pulling back. "We have to go. Goodbye Scott. Goodbye Byron."

"Ladies," Scott replied with a slight bow.

As they made their way into the mall, Scott nudged my shoulder.

"There you go, stud."

I grinned and took a deep breath, reveling in the moment. I had no way of knowing this would be the apex of my interactions with Sarah.

The beauty of limited perspective...

{ Age 16 }

I TAPPED THE BRAKE LIGHTLY to steady the tires on the slush, and then lightly pressed the gas again to push the station wagon forward. This temporarily halted the fishtailing.

"Damn, Byron," my friend Greg said, his hands nervously gripping the top of the dashboard. "How the hell are you driving on this?"

"No idea," I replied, chuckling.

I had just gotten my license a week before, and now we were headed to an all-night bowling party in an ice storm. The loose, unwieldy steering in the family station wagon only heightened the adventure.

"Just get us there," Greg said, clenching his jaw. "It's only like five minutes away now."

The sleet smacked against the windshield as I strained to see the road in front of us. My driving skills were being severely tested right away—such is life. A good part of me was enjoying it.

Finally, to our immense relief, the AMC Lanes sign came into view, and I eased into the parking lot only to find that it was a solid sheet of ice. I employed my magic balance of gas and brake as best I could, but the station wagon eventually entered a very slow slide that ended in a gentle collision with a light post. We jumped out to check the damage, which was fortunately almost unnoticeable.

"Well, at least we're parked," Greg said, laughing. "But how are we getting out of here?"

"We'll worry about that later," I said. "Let's go inside."

As expected, attendance was light, with no one we really recognized, so we quickly claimed a lane, grabbed some pizza and soda, and got down to business. After a few games, we figured out how to spin the ball, and soon we were dramatically curving our rolls nearly into the gutter and then back to hit the center of the pins. By the fourth game, our scores were around 150.

"We're like pro level now," said Greg as we sat eating on a break.

"Totally," I replied, smiling. "I wish we had an audience."

Over the course of the next five or so games, we stopped talking entirely and entered a sort of automatized dream state where bowling became the microcosm of all reality. We had perfected the spin, and our scores kept climbing higher and higher, eventually reaching 200 and above. All that mattered was the open lane, the curving path of the ball, and the clatter of the pins. Nothing distracted or concerned us, and after every strike we just bumped fists and swapped places at the foot of the lane.

During one game in particular, I could not seem to miss. Every roll was a thing of beauty, curving in a precise arc to smack the pins at the perfect angle. I bowled eight strikes in a row before I left a pin standing.

"Damn, Byron," Greg said, pausing to look up at my score.

"I know," I said, grinning and glancing around to see if anyone else was paying attention.

No one had noticed. In fact, most of the other attendees were either playing video games or passed out asleep on the floor. Suddenly I was overcome with dizziness and nausea. I dropped my ball and reached for the bench just behind me.

"Byron, what the hell?" Greg asked with obvious concern as I sat down heavily.

"I just feel dizzy all of a sudden," I replied, my hand on my forehead.

I was seized by an overwhelming, inexplicable feeling that I'd been here before, in this alley, on this winter night, bowling this particular game.

"I've done this before," I said flatly. "We've done this before, you and me."

"What do you mean?"

"Don't you ever have déjà vu?"

"Yeah, sometimes. Are you having it now?"

"Well, it's kind of going away now, but it was unbelievably strong after that last roll. It freaked me out."

"Whoah," Greg said, sitting down across from me. "That's nuts dude."

I took a few deep breaths and peered around the alley. Again, no one had noticed anything. The dizziness and nausea were nearly gone, and in their place was a deep but not unpleasant fatigue.

"I feel a lot better now, but I'm gonna take a quick nap and then we'll finish this game," I said, lying down on the bench. "That cool?"

"Sure thing," Greg replied. "I'll just go play some video games."

As he sauntered off, casually jingling the coins in his pocket, I turned onto my side and tucked my hands under my head. I felt exhausted but also strangely peaceful, as if everything was in its proper place.

{ Age 17 }

O N A SUNDAY MORNING IN MID-JUNE, I was sitting at the dining room table eating a bowl of Golden Grahams and watching a sparrow hop gingerly along a branch of the maple outside the front window. It was the day after my high school graduation, and I was alone in the house. I had no concrete plans for the day. In fact, I had no concrete plans for the summer except my job washing dishes at the retirement community down the street. The months ahead stretched out endlessly in my mind like an open field, followed by years of college, and then God knows what after that.

My reverie was interrupted by a sharp knock at the front door, and I sighed as I realized who it likely was—our prying, hyperactive 10-year-old neighbor.

"What's up, Jason?" I said flatly as I opened the door.

"Hey Byron, are you home?" Jason asked brightly, blinking up at me.

"Yes Jason. I answered the door, didn't I?"

"Oh, right. That's true," he answered, giggling. "You have to be here if you opened the door, right?"

"Correct."

"Can I come in for a second?"

I reluctantly led him inside and pointed to the chair across from me at the table.

"You eating Golden Grahams?" he asked.

"Yup."

"Cool. I love that stuff."

I just nodded and took another bite.

"My mom says you graduated yesterday," he continued. "Did you?"

"Yes."

"Are you happy?"

"Yes, very happy."

"That makes sense. I'd be happy too. What are you going to do now?"

"You mean today?"

"Yeah. I would have my own personal party. If you have one, will you invite me?"

"No party today."

"Well that's too bad," he said, looking confused. "What are you going to do then?"

"Probably go meet some friends somewhere."

"Are your friends like you?"

"What do you mean?"

"Do they act like you? Do they talk like you? A lot of times friends are just like each other."

"I guess they're kind of similar to me. They like doing a lot of the same things."

"Oh, that's cool."

I stood up to bring my empty bowl to the kitchen.

"Ah nice, you finished your cereal?" Jason asked, standing with me.

I said nothing as I walked to the sink and poured out the leftover milk.

"You ever think about what would happen if suddenly no one knew who you were?" Jason asked, following me. "Like one day you woke up and your parents didn't know you, and your friends didn't know you, and your dog didn't know you."

"Not really. Have you?"

"Well, I had a dream about it last night," he replied. "But in my dream it happened to you too. We were real sad about it. We were sitting in your backyard there, talking about how we wished people would just snap out of it and say they knew us again. And then we started to think *we* might not even know who we were anymore. That scared us a little."

"That's a fascinating dream," I said, guiding him toward the front door. "I wish I could talk more, but I have to go take a shower now and get ready to meet my friends."

"Oh cool, that makes sense," he said, unfazed. "I just wanted to tell you that dream. Thanks for listening to me."

"Sure thing," I replied, holding the door open for him.

Ease

After Jason left, I walked upstairs to my room and sat down on the edge of the bed. A tiny moth was crawling slowly across the sheet next to my leg. I brushed it away and it flew off toward the window.

I thought about the infinite number of choices I could make from this point forward. The previous stage was over, and any given choice from this moment on could permanently alter the trajectory of my life. The weight of this made me slightly queasy. I flopped back on the bed and closed my eyes, letting the sense of possibility wash over me. When I opened my eyes again, the moth was fluttering directly above me, tracing patterns in the air.

{ Age 18 }

I MET LIZ ONE SUMMER NIGHT in my friend Jill's living room on the west side of Baltimore. She was sitting cross-legged under a floor lamp, quietly knitting what appeared to be an oversized ski mask.

"Liz, this is Byron. Byron, this is Liz. You guys should probably get together," said Jill with her typical bluntness. "It would make a lot of sense. Liz is an artist. A real one."

Liz gazed up at me with a slight, bashful smile, her hand smoothing back her unruly brown hair. She seemed almost impossibly delicate on first impression, but with a subtle undercurrent of concentrated energy. I was fascinated.

"How do you two know each other?" I asked.

"She just appeared in my life," Jill replied with a knowing grin.

Later that night, Liz and I were left alone in Jill's bedroom. The house was an old, ramshackle Victorian, and the master bedroom was massive, but lit only by a dim lamp on the nightstand. I was sitting on a plush green armchair in the corner while Liz reclined on the bed. Her knees were bent toward the ceiling and her loose, lacy white dress had fallen down around her waist, leaving her thighs exposed.

"So..." I began hesitantly. "How's it going over there? You comfortable?"

"I'm pretty comfortable, thanks," she replied, glancing over at me with a shy smile. "How are you? Are you happy with how everything's going?"

"What do you mean by that?" I asked, chuckling.

"Jill seems to be trying to set us up."

"Oh yeah, that..."

"She's a trip."

"Yes she is."

"So, are you happy?" she asked again.

"Yeah, I think so."

"Nervous?"

"Nope," I lied.

"Good," she replied. "I'm a little nervous. That's typical for me, though. I get it from my mom."

"Damn parents."

"Seriously. My mom's a fucking wreck."

She paused and waved her hand in the air, creating a fleeting shadow arc on the ceiling.

"When you were a kid, did you ever think adults might be wrong about everything?" she asked.

"Sometimes," I said, smiling to myself. "Most of the time I just assumed they knew exactly what they were doing, all the time. But then sometimes it seemed like they were just making everything up as they went along. Like they were just pretending to know and they'd all secretly agreed not to call each other on it."

"Right," Liz replied, laughing. "No one knows."

She turned her body toward me, her eyes gleaming.

"But isn't that exciting in a way?"

"Definitely."

"If they don't know, that means everything's probably different than what we've been told. Nothing's set in stone."

"Right!" I said excitedly, sitting up straight in the chair. "And all that certainty that's fed to us by school and the church and the government is exposed as just a bunch of bullshit, which I've always known deep down."

"Oh, have you?" she asked, laughing again.

"I guess so, yeah," I replied, blushing slightly.

She turned over on her stomach and buried her head in Jill's pillow, then quickly flipped back over and stared up at the ceiling.

"So what do we do now?" she asked, almost to herself.

"We, meaning you and me?" I asked.

"Yeah."

"Well, we could do anything, right?"

"Sure we could," she replied, smiling. "Anything we want. No definitions."

She abruptly sat up in the bed and stared at me.

"Come over here and sit with me," she commanded, her eyes shimmering.

I made my way to the bed, pulled off my shoes, and sat down cross-legged facing her. She edged over to me, her bare knees touching mine, and gazed deep into my eyes. We stayed like this, silent and motionless, for a seemingly interminable moment...

A few weeks later, we were eating Chinese takeout together at Jill's kitchen table. Liz had just moved into the house, and her boxes of kitchen supplies were stacked beside the sink. By this time, I was in love with her and she was almost all I could think about.

"You can stay here tonight, if you want," she said, casually taking a bite of broccoli.

"OK," I replied, my chest clenching up.

"I want you to."

"Well how can I resist, then?" I asked with faux calm.

"You can't," she answered, smiling. "Well, you shouldn't."

She stood up and motioned for me to follow her, and we made our way down the hall to her new bedroom. Once we were inside, she shut the door and began unzipping her jeans.

"I think this is what we should do now," she said, leveling her gaze at me.

My heart was pulsing hard against my ribs as I watched her methodically strip down to nothing. I was standing there motionless, almost paralyzed. When she was naked, she walked slowly over to the unmade bed and stretched out on her back, her legs spread wide apart. I finally begin to undress, my hands trembling.

"Just breathe," she said softly, gazing over at me with a hint of a smile. "Don't worry about anything."

{ Age 19 }

I T WAS AN OVERCAST DAY in early spring, and as I walked south on Bond Street in Fells Point, I heard a sharp clattering sound followed by a dull thud. As I turned the corner onto Thames, I saw a crowd gathering around a man lying flat on his back on the sidewalk. He was wearing stained blue overalls and a white hard hat, and there was a dark stream of blood flowing from his mouth. His eyes were wide open, staring up at the sky.

"Who called 911? Did anyone call 911?" a middle-aged woman kept frantically repeating as she stalked around the crowd.

The man's shallow breathing was growing more labored by the second, and his lungs were starting to emit a bone-chilling rattle.

"What happened?" I asked the man next to me.

"Fell off the roof," he said, pointing up three stories. "He was fixing something up there, apparently."

"Holy shit," was all I could think to say.

"Who called 911?" the panicked woman yelled again. "I don't have a phone. Has anyone called 911?"

"I did," the man next to me said calmly. "Paramedics are on the way."

"OK, that's good," she replied a little more softly. "Now how do we help him?"

"No one should try to move him," said a younger woman standing next to the injured man. "With a spine injury like this, moving him at all could just make it worse."

She knelt down and began tenderly stroking his hair.

"Hang in there. Help is on the way."

He tried to mouth a response, but there was only a soft gurgling sound.

"Don't try to talk," she said gently.

"Poor guy's lungs are filling with blood," my neighbor said softly. "You can't survive a fall like that."

"It's horrible," I replied almost inaudibly.

"There's really nothing we can do," he continued. "Hopefully the ambulance gets here soon."

I felt useless and almost cowardly. As more and more people gathered at the scene, I chose an opportune moment to slip away.

"So you think he died?" asked Liz later that evening.

She was sitting on a rug in the center of her living room floor, her knitting strewn out all around her.

"Yeah, I'm pretty sure he must have," I replied grimly. "There was a woman there who was stroking his hair and trying to calm him down. It was touching."

"It's fucking depressing."

"It is, but it happens. Death…"

"Are you about to say death is a part of life?" she interrupted.

"Yeah, I guess."

"How perceptive."

"Why are you getting sarcastic?" I asked.

"If that's how you want to read it…"

"You've been doing this for months and I don't know why. You just switch up your tone out of the blue. It's impossible to figure out your moods."

"How sad for you, that you can't figure me out."

"That's not what I mean."

"Seriously, why did you have to tell me this today?" she asked, her voice rising. "I didn't need to hear about someone dying today. My day has been shit, literally."

"Because it just happened and I thought I'd share it," I replied, agitated. "It was pretty upsetting."

"Fine, got it."

"Why are you mad?"

"I don't know."

"Well that doesn't help me."

"I'm not trying to help you. I'm trying to create things and I want to eliminate the distractions."

"And I'm a distraction?"

"Sometimes. Honestly, I probably shouldn't be in a relationship. I'm not happy in a relationship, or at least not in this relationship. I'm off all my meds now, and my mind is clearer than it's ever been, but then you come along and say something that clouds it up."

"Trust me, I'm not what's clouding up your mind," I replied, my chest tightening up. "I always give you the space you need."

"You think you do, but you don't," she said coldly. "You can't help it. Like I said, I shouldn't be with anybody."

"So that's it? You're ending it?"

"I guess so," she said, crossing her arms and glaring down at the floor.

"This is really how you want it to end?"

"Sure, why not? It's as good a way as any. Breaking up always sucks."

"Yeah, but it can be reasonable. You're not being reasonable, and you haven't been for months now."

"You love to judge me, just like everyone."

"Bullshit," I said angrily.

"I feel like I'm creating pieces now that are truly tapping into something big," she replied almost pleadingly. "Can't you see that? Do you want to distract me from that?"

"No, of course not."

"Well then, let's just end it."

"If that's what you want," I said, abruptly giving up.

I stood up, grabbed my keys, and stomped out the front door, slamming it shut behind me. When I got in my car, I rammed my forehead into the steering wheel and screamed at the top of my lungs.

I drove around for hours that night, ruthlessly cycling through everything in my mind, but ultimately there was nothing I was going to figure out. It was over.

{ Age 20 }

I T BEGAN AT NIGHT—almost every night that winter—around 10 PM or so. As I sat reading in bed, I felt a deep nausea build in my stomach and slowly move up into my throat. I typically felt like I was about to throw up, but never did, which was almost worse. At first I thought it was just something I ate, or perhaps too much coffee, but shifting things up over a few weeks changed nothing—the situation only deteriorated.

Steadily, the nausea came on earlier and earlier in the evening, until I consistently began to feel it around 7 or so. It also began to come on in the mornings, slowly extending outward from the time I woke up into the early afternoon. Eventually I was left with about four nausea-free hours a day. At that point, the only meal I ever enjoyed was dinner. For breakfast and lunch, I simply forced myself to eat, gulping down bites without any pleasure. As could be expected, I quickly lost a significant amount of weight. I was already thin, so this made me skeletal.

Another symptom soon began to emerge as well— intense abdominal cramping every ten minutes or so. Sometimes the cramps were mild, as they might be during a vigorous run. Other times they caused me to double over in agony.

At first I was diagnosed with an ulcer, but when a series of courses of antibiotics and antacids had no effect, I was retested and diagnosed with Crohn's disease.

"Think about it this way—at least you have a name for what you're going through," the doctor told me as I sat in his office. "It's not a mystery anymore."

"I guess that's true," I replied, mustering a slight smile.

I'd heard horror stories of people with Crohn's essentially shitting their guts out and ending up with colostomy bags, so I was not exactly pleased with this diagnosis.

"Once we have a name for something and know what it is, we can treat it," the doctor continued in a calm monotone. "There are some very effective drugs out there—some short term, and others more long term."

"OK," I said lifelessly.

"We could start by trying a steroid like prednisone, which will help reduce the intestinal inflammation right away. We'll also probably put you on an anti-inflammatory mesalamine drug like Pentasa for maintenance, and maybe an immunosuppressant like 6-MP..."

As he droned on, I suddenly left my body. For a few seconds, I was floating in darkness, and then an image materialized below me. I was looking down on my body, which was perched on the toilet in a bathroom I didn't recognize. There was a trail of blood and shit on the bathroom floor. My face looked panicked, and older.

"Byron, what do you think?"

"Of what?" I asked, snapping back to the present.

"Of trying out the prednisone to start, like I suggested. We'll start with a decent dose to zap the inflammation, and then taper you off once you've stabilized a bit."

"OK, sure. Sounds good."

What did I care? I'd just seen my future, and it was hideous.

I left the doctor's office in a stupor, full of conflicting emotions—anger, relief, confusion, anxiety, but mostly just sheer depression. The world seemed absurd and almost diabolical at that moment, engineered to cause pain.

{ Age 21 }

I STUDIOUSLY AVOIDED LOOKING at myself in any full-length mirror, especially naked. Whenever I did, I instantly regretted it. My arms and legs were like twigs, and my chest was deeply sunken in. My cheeks were covered with acne and puffed out a bit—the familiar prednisone look—and my belly was noticeably distended. My temples were indented inward like tiny caves, which caused my eyes to pop out intensely.

"You look fine," my friends would tell me. "A little skinny, but fine."

"Bullshit."

"No, you do."

To have a chronic illness is utterly isolating. The healthy folk around you try their best to empathize, but there's simply no way for them to know how you feel. It's not their fault, of course. It's no one's fault.

I walked around the UMBC campus in a daze, watching the groups of happy, healthy students in the prime of their lives. Luckily, I didn't have much leisure time to feel sorry for myself. By default, daily life was stripped down to its essence, requiring my utmost concentration. My principal focus was on how my body felt in each successive moment. If I felt reasonably decent, I expanded my thoughts outward to whatever school-work needed to be done, and then perhaps even further out to basic social concerns. If I was in pain, that was my sole focus. Pain was my center.

One morning, I woke up in my bedroom in agony. I'd had countless intestinal cramping episodes before, but this was the strongest I could remember. I curled myself into a fetal position and sucked in deep breaths, tears streaming down my cheeks.

As the pain coursed through me, I noticed that the early morning sun was reflecting in the upper corner of the mirror on the back of my closet door. From my perspective, it was a tiny triangle of light, nearly blinding me if I stared at it too long. Out of desperation, I willed myself to breathe into it. As I did, I felt the light envelop me and begin to absorb my pain, transmuting it into warm, purified energy that streamed out into the world. Soon, time was gone, my body was gone, "I" was gone. The only reality was this dazzling fragment of light, encompassing everything.

A deep and familiar voice then entered my consciousness.

"There is nothing to fear. This is what always has been and always will be."

Eventually I came back into my frail, spent body lying on the bed. The sun had risen higher, and the reflection was gone.

A few months later, I came across a passage in Dostoevsky's *The Idiot* that made me break down in tears. It was about a man on the verge of being executed.

"He wished to put it to himself as quickly and clearly as possible, that here was he, a living, thinking man, and that in three minutes he would be nobody; or if somebody or something, then what and where? He thought he would decide this question once and for all in these last three minutes. A little way off there stood a church, and its gilded spire glittered in the sun. He remembered staring stubbornly at this spire, and at the rays of light sparkling from it. He could not tear his eyes from these rays of light; he got the idea that these rays were his new nature, and that in three minutes he would become one of them, amalgamated somehow with them."

I was beginning to understand.

{ Age 22 }

BLOOD WAS SPURTING EVERYWHERE—on the nurse's scrubs, on my gown, on the curtain, on the wall. I was being prepped for surgery, and the nurse had not properly secured the line for the IV.

"Damn it!" she hissed as she tried to stem the bleeding.

I was about to have a bowel resection. They were going to remove a 12-inch section of small intestine that had scarred over so much it was about to close off, and the gushing blood was not an auspicious omen.

"I'm really sorry about that," the nurse said once everything was secure. "I've never had that happen before."

I just smiled wanly.

Later that afternoon, the anesthesia had completely worn off and I was in agony. My entire abdomen was hard as a rock, and I was literally writhing with gas pains. They had me on a fentanyl drip, timed to release a dose every 15 minutes if I pressed the button, which I did without fail. When the dose came, I'd get a bit of relief for a few minutes, but by about minute five, I was in hell again.

Ease

"This pain medicine isn't doing anything!" I wailed to the nurse.

"You're on a very high dose of fentanyl," he replied. "It's doing something, I promise."

All night, I shifted my body into every conceivable position to try to get some relief, but nothing helped. There was no sense of focus or liberation with this pain—it was simply torture. Sleep was impossible.

For four days, the pain did not let up. The doctors theorized it was because my body, for whatever reason, did not wake up properly after the anesthesia. This allowed an excess of gas into my stomach and intestines, above and beyond the gas they introduced to assist the surgery.

"It really is pronounced bloating," the on-call doctor said one morning.

"No shit," I replied, grimacing.

Friends and family members filtered through the experience, but meaningful conversations were few. Mostly people just sat silently next to me, watching TV and listening to me moan. As much as I appreciated their presence, I was always happy when they left. Something in me sensed this was meant to be a solitary experience.

On the fourth night, I was given a stomach-emptying medicine called Reglan in an attempt to re-

duce my nausea. Within five minutes, I began to hallu-
cinate. At first, the images were innocuous swirling
patterns, but they soon turned horrific and gory. I saw
piles of twisting and churning skin, intestines, eyeballs,
and brains. Gruesome beings formed out of the piles
and shuffled toward me, seemingly eager to absorb me
into themselves. In desperation, I hoisted myself up
from the bed and staggered out into the hallway, drag-
ging my IV cart along with me. The hallway floor was
one huge, glowing whirlpool of blood and body parts. It
was hopeless—there was nowhere I could go to escape.
At that moment, I was unhinged enough to seriously
consider trying to pry open the window at the end of
the hallway to throw myself out of it.

"What's going on, Byron?" asked the nurse, coming
up behind me. "You should be in bed."

"I'm seeing things!" I said frantically. "Disgusting
shit, like blood and guts and bodies coming toward me.
They just keep coming and won't stop!"

"Well, I just gave you that Reglan. It must be a reaction. You're hallucinating."

"What can we do?" I asked plaintively.

"Nothing, really," she said calmly, leading me back
to the room. "It just needs to pass through your system.
It shouldn't take more than 20 minutes or so."

A few minutes after the nurse placed me back on the
bed, I suddenly felt like I was going to throw up. I
made my way to the bathroom and started puking up a

foul, yellowish liquid. I'd had no solids to eat, so I had nothing in my stomach except bile. Once the bile was all gone, I just knelt in front of the toilet and dry heaved over and over. It felt like the stitches in my stomach were being ripped open.

Eventually the on-call doctor materialized above me. He leaned down and gently patted my back.

"It's OK, it's going to pass," he said calmly. "I promise it will pass."

Indeed, the dry heaving soon stopped, and I noticed I was no longer hallucinating. The night light in the bathroom was a greenish yellow, casting an appropriate hue over the scene. I almost laughed at the absurdity of my position as I gazed up at the doctor. What could he be thinking about this pathetic creature cowering beneath him? I was alone and helpless, reduced to nothing.

{ Age 23 }

M Y RECOVERY WAS SLOW but steady, and I spent most of my time reading, thinking, or staring off into space. After a few months had passed and I was no longer quite as skeletal, I was ready to venture out into the world again. I had been thoroughly destroyed—body, ego, mind—and now it was time to reconstruct myself.

At first I just met up with friends one-on-one or in small groups, mainly for food, which I now thankfully enjoyed again. I had been isolated for so long that I had to relearn the art of basic social interaction.

"Am I making any sense?" I asked my friend John one evening at dinner.

"What do you mean?" he replied, laughing.

"I feel like I've been alone for so long that maybe I don't make sense to anyone else anymore."

"You make sense, man. You're good."

"You know all I've really been doing is reading? Which is good in a way, but it can also drive you crazy. Everything gets too internal."

"I hear that. Well, get external and come out to my party on Saturday."

"Maybe."

Ease

"What do you mean, maybe? You've been through some shit, my friend. Come out and have fun."

"Fine," I said, chuckling.

The party was fairly tedious for me until Marion and I spotted each other. I was attempting to explain what had been going on in my life to a group of John's friends, with mixed results. The subject matter of the conversation was unavoidably awkward, and I just kept wading deeper into the weeds. Everyone was patient and sympathetic, but I could tell they mostly just wanted my recitation to end.

After staring at me uninterruptedly for a good two minutes, Marion marched over, providing me an out. She probably took about ten steps to arrive, but the moment seemed endless. An eerie, deeply familiar sensation began to build in my chest.

"Do I know you?" she asked when she finally reached me, her green eyes gleaming.

"I don't know how you would," I said, testing.

"I really think we've met before. You're friends with Shannon, right?"

"Yes, but I don't think that's it. Somehow your stare is familiar to me, though. You know it's a bit intimidating, right?"

"Ha!" she replied, laughing. "You can't take it? I expected more from you."

"Sorry to disappoint."

"Are you scared of me?"

"No," I said. "Should I be?"

"Well, people are typically scared of directness."

"I agree."

"This conversation isn't too intense for you, is it?" she asked teasingly.

"No. How about for you?"

"Fuck no..." she replied, glancing over my head to scan the room.

We'd reached that precarious pause in most initial conversations when things could go either way. If a friend had called for me, or someone had dropped a glass, or a stray memory had come floating into her head, the encounter might have simply sputtered out and died right there, just like innumerable similar encounters occurring every minute of every day.

"OK, I'm going to go catch up with some friends over there," she would have said. "Hopefully we'll see each other again sometime."

But that's not what happened, of course.

"I forget, do I know your name?" she asked with a quizzical expression.

"It's Byron."

"I feel like I already knew that. I'm Marion."

She pressed a lock of her long black hair back behind her ear.

"So what's your situation, Byron?"

"Meaning what?"

"Meaning, what do you do with yourself?"

"I just do what everyone else does," I replied, smiling.

"I call bullshit," she said, her eyes sparkling. "Never mind, I'll get it out of you later."

She paused for a moment to intently examine my face, as if completing her appraisal.

"I'm actually about to get out of here. Do you want to come with me?"

"Where are we going?"

"Do you care?"

"No," I said, quickly downing the rest of my drink. "Let's go."

"OK then," she said, grabbing my hand and leading me toward the door.

Later that night, in her bedroom, we stood naked facing each other. Her body was so beautiful it almost overwhelmed me.

"What's this scar?" she asked, gently tracing the red line next to my belly button with her index finger.

"I had surgery four months ago to remove a section of my intestine," I replied almost apologetically.

"Interesting. Was it painful?"

"Yes."

"Well, that's done, and now you're here with me."

Stephen Intlekofer

She held her palm flat against my belly and stared into my eyes, then slowly moved her hand down between my legs.

"Just relax into it," she said, grasping me gently.

{ Age 24 }

I T WAS A PERFECTLY CLEAR, silent morning in mid-January, and Marion was wandering along the trail ahead of me, whistling some random tune. Her footprints were evenly spaced behind her in the thin blanket of snow from the night before. We were hiking through a small canyon between looming rock walls in Arches National Park, and the sound of Marion's whistling and our crunching footsteps bounced around and echoed back to us. We essentially had the place to ourselves.

"What else do you need?" she asked, suddenly stopping to turn around and look at me.

"Huh?"

"You, the general you. What else do you really need?"

"I guess nothing."

"That's right."

She turned back around and continued onward. It was below freezing, but the air was so still and the sun so strong that we were completely comfortable.

An hour later, we were gazing up at the majesty of Delicate Arch, its outline delineated against the pristine blue sky. There were perhaps ten other people there with us on the wide expanse of rock, all standing and silently pondering.

As I contemplated the precarious left leg of the arch, I felt an immense gratitude for my life. I was finally healthy again, for the most part, and I was in love.

"Think about how long it took for that thing to form," Marion said softly, almost whispering.

"Ages," I replied.

"When do you think that left part will collapse?"

"A few hundred years, I guess."

"Maybe."

To the right of us, about fifty feet away, a middle-aged woman in a dark red coat raised her hands above her head with her palms to the sky. She closed her eyes and began to hum loudly as she swayed from side to side.

"Energy work," Marion whispered, grinning.

I stifled the urge to scoff, which was my default for these types of displays. After about 30 seconds, the woman turned our way, fixed her gaze on me, and started walking slowly toward us.

"She's coming over," I said through my teeth.

"Haha, yes she is," replied Marion, chuckling.

The woman was short and stocky, with flowing black hair flecked with gray and a long, pendulous nose. When she finally reached us, she looked only at me.

"Hi," she said, smiling broadly. "I sensed you looking over at me and thought I'd swing by to say hello. I recognize you."

"Really?" I asked. "From where?"

"I have no idea, but you look very familiar. Have you ever been to Santa Fe? That's where I'm from."

"No, I've never been there. I've always wanted to go, though."

"Are you sure you've never been?"

"Yes," I answered, chuckling. "Pretty sure."

"But are you positive, Byron?" asked Marion, smiling mischievously.

"Yes Marion, I am."

"Well, I guess I'm mistaken then," the woman said. "I often am."

"Can I ask you what you were doing over there?" Marion asked. "It looked interesting."

"I was calling in the energy of this portal," she answered straightforwardly.

"You mean the arch?"

"Yes. That probably sounds hokey to you."

"No, not at all. What happens when you call in the energy?"

"I feel calm and centered," the woman answered. "And sometimes I receive messages."

"What kind of messages?" asked Marion.

"It varies. Transmissions from various star systems."

"Did you get a message just now?"

"Yes, I was told to walk over here and talk to him," she replied. "I wasn't sure how to begin the conversation, so I made up the part about recognizing him."

"What are you supposed to talk to him about?" asked Marion, now completely intrigued.

"I received a vision of a desert at night," she said, turning to me. "I saw it from above. You were walking in front of a long line of people, and all your bodies were glowing. The people behind you all looked exactly like you."

The woman paused and bowed slightly in my direction.

"Wow! Anything else?" asked Marion excitedly, her eyes wide.

"That's pretty much it," she replied. "It was a quick one."

"How often do you have a specific vision like that about someone?" I asked impassively, trying to hide my interest.

"Hardly ever," the woman answered with a cryptic smile. "You must be special."

Later that night, in our motel room in Moab, Marion was reclining in her pajamas on the pink bedspread as I brushed my teeth.

"That woman said you're special," she said with mock seriousness. "What do you think about that?"

I rinsed off my toothbrush and examined my face in the mirror. It was looking much less gaunt these days, which pleased me.

"I think we should go visit her in Santa Fe," I said. "All we need to do is find the local portals, and there she'll be."

"I'm all for it. I loved her."

"Of course you did."

I walked over to the bed and flopped down next to her. We let our bodies relax as we stared up at the white-tiled ceiling, tired and content.

{ Age 25 }

MY FATHER AND I WERE ON OUR WAY to Ikea to pick up a bedframe for my new mattress. I was driving my friend Bill's van with its blown-out shocks, so we were both bouncing comically in our seats whenever we hit even the slightest bump. We'd been silent for a few minutes, and I could sense my father was gathering the strength to broach something difficult.

"So have you thought any more about joining us for church on Sunday? It's Easter, and I'm sure your mom would love to have you there. So would I. Marion's welcome to come too, of course."

"Thanks for the invite, but I don't think so," I replied as gently as I could. "I think church is over for me, at least for now."

"Can I ask," he ventured, having expected this answer, "is your problem more with the church as an organization, or with the basic doctrines of Christianity?"

"Both, really. I'm definitely not interested in anyone preaching to me about anything, but I guess my main issue is with any religion claiming to be the one and only truth. As in, Jesus is the only way to salvation and if you don't accept him, you're lost. I know it probably kills you to hear me say this because people who don't believe in Jesus as their savior are going to hell, right?"

"Well, to me it all comes down to the person of Jesus. What do we make of a human who claimed to be God? I think his very presence on Earth requires us to make some sort of a decision. What if he was telling the truth?"

"I have no problem with the person of Jesus. He was a great teacher."

"But he claimed to be more than just a teacher. He said he was God. If he wasn't actually God, wouldn't that make him either a lunatic or a liar, as C.S. Lewis put it?"

"Well, what if he just saw things clearly?" I asked. "All his barriers were removed and he saw that everything and everyone is part of God, or whatever name you want to put on it."

"You mean like pantheism?"

"Sure, if you want to put a label on it."

The van jolted suddenly as it rode over a huge pothole, and we both nearly smacked our heads on the ceiling.

"Nice shocks in this thing," my father said, laughing.

"I know. Fun isn't it?"

"So do you believe every religion leads to the truth?" he continued, undeterred.

"Not necessarily. Religions can actually keep people from seeing the truth."

"How so?"

"By directing them through one doorway only, like Christianity does with Jesus and the Bible. There are infinite doorways to the truth."

"I don't know about that," my father said, shaking his head. "Where's the solidity there?"

We had reached the Ikea parking lot, and I eased the van into an open space and turned off the engine.

"Look dad, we're never going to agree on this. You believe something I don't believe, that I will probably never believe. The sheer certainty in it kind of repels me, actually. How do we know? How can anyone claim to truly know anything, really? We're just here on Earth, totally confused, limited to our five senses."

My father grimaced slightly and adjusted himself in his seat. I felt like I was physically hurting him.

"But where does that leave us if we don't have a base?" he asked in an almost desperate tone.

"I'm not sure," I said softly, a bit taken aback.

"I can't accept that we don't have a base, that there's no solidity. I refuse to accept that."

"Maybe the base is just that we're human, and we're all in the same boat."

"But humans die. We're just here to live for a bit, then die and be forgotten? There's no larger purpose? I refuse to accept that. God created humans for a purpose."

"What purpose?"

"Well, according to the Westminster Catechism, which I think you memorized as a kid in Sunday school, the chief end of man is to glorify God and enjoy him forever."

"So he created us just to worship him?"

"And to enjoy him. That's equally important."

"And what is God to you? What if God is just the energy behind everything?"

"There's pantheism again."

"Don't label it," I said sharply. "That just lets you conveniently dismiss it."

"For God to have created everything, he has to be separate from everything."

"But what if everything came from nothing? What if creation is spontaneous?"

"I refuse to accept that," he said again, his lips pursed in a slight frown.

"What if nothing is directed and everything is random, including creation?"

"Do you really believe that?" he asked skeptically.

"I don't know," I said flatly, pulling the key out of the ignition.

I opened my door and stepped down to the asphalt.

"Now let's go inside and get this bedframe."

My father sighed deeply, and then smiled.

"OK, let's go," he said cheerfully.

I realized at that moment how much I loved him.

Later that night, Marion and I were sitting on the couch in my apartment drinking whiskey. We'd scrapped the idea of assembling the bedframe and had just left the mattress lying on the floor. We were both fairly tipsy.

"But how does that happen?" I asked, laughing. "How did no one tell you?"

"People did tell me. I just refused to listen. I was in denial."

"Did you still go and sit on his lap and ask for presents? At 13 years old?"

"No, I did not, smartass."

"Well, that's good. At least you had some sense."

"I had plenty of sense. I held onto the magic way longer than you did. Who needs cynicism at that age? Or ever, really?"

"I guess that's true. But it was kind of humiliating, though, right? When your friends found out?"

"They never found out. No one knew, not even my parents."

"Only you and Santa knew."

"Right," she said, giggling.

I grabbed her hand and tried to pull her over on top of me. She laughed loudly, hiked up her dress, and straddled me with her legs.

Ease

"I love you," she whispered tenderly as she leaned down to kiss me.

{ Age 26 }

FOLLOWING AN IMPULSE OF MARION'S, we went to India and got married. We wanted no part of a traditional American wedding, so we arranged for a ceremony in Rishikesh at a temple on the banks of the Ganges, with a young employee from our hotel as the sole witness. Three days later, we arrived in Dharamsala in the foothills of the Himalayas, exhausted after an all-night train ride.

We roused ourselves around 3 PM and headed out of the room to grab something to eat. Our guest house was built into the hillside, as most buildings are in Dharamsala, with numerous steep stone staircases. At the top of one of these, I briefly turned my head to say something to Marion and caught my foot on a raised portion of stone. As my body lurched forward, I desperately reached out for handrails only to find that there were none. As the bottom of the staircase rose up to meet me, time paused for a brief moment.

"This is bad," was my only thought as my body floated through the air.

My face then hit the concrete with a sickening thwack, and everything went dark.

When I woke up, I was lying at the bottom of the stairs with blood streaming out of my nose, into my mouth, and down my chin. Most of my face was numb. I immediately looked up at Marion, who was standing horrified at the top of the stairs. I pointed to my mouth and bared my teeth.

"Are they still there?" I said as loudly as I could.

"Yes!" she yelled breathlessly.

As I looked around, I realized there were several by-standers, all of whom looked appalled. I also realized I was swallowing a good deal of blood, which was pouring down the back of my throat. The guest house proprietor suddenly appeared above me holding towels and cotton balls. He shoved cotton in both of my nostrils, tipped my head back, and began wiping blood off my face with the towels.

"Are you OK?" Marion's voice asked hesitantly.

She was now standing over me looking extremely distressed.

"I think so," I said with difficulty. "I think I only hit my nose. I keep swallowing a lot of blood though."

My body was shaking uncontrollably and my mind was spinning. I found some prayer flags in the distance to focus on as I willed the bleeding to stop. After a few minutes, the frontal bleeding began to slow a bit, and Marion and the proprietor helped me to my feet.

"There's a clinic in town," he said. "I'll call a taxi to take you there."

Later that evening, Marion and I were walking back from the clinic through town. The nurse had taken an x-ray with an ancient x-ray machine and given me antibiotics and pain medication. My total bill was 900 rupees—about $4.50 in U.S. money.

I looked ragged and disgusting, with cotton stuffed up my nostrils and my shirt covered in blood, yet nearly every person we passed stopped to ask how they could help. Eventually a smiling older Tibetan woman insisted we come to her restaurant, which had just closed for the day. When we got inside, she and her husband swiftly transformed a window bench seat into a bed and propped me up on pillows to rest.

"You stay here and I'll make you soup," she said. "And he'll go get you some more cotton for your nose."

Their kindness brought tears to my eyes.

"You're lucky, you know," said Marion, grasping my hand.

"I know."

"I thought you were dead."

"I think I probably would be if I hit anywhere else on my head."

"What the fuck, Byron?" she said, her eyes glistening. "I would have been a widow."

"After three days," I said, smiling weakly.

"Ridiculous."

"Totally ridiculous."

"Can you breathe through your nose?"

"No."

"Well that means you probably can't taste either. Sad for the soup."

"It doesn't matter."

Our benefactor emerged from the kitchen carrying a huge bowl of steaming soup, her eyes radiating a deep, joyful calm. As I sat up to eat, I chuckled at the beauty and absurdity of the moment. The center of my face was numb, my nose was a swollen mass of cartilage and bone fragments, and I was still swallowing little streams of blood, but I felt euphoric. I was still here.

{ Age 27 }

I EMERGED FROM A SHALLOW SLEEP at midnight, about an hour after we went to bed. Marion was turned away from me on her side, gently snoring. All else was silent except for the soft hissing of the radiator under the window. The zig-zagging, snake-like crack in the ceiling stood out prominently in the glare from the streetlight outside, and I traced its path again and again to try to hypnotize myself back to sleep. Where was this restlessness coming from? For weeks now, a strange and indeterminate feeling had been undermining my daily life, distracting me and causing my mind to churn perpetually. Marion had picked up on it, of course.

"You're not listening, are you?" she'd ask, sighing.

"Yes, I heard you."

"You're lying."

I realized there was no way I was falling back asleep anytime soon, so I quietly climbed out of bed and put on my clothes. I made my way to the bathroom to splash some cold water on my face, grabbed my coat, and headed out into the street.

As I walked down St. Paul, I spotted a basement bar I'd somehow never noticed before. There was no sign

Ease

outside, but when I peered in, I could see a bartender prepping drinks and a few people sitting at the tables. As I stepped down the stairs to go in, someone yelled at me from the other side of the street.

"Do you know what the fuck you're doin'?"

It took me a second to locate a man in a hood and a massive winter coat sitting on the curb across from me. He was leaning so far to his right that he was nearly falling over.

"What did you say?" I yelled back.

"Fuck you," he replied, his words slurring. "You don't know what's goin' on. I do."

"Great, can you tell me?"

"No. No. All you people can't handle it. S'too much. Too much."

He stood up unsteadily and started meandering north on St. Paul. I watched him until he disappeared around a corner.

"Welcome!" the bartender called out loudly as I opened the door. "Welcome to you on this cold night."

"How are you?" I asked, sitting down on an open stool at the end of the bar and removing my coat.

"As good as can be expected," he replied, smiling faintly. "What can I get you?"

"Rail bourbon is fine. Neat."

"Coming up."

As he poured the drink, I gazed around the room. There were about ten people total, mostly couples chatting quietly at tables. There was one solo drinker two stools down from me—a man with thick, unkempt grey hair and a ragged, oversized red sweater who looked to be about 55 or so. He was sketching something in a notebook.

"Here you go, my friend," said the bartender as he placed my whiskey in front of me.

"Thanks, and cheers," I replied, holding up my glass.

"Cheers," he said, raising his glass of water. "Here's to no more problems in life."

"You wouldn't want that," said the grey-haired man without looking up.

"That's what you think, Dick," the bartender said, chuckling.

"His name is actually Dick, I hope?" I asked, smiling.

"Yeah, that's Dick, the philosopher."

"The jester," Dick said with a slight grin.

"OK, the jester," the bartender replied.

Dick looked up from his notebook and fixed an unwavering gaze on me.

"What's your name?" he asked pointedly.

"Byron."

"What are you doing here, Byron?"

"What do you mean?"

"Seems like you just wandered in here. What are you doing here?"

"Leave the man in peace, Dick," the bartender interrupted.

"Let him decide whether he wants to engage," Dick replied.

"I'll engage with the jester," I said, smiling. "I came in here because I couldn't sleep, so I got out of bed and started walking down St. Paul. Then I spotted this place, which I'd somehow never seen before."

"Never seen it before, huh?" said Dick. "That does happen. There are hidden treasures all over this fair city of Baltimore."

"Agreed."

"You say you've been restless?" asked Dick, sucking on the end of his pen.

"Well, I've had trouble sleeping."

"I never really sleep. Well, I sleep 30 minutes every six hours."

"Interesting. How does that work for you?"

"Great, I guess. Gives me a lot of time to think and I never get insomnia. Now, tell me why you're so restless. Are you worried about something?"

"I actually don't know," I admitted. "I'm pretty healthy after being sick for a long time. I just got married to an incredible woman. I have a decent job. I guess I should be content."

"You feel like something is missing?"

His light blue eyes had a bewildering power.

"Maybe," I answered.

"Something you could be experiencing right now, that you may have already experienced before, and that you will likely experience again."

"Is that a riddle?" I asked, laughing.

"Yes," he said, grinning and sitting up straight on his stool. "What does *content* really mean though? What does *should* mean? Your mind's too active."

"Probably."

"When my mind starts churning, I sit by the window in my apartment and look down at the sidewalk. I watch people walk by, and for the short time I can see them, I let myself become them. I see everything from their vantage point and I completely lose any trace of myself. Then when I decide to return to being me, everything is leveled. I start over for a little while."

He closed his notebook and dropped it into a tattered messenger bag by his feet. He then stood up, pulled on an old blue pea coat, and draped the bag over his shoulder.

"Gotta go get my 30 minutes," he said, patting me on the shoulder and nodding to the bartender before striding out the door.

When I got home, it was just after 2 AM. Marion was in the same position, still softly snoring. I took off my clothes and climbed under the covers. Her body was emanating warmth, and I began to let it ease me to sleep.

Ease

I dreamt of a large dog looking down at me as I lay in a field on a summer afternoon. The dog's expression was peaceful and wise, almost human. As we stared lovingly at one another, I could feel my consciousness transferring over, and soon I was gazing down at my own face. Eventually someone whistled for me, and I scampered off in that direction as fast as I could, leaving my old human body behind to live how it wanted.

{ Age 28 }

I WAS PERCHED ON THE EDGE of the couch in the living room, staring down at a stray fleck of paint on the floor. Marion was pacing in and out of the kitchen, obviously seething.

"I don't get why you're so mad," I ventured hesitantly.

I did not want to fight again, but an escalation seemed inevitable at this point.

"You're just so disappointing to me sometimes," she replied ominously.

"Well I'm sorry about that," I said sarcastically. "What about me disappoints you so deeply?"

"Mainly your obliviousness. You're so wrapped up inside your own fucking head all the time, and that's why you do shit like this."

"You mean forgetting our anniversary? I fucked up, yes, but in the end, is it really that big a deal?"

"But can't you see how it's a symbol of a larger problem?"

"Not really. And by the way, you've definitely changed if this type of thing matters this much to you now. You've tightened up and gotten so anal and judgmental about everything."

"That's your own shit coming up, which you're constantly projecting onto me," she shouted, stalking back and forth even more vigorously. "Do some real work on yourself—examine yourself clearly for once. Look at how you insist on contemplating everything until you just end up paralyzed. Look at how complacent you are, which is really based in this deep fear about putting yourself out there in any way. Look at your reliance on this story you tell yourself about being sick, and how that bleeds over into every area of your life. Look at all your rationalizations and blindness about yourself. For example, your secret fixation on this idea that you're somehow special, that you have this incredible gift you'll release into the world one day. Where is it then? Are you just sitting on it? The truth is you're so fucking terrified of failure that you'll probably never do anything with your life."

She paused for a moment, breathless.

"Wow," I said sarcastically. "You had all that stored up? Such bitterness and resentment. I'll hold off on reciting what I hate about you, how about that? I'm not cruel like you."

Marion collapsed down on the couch next to me and ran both hands violently through her hair.

"I don't mean to be cruel," she sighed. "Maybe it's just this 24 hours a day, 7 days a week thing I can't do. It's too much time with another person. Everything becomes so fucking mundane and all the flaws become clear. For whatever reason, my mind fixates on the flaws. I can't help it."

"You seem miserable," I said flatly.

"I'm not miserable. I'm confused."

My anger was suddenly replaced by a deep sadness. I felt like crying, but held myself back.

"Well then, what do we do now?"

"I have no idea," she replied, sounding exhausted.

Later that night, we were lying silently in bed in the dark, staring up at the ceiling.

"I can't sleep, can you?" she asked gently after a few minutes.

"No."

"I'm sorry for being cruel earlier. I was overtaken by this destructive impulse. I would have latched onto any reason—the anniversary thing just happened to be handy. I literally wanted to destroy you. I think I still kind of want to, actually."

I considered that for a moment.

"Why?" I asked hesitantly.

"I don't know. I honestly don't. I guess maybe part of me thinks that if we destroy each other, we can start from scratch. Everything will be new. No baggage from before we got together. Nothing except the present moment."

"You're reading that Laura Day book again, aren't you?" I asked.

"No," she answered, chuckling. "Well, yes. But that's not it, I swear. It's something deeper. It's a compulsion."

"So you think we should try to destroy each other?"

"Is that insane?"

"Sort of."

"We're well on our way, right?"

"Uh, yeah," I said, laughing.

"Then what's the next step?" she asked.

"Fuck if I know. It's uncharted territory for me."

"Me too."

We lay there in silence for a moment, reflecting.

"Honestly, I don't know if I want to go too much deeper into this," I said, finally. "This mutually assured destruction or whatever it is..."

"You're scared," Marion said, turning toward me.

"I guess I am."

She wrapped her arms around me and gently kissed my forehead.

"No matter what, I love you," she whispered. "That's deeper than any of this."

{ Age 29 }

SO THIS IS IT?" I asked sadly, staring down at the papers.

"I guess it is," said Marion, her bottom lip quivering.

"It seems stupid," I said, sitting back on the couch. "So formal."

"But we both agree we have to do it, right?" she asked, gazing over at me.

Her round green eyes were glistening with tears.

"Yes, we both agree."

"It doesn't mean we don't still love each other. We just need to end this part of the relationship."

"I'm tired of fighting," I said, looking out the window at a squirrel paused on a branch. "I'm done with it."

"Me too."

"But are you really done? Don't you remember you have a pact with yourself or the universe or whatever to destroy me?"

She laughed and pushed her hair behind her ear, exactly the way she always did.

"There's no pact, silly. And yes, I'm done."

Ease

Dolly Sods is a stretch of legitimate wilderness at the northern end of the Monongahela National Forest in West Virginia. Craving solitude, I headed there for a solo camping trip the week after the divorce.

It was late September, and the day had started off warm and clear, but as I traipsed along a trail through a massive patch of ferns, the temperature abruptly took a precipitous plunge and it began to drizzle steadily. This is typical of Dolly Sods, which has its own contained, ever-shifting climate, completely separate from the outside world.

I sat down on a log to change out of my shorts and into long hiking pants. The water was beading up on the leaves of the ferns, forming tiny reflective spheres. I sat for a few minutes watching the spheres multiply and slide off the leaves. My mind was blessedly blank. Eventually I got to my feet again, strapped on my backpack, and continued down the trail.

After an hour or so, the rain stopped, and I wandered into an open area of large scattered rocks and multicolored moss that resembled the moors of Scotland. It was now mid-afternoon, and the sun was pushing through the remnants of a dark bank of clouds above my head. A large beam of sunlight illuminated a group of rocks in the distance, bestowing on them an almost heavenly glow. There were no other humans in sight, and I had passed no one else on the trail to this point. I leaned back and closed my eyes, pulling a long breath of fresh air deep into my chest and down into my stomach. I released it with a loud yell that echoed out among the rocks.

"Aaaahhhhh!"

I then surprised myself by starting to sob uncontrollably. I dropped my backpack to the ground and sat down on top of it, my chest heaving. Images of my life with Marion began to appear in rapid succession. They were all jumbled together and layered thickly on top of one another, nearly impossible to decipher. I closed my eyes and let them wash over me.

Eventually the images began to separate and solidify into distinct memories, each communicating its essence in a brief moment. Oddly, there were a few scenes I did not immediately recognize, with the two of us in seemingly unfamiliar locations. Had I conveniently blocked some things out? In any case, I absorbed them all without judgment, allowing each one to linger for its appointed time and then disappear.

After what seemed like hours, I opened my eyes again and stood up. The clouds were now mostly gone and sunlight was streaming all around me. I picked up my backpack and eased the straps over my shoulders. My body felt lighter. As I started on my way across the moors, I noticed a large group of vultures elegantly circling overhead.

"Did you think I was dead?" I yelled up at them, laughing.

Ease

They just kept circling, undeterred.

{ Age 30 }

I FLIPPED ON THE COFFEEMAKER and sat down at the kitchen table to wait. As the sounds of percolation began, I stared out the window at the street below, where an old woman was slowly pushing a shopping cart filled with glass bottles for recycling. She paused to watch a pigeon peck at some food on the sidewalk.

I was living alone in a new apartment, trying to establish some sort of "normal" routine. Marion and I were no longer in contact. We'd both decided to make a clean break to let things settle and see where we ended up. I knew she was still living somewhere in the Baltimore area, but I didn't know where. I still thought about her daily, if not hourly.

As I sipped my coffee, I pondered the looming work week. Five days in the office filled with long, pointless meetings and insipid conversations with random co-workers. Then after work, hours of mundane time to myself, which I'd fill with drinking or reading or watching TV or wandering around the city...

"So basically I'm dead fucking tired today," sighed Jimmy, my cubicle mate, as he sat down with a fresh mug of coffee. "Had to go rescue my grandmother. She locked her keys in her car. She's going senile. We waited for triple-A for about four hours, so I didn't get home 'til 1 AM."

"Damn," I said, shaking my head sympathetically. "Nice way to spend a Sunday evening."

"Tell me about it. I mean, she's great and all. She's actually a totally pleasant companion. But man, she forgets everything. She really shouldn't be driving anymore, but she'd be devastated to get that taken away. Do you have any grandparents still around?"

"Nope, all dead now," I replied.

"Sorry."

"It's fine. They all lived good long lives."

"I wonder about that. When you've lived a good long life and you're about to die, are you ready to go? Or do you want to keep living no matter what?"

"My grandmother was done. She wanted to die, mostly because she couldn't breathe anymore from the emphysema. My grandfather, her husband, died suddenly of a heart attack before I was born, so he didn't have time to reflect. My other grandmother had heart problems and went kind of senile, so she didn't really know what was going on. Her husband died of congestive heart failure. He wanted to go, too. Couldn't breathe."

"Damn that's heavy," said Jimmy sadly. "I guess the body mostly decides in the end, huh?"

"Pretty much. Apologies for the unrelenting bleakness there, but you asked..."

"I did indeed. Well, in lighter news, happy hour Wednesday! You coming?"

"It depends. Are you getting trashed again and puking on my shoe?" I asked, chuckling.

"No! I swear I'm keeping it together this time."

"I don't believe you."

"You shouldn't," he replied, grinning. "I wonder if Allison will be there. I could deal with that."

"You're into her?"

"Oh yes, but I think I fucked it up last week by puking in front of her. What do you think?"

"She did kind of frown and hurry off when it happened. But hey, you got that out of the way, right?"

"Shit. Well, every day is a new day. When I see her, I'll just pretend it never happened."

"That's always a solid plan," I said.

He spun his chair back around to face his computer.

"Well, back to work, whatever that means."

It was 11 AM on a Monday morning in April—a moment as restrictive and expansive as any other.

{ Age 31 }

D AN LEANED FORWARD over his nearly empty plate of pasta and leveled a particularly concentrated stare at me.

"I have to tell you something you might not like."

"OK," I replied hesitantly.

The dinner had already been intense, with Dan laying out all the aspects of the "ascendant life philosophy" he was hatching. His enthusiasm was limitless, and my brain was now exhausted.

"It's about Marion," he continued. "She's with someone now. They just got married, quite abruptly."

"OK," I said again, a lump forming in my throat.

"And she's pregnant."

"I don't believe it," I instinctively responded, taking a sip of wine with a shaking hand.

"It's true. They live in Catonsville. His name's Jameson and he seems fairly normal, actually. Even a little boring."

"Bullshit. She couldn't stand being with a normal, boring guy."

"I swear it's true. I had dinner at their place last week. I suspect you're just in denial."

"No, just processing," I replied, trying hard not to betray how thrown off I was.

"Denial is understandable, and forgivable."

"I appreciate that, Dan," I said sarcastically.

"Marion's very complex, as you know," he continued, unfazed. "There's really no way to know why she'd choose a guy like that."

"To take a break," I said under my breath.

"What did you say?"

"Nothing."

Dan then went on to pontificate expansively about the nature of human relationships. I simply tuned him out, polished off my wine, and signaled for the check.

Before bed that night, I sat at my kitchen table with a bottle of Four Roses bourbon. As I downed shot after shot, I pictured Marion calmly chatting with her husband in their living room by the fire as they planned for the baby's arrival. This made me alternately furious and depressed, so I drank more. Eventually I was able to stumble down the hall to my room, where I threw myself down on the bed fully clothed.

I fell asleep almost instantly, and I soon found myself walking through a dense forest at night under the light of the full moon. I had no idea where I was headed, so I chose my path purely instinctively. At times, a bright golden glow appeared in the distance just above the tree line. Over and over, I made my way toward it, only to have it disappear as I drew near. Eventually I gave up trying to forge a distinct path and just started wandering aimlessly, ignoring the glow whenever it appeared. Although I started doing this out of sheer frustration, I soon found a strange comfort in being lost.

Suddenly my body was whisked into the sky and suspended a few hundred feet up. From this vantage point, the entire forest was visible in the moonlight, and I could spot hundreds of paths winding through the trees. Most of these paths meandered along in seemingly random patterns, veering away from one another for miles only to curve back around and meet, then veer off again. Some paths were simply closed loops, and others were dead ends.

After a few moments, the ground began to shake, swaying the tops of the trees back and forth. The shaking became progressively more violent until the earth started to swallow the trees en masse. Everything churned and swirled, twisting into a massive stream of dirt and debris that moved swiftly along from one end of the horizon to the other. Eventually this stream became almost translucent, seemingly composed of pure matter and energy and flowing with incredible speed. Before long, the stream was all I could see—everything had been absorbed into it.

As the stream continued to gain momentum, complex forms, both animate and inanimate, hopped out and then back in, created and destroyed in moments. From my removed perspective, this process seemed almost playful, and it continued unabated for what felt like hours or even days.

Ultimately, though, the observation period ended and I began to move toward the stream, my arms involuntarily stretching out as far as they could to meet it. The moment my fingers touched its surface, I awoke coughing and choking in my bed.

I sat up to catch my breath, and as the coughing subsided, I began to realize what and where I was—a human on a bed in an apartment somewhere on Earth... drunk, alone, and lost.

{ Age 32 }

I WAS SITTING AT MY DESK at work, staring blankly at a mass email from my boss.

"Your phone's ringing," Jimmy said, knocking me out of my stupor.

After half-heartedly untangling the phone cord for a few seconds, I pressed the button for line 1.

"This is Byron," I answered mechanically.

"Hello Byron," said a familiar voice.

"Marion?" I said, my voice nearly cracking.

I hadn't heard anything from her in over two years.

"Yup. How are you?"

"I'm OK. It's been a while."

"Yes, it sure has. I think about you a lot, actually."

"Really?" I asked skeptically, trying to keep my voice soft.

I could tell Jimmy was trying to appear nonchalant, like he wasn't listening.

"Yes," she replied.

"You have a kid now, right?" I asked.

"Yup. His name's Miles."

"Well, congrats."

"Listen, I think we should meet," she continued. "How about tonight at Brewer's Art?"

"OK, I guess that could work," I replied, taken aback.

"Around 8?"

"Sure."

"See you then," she said, hanging up.

I put the phone down and leaned back in my seat, my chest still clenched tight. Jimmy was typing away on his keyboard, attempting to seem busy.

I got to the bar first and ordered a bourbon. I'd been drinking quite a bit lately, so the first few sips brought me to a peaceful equilibrium. It was a Tuesday evening and the crowd was sparse, mostly younger couples chatting quietly. After about ten minutes, Marion walked in the door, looking just as beautiful as ever. She spotted me and smiled, striding over with her typical assurance and stretching her arms out wide to give me a hug.

"Thanks for meeting me," she said as we settled on our stools. "It's great to see you."

"You too," I replied, forcing a smile. "What do you want to drink? White wine, as usual?"

"Naturally," she said, grinning.

I signaled the bartender and ordered for her.

"Like I said on the phone," she began. "I've been thinking about you a lot."

"Oh?"

"Yes. I feel like we essentially left things in chaos and it was mostly my fault. I just hammered on you about everything until neither of us could take it anymore."

"I deserved some of it," I said, gazing down at my glass. "You challenged me."

"But it was too much. I have a lot of destructive energy. Always have. I've been working on just letting it pass through me instead of directing it at people."

"And how is that working out for you and the family?"

"Not bad. I do feel like I'm only partially me, though. I've sacrificed something."

"Is it worth it?"

"For Miles, yes, absolutely. He only just turned one but I swear he's special, Byron. Something's going on there. I want you to meet him sometime."

"What about for the husband?"

"Yes, I suppose it's worth it. Jameson's a good guy. Solid. Very conventional. He can put up with a lot."

"But not what I had to put up with?" I asked with a sly smile.

"No, like I said, I'm not like that with him."

"How nice for him."

"Anyway, I had a dream about you last night, and I woke up feeling like I really had to see you today. I think we should talk to each other. No more of this falling completely out of touch."

"I'm fine with that," I said, steeling myself with a long sip of bourbon. "But I should tell you I'm probably still in love with you. Can you deal with that?"

She laughed and pushed her hair behind her ear, as always.

"Yes, I can deal with that. I'm probably still in love with you too, but I'm pretty sure it's not meant to be in this lifetime. It's not going to work, for whatever reason..."

"Fuck that," I said firmly, almost angrily. "Who knows what's meant to be? We determine."

"Maybe partially, I guess. But we're really just these puny creatures being tossed around by forces that don't give two shits about our individual destiny. I would think you'd agree with that."

"Then no free will in your book?"

"Oh we have free will. We can make any little daily mundane decision we want, but on a grand scale we're being pushed in a certain direction by our patterns, our chemistry, and by simple timing. For example, if we were just meeting now, at this age, both single, and I had been through my first real relationship already and destroyed that person..."

She paused and we both laughed.

"If I had destroyed that person already," she continued, "I might have been able to suppress that impulse for you, and we probably could have made it work."

"But you wouldn't be your true self. I wouldn't want that."

"Even after all the shit we went through? You want that person?"

"I don't want the constant fighting... at all. But yes, I want that person."

Tears welled up in her eyes as she stared at me.

"Why couldn't I just behave?" she asked plaintively.

"Don't beat yourself up," I replied, smiling sadly. "I am incomplete. I can't seem to figure out what the fuck to do with myself. I have these dreams and random moments that show me everything. They're essentially mystical experiences, I guess, and I have no clue how to reconcile them with daily life. So now I'm just confused and restless all the time."

Marion reached over and took my hand.

"Don't try to figure it out. I know your mind. It's always churning, and any mind trying to process all that craziness is going to get stuck or break down. If you can, just relax and let it be."

We kept talking for over an hour, touching on many disparate subjects with the joyful, effortless flow of our early time together. Finally, she stood up to go.

"I'm so glad we did this," she said, beaming. "So glad."

"Me too," I said with a tinge of melancholy.

I didn't want it to end. She hugged me tight around the neck and gently kissed my ear.

"I love you," she whispered.

"I love you too," I whispered back.

After she walked out, I ordered one last bourbon. As I sipped it, I stared unblinkingly at my reflection in the mirror behind the bar.

Late afternoon that Friday, I got another call at work. It was Dan, and his voice sounded hesitant and feeble.

"Sad news, Byron. Horrible news."

"Tell me," I said flatly.

"Marion is dead. Her car flipped over on 695 this morning and she died instantly. Broke her neck."

"She was alone?" I asked clinically, not yet processing.

"Yes."

"OK, thanks for letting me know."

I hung up the phone and stared blankly at my computer screen. The cursor was blinking inside a cell of an utterly pointless spreadsheet. I felt nothing except a compulsion to escape. I stood up and walked out of my cubicle, down the hall, and out the front door of the office. I got in my car and drove to the first dive bar I found, where I drank well into the evening. Around 11, I passed out on the floor of the bar's bathroom, drenched in my own vomit.

{ Age 33 }

T HE DAY BEGAN, LIKE SO MANY BEFORE IT, with me waking up fully clothed and completely discombobulated on my bed, drool covering my cheek and pillow. I remembered snippets of the night before, mainly pouring my heart out to some redhead at the bar. What was her name? I don't think I even asked, not that it mattered. Did we fuck in the bathroom stall? No, we didn't. I puked on the toilet seat, and she justifiably pushed me away and stalked off.

There was a half-empty bottle of bourbon next to the bed on the floor, so I must have continued drinking when I got home. As I stumbled to the bathroom to piss and also likely puke yet again, I caught a glimpse of myself in the mirror and shuddered.

Later that afternoon, I lounged listlessly on my couch drinking bourbon and staring at the wall. It was Saturday, which meant no work. I contemplated what to do later that evening. Dinner somewhere? Maybe Thai? That sounded comfortingly normal.

It had been six months since Marion died, and I felt completely alone in the world. I had shut out my old friends entirely, and I constantly invented intricate excuses to avoid seeing my parents. Naturally they were concerned, but I'd somehow managed to convince them I was doing OK. How I'd held onto my job, I had no idea. My boss Julia had to notice I was half-drunk most of the time. I was good at bullshitting, though, and I always had a set, satisfactory answer for the questions she liked to ask. Jimmy knew what was going on, of course, but he strategically ignored it.

I stood up and tottered unsteadily over to my bookcase, where my eye was drawn to an old copy of the Bible I'd sentimentally held onto from my childhood. It had my name engraved on the front, commemorating the day I became an "official" member of the church at age seven. I randomly flipped to the book of Ecclesiastes, to a verse in chapter 6: "For who knows what is good for a man in life, during the few and meaningless days he passes through like a shadow? Who can tell him what will happen under the sun after he is gone?" I chuckled at the dark humor and thought about the nearly full bottle of Ambien in my medicine cabinet. It had been tempting me for weeks now.

After dinner at the Thai restaurant, I plopped down on my familiar seat at the bar near my apartment. I was already quite tipsy, and Charlie, the bartender who knew me well, eyed me apprehensively as I waved him over.

"Hey Byron, how are you my friend? You solid tonight?"

"What do you mean by solid?" I asked suspiciously.

"I mean, are you OK?"

"Is anyone OK, Charlie?"

"You know what I mean."

"Yes, I'm OK. Please bring me a bourbon, neat."

As he poured my drink, I glanced around the bar to see if I recognized anyone. I did not—no regulars yet.

"What do you think about all this, Charlie?" I asked as he placed the glass in front of me.

"What do you mean by all this?"

"Everything. You working here, pouring drinks, going home and sleeping, waking up. Living, basically."

"I'm not sure what you're getting at," he replied brusquely. "It's life. It's what happens. That's it."

"Nothing more?" I asked.

"No, nothing more. I have no idea why we're here, do you? Because if you do, please tell me."

"We're here to suffer and die while getting teased with glimpses of beauty in the meantime. It's a ridiculous game."

"Ouch," came a raspy female voice behind me. "Is that it?"

I turned to see an older woman wearing a long, plush white coat and carrying a fancy sequined purse. She slowly removed the coat and handed it to Charlie, who hung it up behind the bar. As she situated herself next to me, I caught a whiff of strong Chanel perfume, the same one my grandmother used to wear on special occasions.

"White wine spritzer please, Charlie," she said, adjusting the front of her dress.

"Sure thing, Gladys," he replied, grabbing a wine glass. "Great to see you."

"You too. And who is our nihilistic friend here?"

She looked over at me with a cryptic grin.

"I'm Byron," I said, raising my glass.

"Well Byron, I would say good to meet you, but you seem to be beyond all that."

"Ha!" I answered, laughing. "Good to meet you, Gladys."

"So, why the acidic world view?" she asked, her eyes narrowing.

I shrugged my shoulders and returned her stare.

"It's a pose, I know. Do you have a better idea?"

"Yes," she answered, smiling.

She took her drink from Charlie and raised it to her lips.

"Mmmm," she said as she placed it down on the bar. "Well done."

She gazed up at the ceiling for a moment, savoring the experience.

"We are given the capacity for love," she continued, still looking upward. "What does that mean?"

I polished off my bourbon and signaled to Charlie for another.

"It's just instinct," I replied flatly.

"No, I disagree. Love is the representative of divinity."

I noticed that Charlie had now paused to listen in.

"How have I never seen you in here before?" I asked, diverting the conversation. "I'm here all the time."

"No idea," she replied, looking over at me again.

She took another long and pleasurable sip of her drink.

"Have you ever experienced love?" she asked as she gently placed the glass back down. "I mean, have you truly experienced it?"

I had an overwhelming, cowardly urge to get up and leave, but I stayed with the moment.

"Yes," I answered, my voice catching. "I have."

"You're thinking of one person in particular?"

"Yes."

"Here's my thought on the way love works, accumulated over the many years I've been alive. Love is the infinite divine energy that can never be confined. We try to limit it, but we can't. We try to compartmentalize it as something that's only associated with blood relation or friendship or physical intimacy, but it refuses to fit in any box. Any time you truly communicate with another person and let them change you in some small way, you experience love. Any time you are truly

present with another person, without baggage or preconceptions, you experience love. It has no limitations.
It is the reason we're here, as conscious humans. We
are meant to savor it every moment of every day."

She paused and smiled wistfully.

"Does any of that sound sensible to you?"

I just nodded my head, my eyes welling with tears.
What a fool I was.

"Well there it is," Charlie said matter-of-factly as he
turned around to pour my drink. "Gladys tells the
truth."

I kept drinking on into the night, but I paced myself
a bit so Charlie wouldn't kick me out. At 2 AM, I
stumbled out into the street, pissed in an alley, and
then sat down with my back against a wall and dozed
off.

I woke up on my side about an hour later, drenched
in sweat with my head pounding. I stood up unsteadily
and started wandering in the general direction of my
apartment. I made it as far as the first-floor hallway,
where I gave up and collapsed next to the storage area
underneath the stairs.

{ Age 34 }

I T WAS A CLOUDY SUNDAY in late October, a little chilly for the time of year. I was wandering down by the harbor, taking covert swigs from a flask of bourbon tucked in the inner pocket of my coat. As I watched the wide spectrum of people float by, I felt like I was slowly emerging from the haze of the previous two years. Yes, I was still drinking during most of my waking hours, but that wouldn't last. My enjoyment of it was finally waning. I was ready for the next stage. Well... nearly ready.

As I meandered along growing more and more inebriated, I began to focus my attention on small details—a pebble on the concrete, a weathered penny, a Burger King wrapper, a smashed cigarette butt, a glob of spit. I felt connected to these things—we inhabited the same time and location. Soon they'd all be gone, replaced by nearly identical items that few would notice.

"Can I bother you for some change?" came a gruff male voice. "Any change you got would help. Anything at all."

I looked up to see a rail-thin, white-bearded man wearing an oversized army jacket and a faded Orioles baseball cap. He was standing by a trashcan holding a sign that read "We must have mercy on each other in this last daze. Please help a fellow human if you can." He stared at me plaintively as I approached.

"A quarter? Anything?"

I reached for my wallet, pulled out a $20 bill, and placed it in his outstretched hand.

"Thanks my friend!" he said, his eyes lighting up. "God bless ya, ya hear?"

"What do you mean by last daze?" I asked him.

"Well, it's the last time we'll all be half-asleep here together, like in a daze."

"Why the last time?"

"Last era of this, I'm saying. Then either we all die, or we all wake up and see shit clearly."

I held my flask out to him and he smiled and shook his head. I shrugged and took a long swig.

"Like to numb yourself?" he asked with a sly grin.

"Yup. I'm weak. Can't seem to face daily life without it."

"Been there," he replied. "Been drunk half my life. I can't remember shit."

"But no more?"

"No more. I want to see things clear. Clear is the only way."

"And what have you noticed, seeing things clearly?"

"That everyone's distracted by petty bullshit. All the time. You should hear what I hear. I'm a bum, so I'm invisible."

"People are just stuck in their fragile little bubbles," I mumbled.

"It don't matter anyway," he said. "Too hard to talk to people over that distance."

We stood silently for a few seconds, contemplating the passersby.

"So, what'd you used to do?" I asked.

"You mean a job? I worked the steel mill at Sparrow's Point for a stretch back in the 70s and 80s. Got laid off. Did some carpentry for a while. Then kind of drifted away from everything."

"Why?"

"Just got tired. Couldn't make ends meet. On top of that, had a woman screw me over with my best friend. Started drinkin' a whole lot."

"Ah... What's your name?"

"Frank."

"Mine's Byron."

"What's your story, Byron?"

"I don't have a story. I'm stuck in an endless cycle."

"Depressed, huh?"

"I guess that's it. Just sick of my own limitations."

"We all got flaws. Gotta come to terms with 'em. That's the key."

"I suppose that's right," I replied, kicking at a cigarette butt.

"No other choice, really, except give up."

I shredded the cigarette butt with my shoe, and then turned to Frank and held out my hand. He seemed confused, but shook it anyway.

"I want to let you know, Frank, that I care about you," I said. "I'll be back around to see you again sometime, I promise."

"That'd be great, but no offense to you, I tend not to trust no one. People hardly ever do what they say. I'd be glad to see you again, though, if things break that way."

"Things will break that way," I replied, patting his shoulder. "Bye for now."

I walked away whistling a tune from a music box I'd had as a kid. It came to me out of nowhere.

{ Age 35 }

I WOKE UP TO THE SUN shining on my eyelids. It was peeking over the rim of the bedroom window and reflecting off the mirror above my dresser. I breathed deeply and sat up on the side of the bed. As I gazed out the window at the rows of freshly tilled soil awaiting the growth of the soybeans, I mouthed a brief prayer of thanks for this luminous spring morning, seemingly so distant from the commotion and confusion of the city.

I was living on my friend Nate's farm near Chestertown on the eastern shore of Maryland. He had a vacant, somewhat dilapidated house on the property that he was willing to rent to me cheaply, so I jumped on the opportunity. My daily life was markedly different here—much less neurotic and confining, and consequently a bit less alcoholic. I worked from home editing manuscripts for the same company I worked for in Baltimore, and my schedule allowed me to nap or take long walks whenever it suited me.

In the kitchen that morning, I fried up some eggs from the farm's chickens for breakfast and sat down at the table to eat. As I watched the steam rise off the eggs and coffee, I thought of all the time I'd wasted over the course of the past few years. Was there a point to regretting anything, though? I took a sip of coffee and let it sit in my mouth, savoring the taste. No, there was no point.

After breakfast, I headed out to the front porch to spend some time on the tattered rocking chair that Nate's late grandfather had left there. On sunny mornings, I liked to sit and rock a bit before I started working. On this day, I closed my eyes and listened to the birds, trying to separate and isolate each intertwined song. When I opened my eyes, a woman in a straw sun hat and a long white dress was walking down the dirt driveway toward the house.

"Hello!" she called out cheerfully as she drew near. "Are you Byron?"

"Yes," I answered, rousing myself from my bird trance.

"I'm Katherine, a friend of Nate's from down the road. I'm way overdue for a visit to say hello. You've been here a few months now, right?"

Her entire manner was preternaturally calming, and her eyes showed no hint of judgment or distraction. She was not traditionally beautiful, but her face was mesmerizing. Her mouth was slightly crooked, and one eye was noticeably narrower than the other.

"Yes, three months now," I answered, smiling.

"I'm not bothering you, am I? Not keeping you from anything?" she asked with concern.

"No, no. I work from home and can start my day whenever I want."

"Well that sounds nice."

"Please, come sit on the porch with me," I said, standing up. "Would you like the rocking chair? It's falling apart but the experience is still pretty damn satisfying."

"Sure," she said, grinning. "I love a good rocking chair experience."

I perched myself on the wooden bench next to her, watching as she smoothed the back of her dress and sank down into the rocker.

"So..." she began, removing her hat to reveal her short reddish hair. "How do you like it here so far? You moved from Baltimore, right?"

"Yes, from Baltimore. I love it here. Mainly the peace and quiet."

"It is peaceful here," she said, rocking gently and staring up at the treetops. "Did you not have peace in the city?"

"No. It was mostly my fault, though."

"Oh?"

"Yes, long story. You create your own hell, right?"

"And your own heaven," she replied. "That's what they say."

"Well I think they're right. Anyway, I've emerged from that for the most part."

"Good. We don't need to talk about the past if you don't want to."

"OK," I said, watching her intently.

She was still gazing tranquilly up at the treetops.

"Do you see that cardinal up there?" she asked, pointing up.

I craned my neck to see.

"Yes, I see it."

"Such a deep red, huh? Beautiful."

"Very beautiful."

She turned to me and scrutinized my face intently for a few moments.

"Would you like to be friends with me?" she asked with disarming sincerity.

"Yes," I replied, smiling. "I definitely would."

"Good," she said, seeming relieved. "I feel like I want to get to know you. I'm 25 now, old enough to trust this sort of feeling. I'm beginning to really rely on my intuition."

"That's good to hear. I'm still learning how to trust mine."

"Deep intuition is usually correct. For most people, though, it's hidden behind a bunch of layers."

"I get the sense you have no use for layers," I said.

"No, I don't. What's the point? This life is short."

"Yes, it is."

Ease

"I should let you get to work," Katherine said, starting to get to her feet.

"No, stay. Please stay for a bit," I said. "I mean, if you want to."

"OK, if you insist," she answered, smiling. "I *am* happy right here."

"Me too," I replied, leaning back against the house.

Katherine began to stop by every few days, usually on weekday mornings. She always approached the house the same way she did that first time, worried that she might be bothering me. I never turned her away, of course. We tended to sit on the porch and talk, but occasionally we'd take a stroll around the farm, pausing to observe any interesting trees or birds or clouds. Being with her felt like a continuous renewal for me, with no beginning or end.

One cloudy morning in early summer, we hiked to the dead tree in the center of the largest soybean field on the farm. I hoisted myself up on a thick, nearly horizontal branch and sat astride it. Katherine was kneeling on the ground below me, examining a large anthill.

"This ant is ridiculous," she said, laughing. "It's carrying a red berry that's like five times its size. But that's what they do, right?"

"Yup, they're strong as hell," I said, laughing with her.

"I love this ant," she proclaimed, leaning in closer to observe.

"How come you never ask me about my past?" I asked, gazing down at the top of her wide straw hat. "Or talk about your past?"

"No need," she answered cryptically. "We're both just here now, enjoying ourselves."

"I still kind of want to know where you came from," I said. "And how you ended up down the road from here."

"I came from around here, from Chestertown, but I'm not always going to stay here. I'll probably leave soon."

"And go where?" I asked, surprised and suddenly a little distraught.

"Oh, I don't know. I don't worry about it. That's the future."

Another morning, early, Katherine sat down at the old piano in the living room and began testing out the keys. The piano had been Nate's grandfather's and it hadn't been tuned in years, maybe decades. She started playing the first few measures of the Moonlight Sonata, very slowly.

"Wow, this thing is out of tune," she said, laughing.

"Still sounds pretty," I said.

"Do you play?" she asked, pausing to look up at me.

"No, not really. I took a few lessons as a kid, but that's it."

"I can teach you if you want. If not now, then later."

"OK, I'd love to learn."

"I'm not very good, but I can show you the basics, I think."

She resumed playing, gently and slowly, as dust motes floated off the keys in the sharp morning sun.

A few days later, on a Friday morning, she approached the house carrying two intricately carved walking sticks. As she neared the porch, she smiled mischievously.

"Are you busy with work?"

"No," I answered, chuckling. "What are those?"

"They're for you, and the next person you might want to take a long walk with. I carved them back in college. The carvings are kind of lame... wizard and fairy stuff."

She leaned over and placed them carefully on the ground at the foot of the porch steps.

"Thanks for these, but I'm confused... why aren't we using them on our walks?" I asked.

"I'm leaving tomorrow to go to Asheville. My friends Marc and Leah are down there, and I can live with them for a bit while I figure things out and look for a job like real people do."

I felt my chest and throat tighten up.

"I'm sad to see you go," I said, my voice catching a little. "But I'm happy for you if it's really what you want to do."

"Why are you so sad about it?" she asked slyly.

"Because I care about you. I like having you around."

"I care about you, too," she said, cocking her head slightly. "But don't worry, this is just the first time."

"What do you mean by that?" I asked, confused again.

"There will be other times. We can try different ways."

"Different ways of what?"

"Meeting, interacting, caring for each other."

"Are you talking about the future?" I asked, smiling teasingly. "I thought you weren't so interested in that."

"Don't worry about it," she said, chuckling. "I'll see you again before you know it."

And with that, she turned around and walked back up the driveway toward the road. She did indeed move to Asheville the next day, leaving me alone again, for the most part.

{ Age 36 }

THE FIRST TIME I ATTEMPTED IT was on an ordinary Tuesday night in February. It was around 11 PM, and as usual, the farm was utterly silent. I had been trying to read the Tao for a bit, but my eyes refused to stay open, so I placed the book down on the nightstand and switched off the lamp. When I closed my eyes, I began to see vague, swirling geometric patterns in a multitude of colors. The patterns soon coalesced to form recognizable objects like chairs, trees, staircases, rocks, insects, human bodies, and so on. These objects were in constant flux, shifting and transforming endlessly, emerging out of the void only to be swallowed up again. I soon relaxed enough to simply let the images wash over me.

Eventually certain distinct forms began to stabilize in my vision, and I was able to recognize specific locations and people. I saw my father and mother, my cousin Isla, friends from college, random people I'd met on the street or at a bar. I soon noticed that if I concentrated slightly, but not too hard, I could cause particular images to appear and solidify for a few moments. First I called up my mother, and there she stood in front of me before abruptly disappearing. I then materialized my father, a hamster I'd had as a kid, my sixth-grade teacher Mr. Nadolny, the station wagon I first drove, and finally, Marion. She appeared for a few precious seconds, staring straight at me, before vanishing. All went to black after that, and I fell into deeper sleep.

Two nights later, the same opening sequence happened again, but this time I was able to proceed to controlled visions more quickly. As before, the key was to shut down the "front" of my conscious mind. If I fixated on anything or exercised my reasoning faculties at all, the controlled image disappeared. The balance was extremely tenuous, and I could sense it would take some practice.

During this particular sequence, I again conjured an image of Marion. She materialized in an open field at night, under a full moon. She was wearing a fancy black dress and a cowboy hat, and her eyes were glowing bright red. She seemed to be mouthing words, but no sound came out. I tried to concentrate so I could catch what she was saying, but the conscious effort caused the scene to collapse into a chaos of twisting patterns and shapes.

About a week later, after a few false starts, I was able to go further. This time Marion was lying next to me under a tree in what appeared to be a massive park. It was evening, nearly twilight, and she was reclining on her side with her hand supporting her head. Her eyes were closed as if she was meditating. I waited patiently for her to open them, and when she finally did, her pupils were again glowing bright red. She smiled joyfully when she saw me, reaching out her free hand to touch my cheek.

"Byron, you're here," she said almost inaudibly.

I started to ask her to speak up, but quickly stopped myself. I knew better now. My job was to simply let things unfold.

"I'm here," I replied.

"I'm happy you're here," she said, a little louder, "for as long as it lasts."

"I'm not worried about how long it will last."

"Neither am I. Nothing is measured here anyway."

She gazed up at the darkening sky and laughed.

"Where is this?" I asked.

"If you think about it too hard, it will go away," she replied, looking back over at me.

I just nodded and said nothing.

"Can you do something for me?" she asked, touching my hand.

"Yes, anything."

"Find Miles and meet with him. Not right away, but soon."

"OK, I will."

"Thank you."

She pushed herself up and sat cross-legged in the grass, facing me.

"Don't worry about where you are or where I am. It all overlaps and meshes together, like this."

She held up her hands with her fingers interlaced.

"You are all over, everywhere, as you already know," she said, smiling.

"I do?"

"Yes, you know."

"But what does that...?" I began to ask, but this was too much.

Everything collapsed around me, leaving me awake and alone in the dark. I switched on the lamp and sat up in my bed, pulling my knees in against my chest and shivering involuntarily.

The next morning, I woke just before sunrise. Following some random impulse, I pulled on my coat and started walking briskly down the long dirt road that led to the main house where Nate and his family lived. As I walked, I breathed the crisp, cold winter air deep down into my lungs. Before long, the sun emerged just above the horizon, shooting beams of light through the branches of the bare trees lining the road. I paused for a moment to observe, the mist from my outbreaths wreathing my head.

"What else do you need?" I asked myself, aloud.

Then I laughed softly, joyfully.

{ Age 37 }

I WAS LISTENING TO BITCHES BREW while I ate my chicken noodle soup for lunch, sinking into that familiar stoned, mystical vibe. As I rinsed my bowl in the sink after finishing up, I gazed over at the album cover on the counter. Miles.

I called Dan's old cell phone number and left a voicemail. It was an automated message, so I could only hope I'd actually reached him. I had no idea where he was these days or what he might be doing. We hadn't spoken since around the time Marion died.

I plopped down on the couch, closed my eyes, and let the music cascade over me. Work could wait.

My phone rang around midnight, yanking me out of a dead sleep.

"Byron, it's Dan. Did I wake you?"

"No, no," I slurred. "Well, sort of."

"Sorry my friend. I don't think much about time out here."

"Where are you?"

"In Colorado, at a retreat center near a little town called Lyons."

"A retreat center?"

"Yes, it's called Beyond. It's run by a beautiful soul named Laura Day. You might know her books."

"Yeah, I remember that name from somewhere."

"You should come out here soon and join us. I think you'd get something out of it at this particular point in your life. I'll just leave it at that."

"Sounds intriguing," I said, now almost fully awake.

"It's much more than that," he replied with his trademark gravity. "Listen, I got your message about Jameson and Miles. Yes, I do know how to get in touch with them. They still live in Catonsville in the same house. I haven't spoken to Jameson in a few years, though."

"What's his number?"

"I'll send it. Why do you want to get in touch?"

"Curiosity."

"Simple curiosity?" he asked skeptically.

"Is that hard to believe?"

"Yes."

The next evening after dinner, I fortified myself with a quick shot of bourbon. I sat on the couch with the phone in my hand, contemplating how Jameson would react to my call. My mind sifted through numerous scenarios, all of them awkward. Finally, I just dialed the number.

"Hello, this is Jameson," came a deep voice.

"Hi Jameson," I began hesitantly. "This is Byron calling."

"Byron? You don't mean *the* Byron?" he asked, almost sounding happy I called.

"I don't know about *the* Byron, but yes, Marion's ex."

"Wow. Well, how are you?"

"I'm OK. How are you?"

My body relaxed a bit. This was not remotely what I was expecting.

"I'm doing reasonably well, I suppose. That's the phrase I use when people ask—doing reasonably well. It works most of the time."

"It sounds legit."

"How did you get my number? I mean, I have no issue with it, but how did you get it?"

"From Dan."

"Aha! Dan. Good old Dan the philosopher. How is he?"

"He's living out in Colorado at a retreat center, apparently."

"Somehow that makes perfect sense," Jameson said, chuckling. "Now, what can I do for you?"

"I have a request that I hope doesn't sound too odd or creepy."

"Shoot."

"I'd like to meet Miles, if possible."

"Hmmm. I don't see why not. Where are you located?"

"I'm living over the bridge near Chestertown. I'm happy to drive to the city to meet you guys."

"OK, how about this Saturday? He likes to eat at Friendly's. Do you want to meet there for lunch around noon? There's one on Frederick Road."

"Sounds good to me," I replied.

"Done, see you then," he said, hanging up.

I tossed the phone on the couch beside me and watched a fat, lazy fly crawl laboriously along the scuffed hardwood floor. So that was *the* Jameson...

I pulled into the Friendly's parking lot around 12:10. As I got out of the car, I started nervously scanning the tables through the window of the restaurant. There were various scattered families and one lone overweight man eating a sundae, but no single father and son. Once inside, I surveyed the entire restaurant as the hostess waited patiently, but I couldn't find anyone who might be them. I let the hostess lead me to a table, where I sat down to wait.

I nervously flipped through the menu while keeping an eye on the door. Finally, after about ten minutes, a man and a boy entered. The man was tall and seamlessly "normal," dressed in a plaid shirt and khaki pants. The boy looked to be about six years old, with curly black hair and wide, searching eyes. Miles saw me before Jameson did, and he yanked on his dad's hand to let him know. Jameson nodded and smiled, and they made their way over.

"Jameson?" I asked, standing up to shake his hand.

"Yes, good to meet you Byron," he replied, smiling. "This is Miles. Miles, say hello to Byron. He was a friend of your mom's."

Miles held out his hand and gave me a limp handshake.

"If you were friends with my mom, you're probably sad she's dead," he said impassively as they settled in across from me.

"Yes, I am sad. Even though it was a while ago, I'm still sad when I think about her."

"Miles, we don't have to talk about dying right now," said Jameson gently.

"Why not?"

"Because we're at lunch at your favorite restaurant. We're going to try to enjoy ourselves and talk to our new friend Byron."

"But dying is fine to talk about. You told me that before."

Jameson sighed and glanced across at me.

"He's a unique one," he said apologetically. "Always has been."

"Like Marion," I replied.

"Oh yes, for sure," he said, grimacing. "Listen, to get it out of the way, I have no issues with you whatsoever. I'm actually glad you called. I think you knew her better than anyone. She talked about you all the time."

"I'm sure you knew her better than I did," I said.

"No, I knew her partially. She never fully opened up to me. I was just a comfortable place for her to rest."

Our waitress appeared to take our drink order.

"I always order Sprite," said Miles as she left.

"Oh really?" I asked, smiling.

"Yes, I like it. It's really fizzy. Do you remember me?"

"Do I remember you?"

"Yes, from last time."

"I think this is the first time we've met, isn't it?"

"No. We talked before, at the mall, with my mom."

"That must have been a dream, buddy," Jameson said, patting him on the head.

"It wasn't a dream," he said, staring at me. "Or maybe it was. I don't know."

He giggled and looked down at the tabletop.

"I guess in the spirit of Marion, we can just toss out the small talk," Jameson said. "I want to ask you a pretty personal question, if that's OK."

"Sure," I replied, surprised at how calm and natural this all felt.

"Were you still in love with her when she died?"

I inadvertently glanced over at Miles before answering.

"Don't worry, I don't gloss over things with him. He's not a normal kid, anyway."

"Yes," I answered. "I was."

"I'm sorry. That must have been hard."

A lump formed in my throat as I stared down at the burger section of my open menu.

"Yes, for sure," I said softly. "And I'm sure for you, too."

"Look, we've both been through the gauntlet on this," he said gently. "We were both in love with her. That connects us."

"For sure it does," I answered, genuinely moved.

Over the next several weeks, the three of us stayed in touch on an almost daily basis. We met a few more times for meals, and I even visited their place one Sunday afternoon. Soon Miles began call me in the evenings, usually after dinner, to fill me in on whatever was in his head at the time. I looked forward to these calls more than almost anything else in my life.

"Byron, hi," he said one evening when I answered the phone. "I'm looking out the window at the grass. It's windy, so it's moving just a little bit."

"Is it pretty?"

"Oh yes, it's very pretty. I also see a bird in the bird feeder. He's drinking the water."

"What color is the bird?"

"He looks red."

"Ah, he might be a cardinal! Those are my favorite."

"If you come back to visit our house you can probably see him."

"OK, maybe I will."

"You need to come pretty soon, before you go away."

"What do you mean?" I asked. "I don't think I'm going anywhere."

"Never mind," he said, giggling. "I dreamed it again I think."

"Oh. You dream a lot, huh?"

"Yes. Do you like trees?"

"Of course I like trees."

"I see a big one right next to the bird feeder. It has a lot of branches. OK, I'm hanging up now. I'll call tomorrow to tell you more."

"OK, goodnight Miles."

{ Age 38 - A }

O NE NIGHT IN MID-AUGUST, I unearthed a box of books I had forgotten about after my move from Baltimore. One of the books lying on top was Marion's old copy of *Destroying the Fortress* by Laura Day. I thumbed through it for a few minutes before stumbling on a sentence that struck me: "Paradoxically, everyone is simultaneously alone and connected to everyone and everything."

A few moments after reading this, I suddenly felt deeply nauseous—a depressingly familiar sensation. I ran to the kitchen sink and waited for the vomit to come up, but it refused to arrive. I just dry-heaved a few times before collapsing down on the floor. As I sat there with my back pressed against the oven door, an intense feeling of dread began to overtake me. The air seemed to be pressing down like a vice on all sides of my body, and horrific images swam into my vision—exploding heads, writhing guts, piles of bodies. Eyes open or closed, it didn't seem to matter. I finally remembered to breathe... deeply, slowly, rhythmically. I concentrated only on the breath, and within a few minutes, the world began to reassemble into something vaguely recognizable.

Later that night, as I was brushing my teeth before bed, I couldn't shake the feeling of impending doom. Apparently something was going wrong with my body again, but I felt a strange sense of fatalism about it all. If this was a Crohn's relapse or something like that, so be it. I had no real choice but to let it play out for a bit.

As I lay in bed skimming the Laura Day book, I remembered my last call with Dan where he'd encouraged me to come meet him out west. This idea suddenly seemed appealing to me. If my health was about to go downhill again, why not have a last quick fling while I felt decent? I could drive to Colorado, have an adventure, maybe meet this Laura Day person whose books had affected Marion so deeply. There were no loose ends to tie up except work, and I could probably push that off for a while. I picked up the phone and dialed Dan's number.

"Byron," came the familiar voice, sounding unsurprised that I called.

"Dan, how are you?"

"I'm good. More importantly, how are you?"

"I'm OK. A bit weird, but OK."

"So is it time for you to come out here?"

"Yes, I think so."

"Good, makes sense. Let me tell you what to do. Locate Lyons, Colorado on a map and make your way there. When you get into town, call me and I'll lead you here. When are you leaving?"

"Probably tomorrow," I replied.

"Are you driving?"

"Yes."

"Excellent. I'll make sure there's a place for you to sleep. You can stay as long as you need to."

"OK, thanks so much Dan."

"One last thing. Try not to have any preconceptions at all about what you'll find here. Bring your beginner's mind."

"OK, I'll try," I said, chuckling.

"All I'm asking you to do is try," he replied. "See you soon."

The next morning, I woke up around 7 and tossed a bare minimum of clothes, books, and toiletries into my backpack. Before walking out the door, I gave Jameson and Miles a call to let them know what was going on. Miles was curious and a little sad, but I assured him I'd be home in a few weeks and that I'd call him from the road. And with that, another journey west commenced.

I decided to drive straight through to Terre Haute, Indiana, partly because it seemed like a reasonable halfway point, and partly because I was always intrigued by the name. Assuming I only stopped for lunch, gas, and a few quick pee breaks, I'd arrive there around 8 PM or so.

As I drove, I fell into a sort of trance. I kept the windows open and the radio off, so all I heard was the persistent roar of the wind and the steady drone of the tires on the road. My mind stayed relatively blank, which felt like a blessing. The simple act of driving—moving forward—was my sole concern.

I pulled off at the first exit for Terre Haute just after 8:15 and eventually found my way, randomly, to the Woodridge Motel. It looked reasonable enough from the outside, so I eased into the parking lot and headed to the office to get a room. There was no one behind the desk, so I rang the bell a few times and stood back to survey the scene. After a minute or so, a young girl in a fluorescent green dress and gaudy pink sunglasses sauntered out from the back. When she reached the desk, she rested her elbows on the edge and stared up at me with her chin in her hands.

"Do you like these sunglasses?" she asked. "I wear them even when it's getting dark."

"Yes, they're pretty spectacular," I replied, smiling.

"Thanks. I have another pair that's blue, but they're not as pretty."

"Are your parents here? They run the motel, right?"

"They're somewhere around here," she said, still staring up at me.

"Do you know if there are any rooms available for tonight?"

"Sure, lots."

"Do you know how much they cost?"

"I think 55 dollars."

"Well, can you grab one of your parents so I can pay for a room and get my key?"

"Are you impatient? My mom says I'm impatient. I can't wait for anything. I get antsy."

"No, I'm not impatient," I replied, chuckling. "At least I don't think so. I'm just kind of tired and hungry. I've been driving all day."

"Do you want a hot dog?" she asked. "I can make you one."

"Thanks so much for that offer. What's your name?"

"Bonnie. I'm 9."

"Well I'm Byron. I'm 38."

"38's still young, don't worry," she replied.

"It is?" I asked, laughing.

"Yes. Listen, if you want to give me the money, I can give you the key to a room."

"OK, I can do that."

I pulled three 20s out of my wallet and handed them to her.

"This requires change," she said matter-of-factly. "But I can't use the register. Mom says."

"No problem, I'll get the change later. Can you give me the key?"

"Sure, sure, hold your horses," she replied, smiling mischievously.

She turned around and grabbed the key to room 7.

"Here, room 7. A nice one."

"Thanks Bonnie."

"Now go to your room and relax yourself. I will bring you a hot dog and lemonade. Do you like corn on the cob?"

"Yes, definitely," I said, grinning.

"Well that's coming too, then."

She abruptly turned around and marched away, leaving me alone in the office.

About 15 minutes later, she did indeed bring the food to my room. She also brought me a plastic ring with a huge fake green emerald.

"This is for you," she said. "It's lucky and peaceful. If you ever get in trouble or get scared, use it."

"Thanks Bonnie," I replied, slipping on the ring and holding it up for her to see. "I love it."

"I don't give these rings to just anyone, you know," she said, waving her finger at me theatrically. "So use it, don't lose it. That's what my teacher always says."

"OK, got it," I said, smiling.

With that, she turned around and strolled off toward the office, leaving me alone to finish my meal. When I was done, I brushed my teeth and climbed into bed, once again completely exhausted. Within a matter of minutes, I descended into a deep, dreamless sleep.

Around noon the next day, I pulled into a gas station just outside of St. Louis. After filling up the tank and grabbing some snacks inside, I sat in the car with my map to determine my next stopping point. I decided to continue on to Salina, Kansas, which was about 6 hours away. As I was plotting the drive, my phone rang. It was Miles.

"Hi Byron. How's your trip?"

"It's going great, Miles," I said, smiling. "Thanks for calling to check."

"Where are you now?"

"At a gas station near St. Louis, Missouri."

"Is that a long way away?"

"Yes, it's near the middle of the country."

"Oh, neat," he replied. "I'm looking out the window at the big tree in the front yard. It's windy and the branches are blowing all around."

"I like that tree a lot," I said, grinning.

"Anyway," he continued, "I wanted to tell you I love you, in case I don't see you again soon."

I got momentarily choked up.

"Well thank you, Miles. I love you too. But I'll see you again soon, I promise."

"OK, maybe," he answered cryptically. "Remember not to be scared. There's nothing to be scared of, no matter what."

"Why do you say that?"

"Just because."

"Alright then. Well, tell your dad I said hello, OK? I'll see you guys soon."

"OK, Byron. Bye."

As I put the phone down, I felt a slight surge of nausea, but fortunately it died down quickly.

I pulled into the parking lot of the Best Inn in Salina just after 7:30. After checking in, I headed to my room to eat the pizza I'd picked up from Coops Pizzeria nearby. Sitting cross-legged on the bed with the pizza box in my lap, I stared out the window at the parking lot while the ceiling fan above my head rattled arrhythmically. What the hell was I doing here, in a random motel room in the middle of Kansas?

After a few minutes, I tossed the half-empty pizza box on the floor and lay back on the bed, gazing aimlessly up at the whirring blades of the fan and the white-tiled ceiling. At that moment, I felt utterly tired and alone. I had nothing, no real accomplishments or ties to the world. My life seemed pointless—a failed experiment.

I turned over on my side, shut my eyes, and hugged my knees into my body. Then I simply breathed... in and out, over and over. After a few minutes, I became calm and almost content. What did I expect to happen, after all? There was only this.

I woke up from a dead sleep at 5:30 AM, my hair sweaty and the edge of my pillow covered in drool. For a few disorienting moments, I had no idea where I was. I struggled to situate the bed in a familiar room, but nothing was lining up. Eventually I remembered I was in Kansas, in a motel just off I-70. If I strained a bit, I could hear the trucks on the highway. I switched on the lamp next to the bed and sat up with my back against the headboard.

After a few minutes of staring at the wall, I began to plot out the rest of my journey. Lyons was a little under seven hours away, so if I left soon, I'd be at Beyond by early afternoon. I had no idea what I'd find there, if anything, but at this point it hardly mattered.

{ Age 38 - B }

WHEN I REACHED LYONS around 1 PM, I pulled into the parking lot of a gas station and called Dan.

"Where are you?" he asked without a greeting.

"In town," I said. "In Lyons."

"Good, good. I'll let Laura know you're close. She's been asking about you."

"Really?" I asked incredulously.

"Yes. She says she's very intrigued to meet you."

"What have you told her?"

"Nothing, actually. Just your name. OK, are you ready for directions?"

By 2:30, I was sitting in Laura Day's cavernous kitchen, nervously sipping a beer while she prepped a late lunch for us. Her instant familiarity with me was baffling, especially since Dan told me that she rarely if ever invited anyone into her house. Outside the window, the branches of the pines were swaying in the slight breeze of the late-summer afternoon.

"Relax," she said gently as she chopped up carrots on a cutting board. "What are you so worried about?"

"I guess I'm confused why you've taken such an immediate interest in me," I replied. "You're treating me like an old friend."

"Does that make you suspicious?" she asked, pausing and fixing her inscrutable blue eyes on me. "Don't analyze it. Leave it alone and enjoy yourself."

As she resumed her chopping, I gazed up at the large skylight in the center of the soaring, arched ceiling. A thin ribbon of cloud was floating slowly by.

"My ex-wife had a bunch of your books," I said hesitantly after a long moment of silence.

"Nice," she replied, smiling. "I'm glad when someone gets something from them. I always feel like disowning them after a few years."

"Why's that?"

"Each one is a snapshot of a temporary way of thinking, and my thinking usually shifts very quickly. I'm not even sure why I try to get it down in writing. I think I'll stop."

"Just like that? No more books?" I asked, chuckling.

"Just like that."

After lunch, Laura led me down the hallway to her imposing living room, with its gigantic fireplace and lofty wood-beamed ceiling. The room had a series of long, plush white couches against the walls, leaving a huge open space in the middle that was covered by a striking, bizarrely decorated rug. In the center of the rug was a spiral staircase that wound its way up to a mammoth, disembodied human eye. From this central eye, dark blue and purple concentric circles radiated out to the edges of the rug. The effect was both hypnotic and unsettling.

"Take a seat anywhere," Laura said, motioning broadly with her arm.

I walked over and sat down in the middle section of the couch to the right of the doorway. Laura sat cross-legged on the edge of the carpet, facing me. The afternoon sun streamed in through the towering windows on either side of the fireplace.

"So..." Laura began, tossing back her thick grey hair. "Here we are."

"Indeed," I replied uncertainly.

"What do you want to talk about? This is your show."

"Is it?"

"Well, sure. You came here."

"That's true, and I'm not even sure why. Dan loves it here."

"Bless his heart."

"But I'm naturally skeptical of all this. I mean, the camp out there. The dining hall. Are you running a commune? A cult? What's the story?"

"You're searching for a label," she said, smiling.

"I guess I am," I responded. "But seriously, what's going on here?"

"A bunch of people are living in the same place, together. They chose to. They came to me. I didn't build it and lure people here. People built everything out there after asking me if they could. If it was up to me, they wouldn't be here."

"What do you mean, up to you? Isn't it up to you? You don't want them here?"

"Not particularly, but I'm not fighting it. As long as they get something out of it, what's the harm?"

"Dan says you hardly ever have people in your house."

"Yeah, it's rare. Do you feel special?"

I laughed and shifted a bit on the couch.

"Seriously though, what's your big interest in me?" I asked.

"Frankly, I'm not sure. I'm drawn to you, for whatever reason. And now that you're sitting here in front of me, I do like you. I appreciate your honesty. In any case, I've learned not to question too deeply."

"I'm learning that, too. There's a limit, and past that limit you just drive yourself insane."

"When I was younger, I questioned everything. My family, my friends, all the social and authoritarian constructs, all the teachers, all my own thoughts and emotions. I didn't trust anyone or anything. But that got exhausting."

"Did someone hurt you as a kid or something?" I asked.

"A few people did, yes. My father was verbally and physically abusive, mainly to my mother, but sometimes to me. Then my mother would constantly berate me at home and in public, passing the ugliness on down. And so on and so forth. So I became cold and distant, utterly analytical. I tore down everything before I could even engage with it. This continued throughout my teenage years up until a certain incident. My mind was working well, almost too well, but I felt dead inside."

"What changed things for you? Was it that incident?"

"Yes, I tried to kill myself when I was 19," she said with a pained smile. "Do you want to hear about it? I've never told anyone."

"Sure, if you want to tell me," I answered, sitting forward.

She paused for a moment to collect herself.

"So I set up a makeshift noose and hung it from a metal beam in the garage of the house I was renting with some friends in Charlotte. It was late at night and everyone else was asleep. I stood on a stepladder, secured the noose around my neck, and paused for a moment. I remember staring through the tiny garage door window at the streetlight outside, thinking that was the last thing I'd see. I kicked the stepladder over and the noose tightened around my neck and I started choking. I just kept watching the streetlight outside. It looked so warm and calm and unbothered by anything.

I began to feel euphoric... light... like I was about to ascend upward into the sky. Then my chest started to feel like it was going to explode. I experienced a moment of pure, unadulterated panic, and then, suddenly, the rope broke and my body collapsed to the ground. I lay there in fetal position coughing uncontrollably for a few seconds, and then I turned over on my back, relaxed my body, and surrendered. For some reason, I wasn't dead. I was alive. And miraculously, in that moment, I somehow began to feel compassion for myself. I felt a deep warmth radiating from my chest that filled my entire body, from my feet to the top of my head. I started to cry, wrenching sobs that shook me from head to toe. I forgave myself in that moment, and I also forgave my parents. They didn't know what the fuck they were doing, just like I didn't know. No one did... No one does."

Laura paused and stared solemnly down at the rug. The rays of the afternoon sun were illuminating her shoulder and the side of her neck.

"So that moment changed me, obviously. It let me live."

She paused again and smiled at me.

"Sorry for the heavy detour."

"Not an issue at all," I responded gently.

"I have no idea why I'm unloading this on you."

"Don't worry about it. I'm happy to listen."

"Why don't you give me a story now?" she asked, rising to her feet.

"I don't have anything as interesting as your story."

"Who cares? Give me anything you want."

"OK then," I replied, stalling for a moment. "Well, when I was around eight, I had a recurring dream that I can still remember. It scared the hell out of me at first, but then I kind of got used to it, the more I dreamt it. I was walking in a forest alone, near dusk. Everything was completely silent except for my feet crunching the dead leaves on the ground. After walking for a bit, I noticed a large tree with a door in its trunk. I went up to the door and knocked. No one answered, so I opened it and saw that there was a staircase descending downward. I hesitantly walked down the stairs and found myself in a huge hollow area below the forest floor. Everything around me was glowing light blue, and when I looked up, the forest floor was see-through like glass. I strained to see in front of me, but the blue light faded quickly after a few feet into complete blackness. Suddenly, a huge, centaur-like figure came out of the darkness, running directly toward me at full speed and swinging a huge axe above its head. At first I was frozen in terror, but at the last second I dove to the side, and the centaur brought the axe down hard on the staircase behind me, which had turned to glass. The stairs shattered into thousands of pieces, and the centaur ran off into the darkness again, leaving me alone and trapped down in this weird netherworld. I typically woke up around this point feeling vaguely sad and lonely."

I paused and glanced over at Laura, who was standing in the center of the rug with her arms folded.

"Fascinating," she said with a slight smirk. "What the hell does it mean?"

"No idea," I replied, leaning back on the couch. "I think I had the dream about ten times before it finally stopped."

"Let's see here... You are out in nature, in normalcy, and then you're lured into some parallel zone of reality. One of the inhabitants of this zone wants to keep you there, so it severs your pathway back. The place feels foreign and opaque to you, gives you a feeling of loss. Symbolically, your mind and your imagination are that parallel zone of reality. You haven't figured out how to integrate that zone with everyday life. The two feel hopelessly separate. Am I getting somewhere?"

"Yeah, for sure," I replied, chuckling.

"Still the case?" she asked.

"Pretty much, yeah."

"If you can relax the conscious mind, imagination seeps into the mundane and becomes intertwined with it. You can stop trying so hard."

"What do you mean by that?"

"Stop categorizing."

With that, Laura sauntered over to a drink cart that sat against the wall near the door.

"Whiskey?" she asked, holding up a bottle of Maker's Mark.

"Sure," I answered.

Above the cart was an intricate tapestry depicting an Aztec priest carrying out a ritualized human sacrifice at the top of a stone pyramid. The priest was wearing a brightly colored costume and mask, and he was thrusting a large, gleaming knife into the chest of the prone victim.

"Nice tapestry," I said, laughing.

"Just a reminder," she replied with a smile.

She handed me my drink and sat down next to me empty-handed.

"Nothing for you?" I asked.

"I'll get one in a minute."

I sipped my bourbon as we sat in silence for a few moments.

"You know you can stay here as long as you want, right?" she said, eventually.

"Thanks very much for that. I'm not sure what I'm going to do at this point."

"Let me guess—you're reaching the end of the previous stage and the beginning of the next, so you're in a sort of limbo. At least that's the story you're telling yourself, no?"

"In a nutshell..."

"My personal story is the wise but flawed teacher, verified by a certain level of outside success, isolating herself to do personal work that will allow her to bestow even more of her hard-won wisdom on the world. Boring and tedious bullshit, but necessary... Every thought we have is just a story, really, and waking reality is just stories nested within stories. And then behind it all, there are the base stories of our existence— we're lovingly created by God in his image, we're meaningless collections of chemicals floating on a speck of dust through the immensity of space, we're the key participants in a vast experiment in consciousness, and so on and so forth. If we get beyond the stories, we're left with simple awareness. That's it."

"Well, shit..." I said, chuckling and taking another sip of bourbon. "You sound so sure of yourself."

"It's an act," she replied matter-of-factly.

Later that night, after a light salad dinner, we were both lying on the rug in the living room, fairly stoned.

"It doesn't really make any sense," said Laura, her arm draped over her eyes, "but I feel like I've known you for a long time. Doesn't it seem like we're having an ongoing conversation in some kind of overlapping time loop?"

"Yeah, it does," I replied, slurring a little. "It really does."

"It seems like we keep coming back to this room, over and over, and everything's winding back on itself. It's making my head hurt."

"Cyclical..." I said vaguely, trailing off.

"It's like a fucked up case of déjà vu. We've known each other before and we will again, but it all seems to be based around this exact point in our lives. You're always in some sort of identity crisis. I'm always acting like a self-important prick in my pseudo-mansion."

"Are we supposed to be teaching each other something?" I asked blearily, propping myself up on my elbows.

"I'm guessing yes," Laura responded, her arm still covering her eyes.

"How many times do you think we've done this?"

"Many, many times. Or not. Maybe just a few."

"So what's the point then?"

"Maybe the point is to learn how to toss out the stories completely. Even the story of how we made our way here to this particular moment, lying stoned on this rug."

"And then what?"

"Then nothing. That's it."

"But what about...?" I began.

"Ah, ah, ah, don't question," Laura interrupted firmly, holding up her hand. "No more fucking questions. I've had enough. You've had enough."

"Yes," I sighed in agreement, letting my head drop back down to the rug.

"This can be it, I swear to God," she said softly, gazing up at the interlaced patterns of shadows on the ceiling. "No layers, no baggage, no history, no future, no patterns, no cycles, no stories. And then you take this moment and string it out so it bisects time and space."

"Very elegant, but you still have to wake up in the morning and go about your business," I replied. "You have to deal with the mundane life, the bodily life."

"But it's all part of this," she said with a wave of her arm. "This contains that and that contains this. It's all nested together, like a set of Russian dolls. Only you never really know which doll's the biggest one, the one that contains everything. They keep switching on you. But once you come to peace with that uncertainty of having no idea where it all ends or begins, you're golden."

I just laughed and shook my head.

"You're calling bullshit, aren't you?" she asked, chuckling.

"No, no, but reaching that place is absurdly fucking hard to do."

"If you keep thinking it's hard, it will never happen," she replied with a sly grin.

With that, she abruptly stood up and stumbled off toward the doorway.

"Good night," she said, switching off the lights presumptuously. "There are like five guest rooms upstairs, or you could just sleep here. There's also my room, of course. It's all open."

I sat up for a moment to watch her leave, and then sank back down on the rug. As I gazed up at the ceiling, now recessed in darkness, my eyes began to grow heavy.

{ Age 38 - C }

I WAS SEVEN YEARS OLD, or thereabouts, sitting alone in the backyard just before sunset with my head in my hands. I had been crying, but I was growing calm now as I watched a line of ants wind its way down a blade of grass and then up another. I couldn't remember why I was upset. In fact, I couldn't really remember anything about the events leading up to this moment.

After some time had passed, I looked up to see a large group of people standing in a circle by my swing set. They were all smiling and talking and gesturing animatedly, but I couldn't make out what they were saying. My parents were there, as were my grandparents, who oddly looked about the same age as my parents. I thought I recognized the others, but I couldn't quite put names to faces. No one seemed to notice me sitting there, so I leaned back on my elbows and placidly observed the interactions of the group.

Eventually, a young girl snuck up from behind and sat down next to me. She appeared to be about nine or ten, with tendrils of curly black hair and wide, bright green eyes.

"Adults are funny," she said, smiling at me. "I see you watching them."

I just nodded and said nothing. The girl seemed vaguely familiar to me, but I couldn't place her.

"They play like kids do, but they don't know it," she continued. "They're not very good at it anymore. They think everything's important. They always talk about how much everything means."

"Well what *does* it mean?" I asked.

"Nothing. It doesn't mean anything, at least the way they play."

"I don't think I believe that."

"That's fine," she said breezily. "You don't have to believe it, but it's true."

"If it doesn't mean anything, then what are we doing here?" I asked, frowning.

"Here? Here is where we learn to play for real."

"I don't understand."

"I'll show you," she said, jumping to her feet and holding out her hand to me.

I hesitated for a few seconds before letting her help me up. As I stood facing her, she placed her index finger on the top of my head and slowly traced a circle on my scalp.

"Just relax," she said, grinning. "I'm opening up your form so you can understand."

I suddenly felt an overwhelming wave of energy move from my feet up into my forehead. It then dis-

persed throughout my body, heating my skin and causing all my hair to stand up on end. I began to feel shaky
and anxious.

"Shhh," she whispered in my ear. "Don't worry
about anything. Just relax and let this move through
you."

"What are you doing to me?" I asked, my voice
cracking.

"Filling you up and breaking you apart," she replied
calmly. "You can trust me. There's nothing to be afraid
of."

I looked down at my arms and saw that they were
beginning to glow. Tiny flecks of skin seemed to be
breaking off and floating away, but there was no hint of
pain.

"Look at the adults over there," the girl said, pointing in their direction. "I did the same thing to them."

The bodies of the adults were also glowing and
breaking apart, their skin dissolving into tiny particles
and floating away into the evening air. They were no
longer talking and laughing, but they didn't seem
afraid or upset. In fact, they seemed completely at
peace.

"I'm teaching them the real game," she said, giggling softly.

"Are they dying?" I asked quietly.

"No, they're learning. When they return, they'll
begin to see things as they really are."

"And what about me?" I asked.

By now, a good portion of my body had dissipated into the air, but I still felt no pain.

"It's the same for you, of course," she replied, tenderly stroking what was left of my arm. "You are learning too, always..."

Ease

{ Age 38 - D }

I WOKE UP IN THE MORNING groggy and confused, my face planted in the rug near the foot of the woven spiral staircase. As I sat up and adjusted to the growing daylight, it took me a few disorienting seconds to recall where I was. I could smell fresh coffee wafting down the hallway from the kitchen, so I rose unsteadily to my feet and tottered toward the doorway.

There was no one in the kitchen when I entered, but there was an open container of yogurt, a box of granola, a sliced grapefruit, and a clean mug next to the coffeemaker. The wall clock read 7:30, and there was a note for me by the sink:

"My dear Byron, I am out wandering in the woods. Please have some breakfast. If you stay, I will be happy. If you go, I will be sad, but only briefly. Love, Laura"

As I ate, I stared out the window at the pathway of young pine trees leading to the door of the house. How many times had I walked that pathway? Did it matter?

I found a pen and wrote beneath Laura's note:

"My dear Laura, I'm headed south, hopefully out into the desert. Thanks for the memories and the hospitality. I'm guessing I'll see you soon. Your (seemingly) eternal partner, Byron."

Just after 2 PM, I pulled into a gas station in Las Vegas, New Mexico. I was oddly craving Combos, which I hadn't eaten in at least 20 years, so after pumping my gas, I headed inside to buy a bag—pepperoni pizza flavor. When I returned to my car, there was a folded piece of paper shoved in the door handle on the driver's side. It was a child's crayon drawing of a bright yellow sun with rays shooting out of it in all directions. Beneath the sun was a stick-figure human reclining on a bed of green grass with a huge smile on its face. The words "I love you" were written across the bottom of the page in charming, barely legible kid scrawl.

By 7:30, I was sitting in a booth at Café a Go Go in Las Cruces. I had just ordered the red enchilada burger and a beer, and a three- or four-year-old boy from the adjoining booth was peering at me and giggling. I heard his parents quietly shushing him a few times.

"That man doesn't want you spying on him like that," the mother said softly but firmly.

At the table to my left, an older couple seemed to be in the midst of an argument. They were both frowning and staring out the window with their arms folded, the half-eaten remains of their meal strewn out forlornly in front of them. When the waitress brought me my beer, the man signaled to her for the check.

"Another joyful meal together..." the woman said bitterly, reaching for her purse.

"And what would you like me to do about it, Doris?" the man replied, sighing loudly.

"I have no idea, Dennis," she answered, defeated.

"That's what I thought."

When their check came, the man slowly counted out his cash and they both stood up and silently walked out. The busboy came up quickly behind them and collected their dishes, glasses, and silverware. He caught me observing him and flashed me a brief smile before returning to the kitchen.

"Hi!" came a high-pitched voice from the adjacent booth.

The kid's eyes and tousled hair were barely visible above his seat. The eyes were gleaming at me unblinkingly. I grinned and waved in their direction.

"Hi!" the voice said again, a bit louder.

"Hi!" I answered back.

The boy's parents were now immersed in conversation, so the two of us were free to interact.

"I see you!" the voice giggled.

"I see you too!" I said, pointing exaggeratedly at my eyes and then his.

"No you don't! I'm invisible!"

"Oh, I guess I'm imagining it then. Maybe I just think I see you!"

The waitress then materialized with my burger, and the kid's head dropped down out of sight. I was nearly halfway finished eating before the eyes reappeared, but there was no more talking this time. As the two of us stared playfully at one another while I polished off my meal, I felt a deep and inexplicable sense of contentment.

By 9 PM, I was reclining on the bed in my room at the Royal Host Motel. The hum of the air conditioner was hypnotizing, and I soon turned over on my side and shut my eyes. Tomorrow I'd head to White Sands to walk the dunes, and then after that, farther south. Down into west Texas and more of the huge open spaces, to Big Bend, and then maybe even farther down... into Mexico... and then perhaps even farther beyond that...

{ Age 38 - E }

I WAS LYING FLAT ON MY BACK in the desert at night, naked and alone, my mind completely empty as I gazed up at the seemingly boundless range of stars. My body was fully relaxed, with my legs spread wide apart and my arms stretched straight out from my sides, palms up. The temperature was cool, but not uncomfortably so, and I felt no impulse to cover myself up.

As time passed, I could occasionally hear a soft fluttering noise nearby, like the flapping of wings, but I didn't turn my head. Eventually I began to feel a disconcerting sensation across my legs, chest, and head, as if some octopus-like being was wrapping its tentacles around me from behind and squeezing me tightly. I looked down at my body and saw nothing amiss, at least at first. After a few moments, however, I noticed the rocks and shrubs around me seemingly growing larger. The pressure on my body became overwhelming as I watched the sagebrush beside me grow into looming trees and the rocks turn into small mountains.

In a matter of seconds, my body was smaller than a pebble, and then a grain of sand. The sensation of constriction was almost unbearable, but I could still see and hear everything. Suddenly, I realized the pressure was my own inner resistance, and I let my body go limp. A feeling of incredible elation surged through me, suffusing me with a warmth and energy unlike anything I'd ever experienced. I was now molecule-sized, and I could see countless particles in frenetic motion all around me. As I released even further, I transformed into one of the particles, colliding with and bouncing off the others at incomprehensible speeds, over and over, faster and faster.

Then, suddenly, there was no more motion, no more light, nothing—only pure void. Here I stayed for an interminable instant, alone. Then came an eruption of blinding light and violent expansion, and I was tossed out in all directions across the newly born universe. Within moments, I was everywhere. My base consciousness—along with innumerable others—was intermixed with every aspect of the perpetual creation, forming out of and along with the fundamental elements of matter.

I was shown the epicenter—a rotating wheel of pure, unadulterated light energy where all existence and all possibility is swallowed up, reintegrated, and rebirthed in the eternal sequence. At the heart of the wheel is an axis of primordial darkness and void, the fulcrum on which it all turns.

Then, abruptly, I was back on Earth, about seven years old, sitting at our dining room table. There was a half-full glass of orange juice in front of me, and I could smell the pancakes my father was cooking in the kitchen. I was still in my pajamas and feeling groggy, like I'd just woken up. I rubbed my eyes and stared down at the table, where the shadow of a leaf was quivering slightly in the morning sun.

"Almost ready in here," came the voice of my father. "Are you hungry for some pancakes?"

"Sure dad," I replied, yawning.

I could hear my mother bustling around the living room, happily whistling the same abbreviated section of a tune over and over. My father smacked the spatula a few times on the edge of the skillet.

"Just a minute more..." he called out.

{ Age 38 - F }

I WOKE UP COUGHING UNCONTROLLABLY, my head hanging off the side of the bed. I was soaked in sweat and my heartbeat was pulsing loudly in my ears. As I sat up, it took me ten or so terrifying seconds to remember where I was. The clock beside the bed read 5:05, and the blueish digital display was shifting in and out of focus alarmingly. Every aspect of my body seemed out of control, overtaken by some chaotic force.

Without thinking, I stood up abruptly and nearly fainted, sinking to my hands and knees on the carpet. After gathering myself for a few moments, I crawled over to the nightstand by the bed and switched on the lamp. Sitting there on the nightstand was the ring with the green emerald that Bonnie had given me. I vaguely remembered pulling it out of my pants pocket the night before. The light and the ring centered me to a degree, and as I leaned back against the side of the bed, I sifted through the possibilities of what might be happening to me. Panic attack? Heart attack? Stroke? Brain aneurysm? As I had been so many times before, I was helpless.

Suddenly, on top of everything else, my bowels began to churn and seethe, and I knew I had to get to the bathroom immediately. I crawled across the carpet and the tiled bathroom floor and hoisted myself up on the toilet. Then came the blood, gushing down into the bowl beneath me.

As the seconds wore on, I began to waver dizzily on the toilet seat, nearly losing consciousness, when for some reason the bleeding abruptly stopped. For an extended moment, I was completely calm and aware. I felt an almost ecstatic connection with everything around me—the tiles at my feet, the towel hanging in front of me, the sink, the tub, the lamp throwing out its soft light, this little motel and everyone asleep in the rooms around me, my own feeble body and mind, my family, my friends, all the random acquaintances along the way, every infinitesimal detail that had led up to this moment, every last being in the world... I even began to laugh—a silent, joyful, empathetic laugh at the absurdity of it all. The games being played, the roles being assumed, the limitations being constructed, every second of every day. I felt a deep love and compassion for everyone and everything...

Then the blood returned, violently, and my lifeless body tipped over onto the floor.

Epilogue

S TEP BACK, AND EVERY MOMENT is the same moment. I am feeding this "back" into the cycle so it can be read by anyone who wants to read it, but you are also here right now, where I am. We are commingled together here, just as we always have been...

Stop trying to figure it out.

Stephen Intlekofer

Made in the USA
San Bernardino, CA
19 December 2016